THE DEADLIER SPECIES

One minute she was the foxy Asian woman who'd sat down next to me. The next minute she was different. Her voice, her hair, her body structure. All different. What was going on?

It struck me just as she lashed out with a roundhouse kick to my temple. I slid inside the arc of the kick and caught her leg, punching into the underside of her thigh. She yelped.

A lycanthrope.

I swore under my breath. Why had I been assigned to kill a lycanthrope? I killed vampires for a living, not were-creatures.

She rolled away, yanking her legs out of my lock.

I ran for the cooler, but she tackled me halfway there, taking me down at the knees. I went face-first into the sand and came up spitting beach.

She grabbed my head from behind and rammed me back into the sand. And then I felt her claws on my lower ribs. She grabbed a handful of skin and twisted it like a doorknob.

And then she opened me up. . . .

*Books in the Lawson Vampire
series by Jon F. Merz*

THE FIXER

THE INVOKER

THE DESTRUCTOR

THE SYNDICATE*

Published by Pinnacle Books

*coming soon

(Please visit http://www.lawsonvampire.com
for more information)

THE DESTRUCTOR

Jon F. Merz

PINNACLE BOOKS
Kensington Publishing Corp.
http://www.kensingtonbooks.com

For Joyce
The only time words fail me . . .

One

For most humans, coming to the North Shore in Hawaii means big waves. It means a chance to surf with some of the best, if that's your game. Or you can just hang out on the beach watching eye candy and supreme athletes mingle in the sand and sun. The scent of sex wax and tanning lotion wafts across the gently sloping beach, seducing you into a mellow state of mind.

For me, the North Shore meant a chance to finish up a case.

A bad case at that.

Details, a vitally important ingredient to any mission, were missing. I wasn't all that surprised. I'd been a Fixer for years, hunting down vampires who break the laws of our society, and I felt almost too used to sketchy second-hand intelligence.

I'd been humping jets for the past three weeks—skipping time zones like a sidearmed rock bouncing across a pond. I felt like shit.

Which again was par for the course.

My target was a woman. I had a grainy surveillance photo that looked like someone wearing Coke-bottle glasses and suffering from acute glaucoma had taken it. I could make out very little.

Which meant I had to rely on informants.

Ask any intelligence operative or law-enforcement

professional about how great it feels to have to place absolute trust in the word of a sleazebag who turns over for a few bucks, and you'll know why I was just so gosh-darned excited about being in Hawaii.

I would have rather been home with my cats.

At least I know what they look like.

A giant tube crashed out about fifty yards from shore taking a few surfers under the swell. I saw boards go flying and feet inverted. Seconds later, they all surfaced intact.

Helluva way to score some thrills.

Maybe I should have swapped jobs.

I felt the crystalline sand grind between my toes. The sun's warmth beamed down on my skin. I was lucky enough to have inherited my father's skin. He tanned well. Whenever we'd gone to the beach, he used to brown nicely.

I'd rather be brown than burned red.

According to the low-grade heroin addict who knew something about my target, she'd begun frequenting this beach since a week back. That would have been right after she'd ditched Bangkok.

I'd been in Pnomh Penh skirting crazy moped drivers and tricycle taxis at the time, trying to find her trail.

A trail that had gone cold.

I turned up in the islands two days after she did. Directed here by my Control back in the States who'd sent word someone had spotted her in Hawaii.

At Honolulu International Airport, the local Fixer met me. He gave me some more information and then turned me loose.

Two days later he was dead.

She'd killed him.

I'd started coming to the beach soon after getting word from the informant who'd worked with the now-deceased Fixer. My first question to him had been to ask what she was doing hanging out on the North Shore.

He'd only smiled and walked away.

He was lucky I let him do that.

I spent every day on the beach. From just after sunup to just after sunset.

Waiting.

Waiting.

Waiting.

I kept my gun with me all the time, even though it was a little tough wearing a piece on the beach. I usually kept it in the cooler next to me. Or else when I slid the Hawaiian shirt on, it went behind my right hip, where I like to wear it normally.

I kept phoning in updates to my Control. No progress. No luck. Nothing.

He kept telling me to stay put.

So I did.

A day later I sat on the beach again watching more surfers carve half-pikes in the frothy ocean, wondering if there were any tiger sharks in the area.

"Excuse me."

My sunglasses did a good job of blocking out the sunlight so I didn't have to squint. Not that I wanted to anyway.

The woman in front of me stood about five feet six inches and weighed maybe a buck ten. She had more curves than a corkscrew, and they were barely contained by the triangles of fabric that made up her bikini.

I smiled. Cleared my throat. "Hi."

She smiled back. I love progress.

"I've seen you here for a few days now."

"Yeah?"

"Mm-hmm. You never go swimming, though."

"I'm allergic to water."

"Really?"

"No. But the truth is a lot more boring than that."

"So you just sit here."

"I just sit here."

"Watching?"

"Some watching. Mostly waiting."

"What are you waiting for?"

"A friend."

She crinkled her eyes. "This friend of yours . . . is it a he?"

"A she actually."

"Really." Her voice dipped.

"Not that kind of friend."

"Really." Her voice lifted.

I grinned. I thought about how funny it would be to tell her the truth. That I was there to put a few bullets into the body of some woman I'd never even seen a clear picture of. Then I realized how utterly stupid the truth sounded. Sometimes life's like that.

"Why don't you sit down?"

She sat. I looked her over. Her long dark hair framed her almond-shaped eyes and smooth creamy tanned skin. Her smile spilled white against the mocha background of her face.

"You're from Hawaii?"

She shook her head. "No. Back in New Jersey actually."

"Filipina?"

"Yeah." She brightened. "Good eye."

"What's a Jersey girl doing out here?"

"You ever been to Jersey?"

"Few times."

"You shouldn't have to ask then."

"Question withdrawn."

"I work here."

"What's work?"

"I'm something of a consultant."

"Self-employed."

"Don't say it like I'm some out-of-work wanna-be entrepreneur who hasn't got a dime in the bank. I'm very much employed. And I make a pretty damned good living."

"Fair enough."

"What about you?"

"Me?" I spread my arms. "I'm just waiting."

"We covered that."

"Yeah."

"Do you think I'm pretty?"

I smirked. "You're not much on subtlety, are you?"

"Life's short. Answer the question."

"I think you're the most beautiful woman on this beach." I glanced around for effect. "Nothing finer around here."

"You're sweet."

"Well, I was kinda put on the spot there."

"How much longer do you have to wait?"

I cleared my throat. "Until my friend shows up."

"And after that?"

"I don't have to wait anymore."

"Good." She turned and looked out toward the ocean. "You mind if I wait with you?"

"I was sorta hoping you'd say something like that."

We watched the waves roll in for another hour. We watched the sun trek west, spilling oranges and reds into the blue green of the Pacific. We sat close together as a breeze kicked up sand and bounced it off our skin.

And time ticked by.

People left the beach.

Until we were alone.

And she looked at me. "Are you through waiting?"

"I'd sure as hell like to be."

"Your friend didn't show up."

"Maybe tomorrow."

"Maybe you should just kiss me now."

I did. I kissed her full lips, tasted the sweet coconut oil, felt her moist tongue part my lips and search for my own. I felt her hands touch the back of my head, fingers roaming through my short bristly hair. Then they slid south. Down my back. Down past my hips. Down lower.

And lower.

She broke the kiss and smiled at me. Her eyes a mere inch from mine.

"I'm glad you asked me to wait with you."

"Why's that?"

She gave me another peck on the lips. Her hands tightened around my butt. "Because it's a lot easier killing somebody at night."

Her words barely had a chance to register before I felt her fingers turn into claws, digging into my butt, ripping, shredding their way north.

Toward my kidneys.

I cried out, twisted under her grasp, and tried to roll away. She tucked her body into mine and rolled with me. I could hear her laughing as we tumbled toward the waves.

"You won't get rid of me that easily, Lawson."

Oh, crap.

It had to be her—the woman I'd been sent to kill.

As we rolled, I brought my elbow up and smashed it into her face. My pistol was back at the cooler. If I could just get to it—

She grunted as I struck her nose. I heard a crunch and figured I'd broken it. I smelled blood a moment later and fought back the sudden rise of saliva in my mouth.

We broke free.

"Are we having fun yet?"

In the dark I could see her almost as well as during the daylight. Vampires can see pretty well at night. Waves crashed at our feet. We circled under the new moon, embraced by a million stars overhead.

She crouched low—between the cooler and me.

And my gun.

And then something else happened. She began to . . . change.

One minute she was the foxy Asian woman who'd sat down next to me. The next minute she was different. Her voice, her hair, her body structure.

All different.

What the hell was going on?

It struck me just as she lashed out with a roundhouse kick to my temple. I slid inside the arc of the kick and caught her leg, punching into the underside of her thigh.

She yelped.

Christ.

A lycanthrope.

I swore under my breath. What the hell had I been assigned to kill a lycanthrope for? I killed vampires for a living, not were-creatures.

She rolled away, yanking her leg out of my lock.

I ran for the cooler.

She tackled me halfway there, taking me down at the knees in a way that would have made a scout for the NFL drool with desire. I went face-first into the sand and came up spitting beach.

She grabbed my head from behind and rammed me back into the sand. I bucked up with my hips and butt, trying to unseat her.

She laughed.

"I've played Ride 'Em Bronco before, Lawson. I'm very good at it."

Maybe. I rolled to the side and she fell off. I straddled her and went for a choke hold, slamming my forearm into her throat and shoving it down trying to cut off air and circulation.

She struggled, but the beach enveloped her, making it tough to get any purchase.

And then I felt her claws on my lower ribs. She grabbed a handful of skin and twisted it like a door-knob.

And she opened me up.

I gritted my teeth as I felt my body rise just a little bit. That's all it took. I felt the knee shot a second later.

It thundered into my groin and my bowels dropped south like a cinder block tossed off a building. I grunted and rolled off her, clutching my crotch.

She rolled away from me, gasping for breath and retching in time to my own.

Her voice hissed across the beach. *"Bastard!"*

The cooler lay twenty feet from me. I turned over onto my stomach. I had to get to it. I clawed at the sand, trying to find the strength to stand.

She was on all fours. She looked at me. "You're good."

I didn't say anything. I just had to reach the damned cooler.

She stood, massaging her throat. "Almost had me."

Ten feet from the cooler.

"I ought to kill you the way I did the other Fixer."

Eight feet.

"I ought to."

Six feet.

"But I won't."

Four feet. Almost within . . . reach.

"Good-bye, Lawson."

I felt the plastic under my hand and tore the lid off. I felt the gun a second later and tore it out, flipping over on the sand, searching for a target.

But she was gone.

She'd disappeared.

Right in front of me.

Almost like she didn't even exist at all.

And if it wasn't for my swollen and bruised scrotum, I might have almost believed she'd been a ghost.

A ghost that had almost killed me.

Two

That was then.

This was now.

They called her Shiva, after the Hindu god of destruction.

I called her a lot of four-letter words. Especially after our run-in in Hawaii.

Shiva was one of those cases I wished I could forget. One of the missions that crept back into my mind—that haunted my memory—usually after I'd had a few glasses of Bombay Sapphire and tonic. When the lights were low and I had some Dexter Gordon filtering out of the stereo.

Like her namesake, Shiva destroyed things.

She killed with the same frosty attitude so common to hardened street thugs or wartime orphans who have had to eke out a life among the death and ruin.

Shiva excelled at killing.

Before the Council sent me after her, she killed three Fixers as easily as the sun comes up. That's a pretty good record for someone not even in the service.

But Shiva had a gift.

And that gift gave her an incredible edge. It made her tougher to hunt and kill than most anyone else we'd ever faced before.

Shiva could change.

Transform.

And she could do it standing right in front of you. One minute she was there. The next, she was someone else. Someone new. And trying to keep track of her was next to impossible.

According to her dossier, she'd been born to a pair of vampire parents in Seattle. She'd been raised with no problems. In fact, the psychological profile attached to the file insisted, everything seemed normal. But as I've often said in this business, just when things seem normal, you'd better hike up your pants or you'll get boned pretty damned hard.

So it was with Shiva.

Digging deeper into Shiva's family history, it became apparent that the phrase "normal vampire" had gone out the window quite a while ago—thanks to two generations previous when one of her uncles had had a one-night stand with a lycanthrope.

That's a werewolf to you and me.

Well, not necessarily a "wolf." Lycanthropes could change into pretty much whatever they wanted to. These days, it was other humans most of the time. But some of them still liked roaming around forests on four legs.

A lot of vampires called them "moondogs."

I had a bit more respect than that.

After all, Shiva had disappeared right in front of me.

And despite my best efforts, I hadn't been able to find her again.

I don't like coming up empty.

I like getting my job done.

I sighed, closed the file, and looked up. Across the table from me sat a wispy thin guy named Niles.

Niles—my new Control.

And I wasn't especially thrilled about it.

Why? For one reason. Controls are—or should I say were—all former Fixer agents. They've been out in the cold, been shot at, and experienced a rough life most others of our kind can't even imagine.

But ol' Niles looked like he'd spent most of his life cowering away in a corner somewhere. He looked like the kind of guy who actually believed the sky was falling or the check was in the mail.

Then again, so did most of humanity.

Maybe I'd just think of Niles as a temp. A fill-in. After all, working with me usually had a way of weeding out the ones who couldn't cut it.

I shouldn't have complained. After all, I'd been on the Council for months about getting a replacement Control. My last one met with an untimely demise when I killed him for treason.

I don't like traitors.

Then again, I'm not exactly fond of wispy guys either.

Niles seemed to be considering how he would navigate the bowl of steaming chicken noodle soup on the table without scalding himself. He took a single spoonful and spent the next three minutes blowing the steam off it. Finally, after giving it a searching look, he extended his lips to the spoon, slurped vaguely, then finally took the rest into his mouth, chewed slowly for about forty seconds, and then swallowed.

I sighed.

This did not look good.

We sat in a small eatery called Mr. Lee's in Harvard Square. I like the place because it's a greasy spoon that happens to turn out damned fine food. It's small, and occasionally given to precocious students who yammer too much about inconsequential things, but that's what young people are supposed to do. I go there for a kick-ass cheeseburger and soda fountain-style Cola. Sometimes, that's just about the best meal you could ever hope to eat.

Niles had blanched when I ordered up the burger.

"Don't you know how bad beef is for you?"

I looked at him. "Since when is cholesterol a problem for us?"

"They're doing studies, you know."

"My teeth are used for eating meat, not grazing on grass. We didn't work our way to the top of the food chain to spend life munching on hay and herbs."

I grabbed the burger and seated us by the booth next to the door. Sure it was humid and uncomfortable every time someone came in, but I was hungry, I had a cheeseburger, and that was as good as my life needed to be at that particular moment.

At least up until Niles dropped the dossier in front of me.

"Know her?"

I cleared my throat. "Tell me something, Niles."

"What?"

I leaned across the laminated tabletop. "Did they tell you anything at all about me?"

"You mean the Council?" He started, hearing how loud he'd spoken, and then leaned in and reduced his voice to a whisper. "You mean the Council?"

"I'm not listed in Internet chat rooms, Niles."

He sat back. "Well, yes, they told me some things about you."

"What—exactly?"

He took another spoonful of soup, but didn't give it the required three minutes of preparatory fellatio and promptly burned himself. When he'd recovered as much as he possibly could barring the sudden appearance of a container of Bactine, he shrugged. "They told me you killed your last Control."

I love it when the Council stresses my positive attributes. Work your butt off for them and they shit on you. Typical. "They tell you he was a traitor—that his execution was justified, warranted, and damned necessary?"

"No." He grinned. "But I looked that up in the file myself."

Score one for Niles. I flipped open Shiva's dossier and looked at her picture. It must have been taken a few years back from the look of it. Long flowing brown hair, blue eyes, arching eyebrows. Overall, a nice package. Albeit deadly as all get-out.

"Yeah, I know her." I pointed to the photo. "This thing's useless. Shiva can look like anyone she wants to. She could be Katie Couric one day and Tiger Woods the next and the only way you'd know it was her is if she played a bad round on the links."

Niles ignored his soup for the moment and sipped his iced tea. "The Council believes she may be heading to Boston."

"The Council told me she was dead."

"Yes, I heard that too."

More lies from the Council. Who woulda thunk it? "Why's she coming here?"

"We're not sure."

"Ah, there's that nifty intelligence-gathering apparatus I love so much."

"They have another agent following her."

"Another Fixer?"

"Yes."

"Who is it? He'd better be damned good or she'll take him pretty quick."

Niles removed a small notebook from his jacket, opened it, and scanned a page. "Agent's name is Jarvis. I was told you two worked together before."

This second piece of news had the potential to ruin my otherwise great lunch. Jarvis. Mr. Gung-Ho. Disco-stud boy with the ladies and the kind of guy smart Fixers don't want to be around. Reason? He was dangerous. Being headstrong does not grant you invulnerability. Jarvis thought otherwise. That's where we differed in opinion. He could operate okay, but no one ever wanted to stand too close to the guy. It was like being next to a lightning rod in the middle of a thunderstorm. You were gonna get struck, it was just a question of when.

I'd last seen Jarvis in Tokyo. I did not have fond memories of that trip.

"Where's he now?"

"En route to Boston. I was told he'd be touching down sometime this afternoon. You want to meet him at the airport?"

"No." I took a long sip on my Coke. "You can get in touch with him?"

"I have his cell phone number."

"Tell him to meet me at the place we met the last time he was here in town. And tell him to make damned sure he's not followed."

Niles looked at me. "Followed? From the airport? Really, Lawson, you don't actually think—"

"Listen to me, Niles, because I am only going to say this one time: Take no chances. Take nothing for granted. If we're going to be dealing with Shiva, then anything is a possibility."

"'We?'" Niles looked like I'd fed him raw beef.

"I didn't mean you. I meant Jarvis and me."

"Oh."

I wiped my mouth, suddenly not so hungry anymore. I made a mental note to stop eating with my Controls. Seemed like my meals always went south as a result of it.

"Say, Niles."

"Yes?"

"The Council, they . . . uh . . . told me you were over in Saudi Arabia finishing up some work."

"Yes."

"What were you doing over there? Exactly?"

He looked happy I'd taken an interest in him. "You really want to know?"

"I asked, didn't I?"

"I was leading a management course for other Controls."

My jaw must have hit the table. My head suddenly hurt. I wondered how much acid I would have had to take to con myself into believing Niles could be any kind of leader or manager. I decided I'd probably have to overdose ten times.

"A management course."

"Uh-huh. Neat, huh?"

It has been my experience that people who use the word "neat" in their everyday vocabulary are to be avoided as often as possible. I also don't like hard-line vegenazis. And I've already elaborated on my hard-line stance against wimpy dudes.

Niles was batting a thousand and we weren't even

on the damned field yet. I love it when my life suddenly becomes so rosy I just about can't stand it anymore.

"There anything else we need to discuss?"

Niles smiled, took a final sip of his iced tea, and shook his head. "No. I'll pass Jarvis the message. Do you want Shiva's dossier?"

I shook my head. There was no need. "I know her already."

I just wished to God I didn't.

Three

Jarvis looked about the same as he had in Japan. A mop of black hair topped his head and bushy eyebrows overpowered his face. We'd nicknamed him Captain Unibrow once, but I don't think anyone called him that anymore. Not since he'd started plucking or waxing or whatever the hell he was doing to keep the fuzzy growth barely at bay.

I watched him thread his way through the bustling crowds outside Boston's Fanueil Marketplace and amble over to where I sat. Behind me, a copper statue of some historical persona who no doubt figured prominently in Boston's history provided some good support. Jarvis eased himself down about six feet away. Leaving just enough space for passersby to think we weren't together.

"Been a long time, Lawson."

I didn't say anything until the overweight woman with three kids managed to waddle past. "Tokyo. You took me to that awful bar named Pussy."

"Poussé actually. I think it was French."

"Only thing French about that place was the champagne." I took a sip of orange juice from the small carton I had with me. "What's new?"

"Heard you lost your Control sometime back."

"I didn't lose him, Jarvis."

"No?"

"No." I turned. "He suffered an unfortunate accident."

Jarvis smiled. "The accident being you, so I heard. Not that it matters now. That guy never sat right with me. Strange vibe and all."

"You met him?"

He shrugged. "Once. Probably better he's gone."

"Better for everyone," I said. "But that's history. Where is she?"

"Straight to business, huh? You really need to take some time out for yourself and relax more. Adopt a European attitude about life. Take a siesta, eat better meals, that kind of thing."

"Who the hell are you—Julie McCoy, the Cruise Director for the Love Boat?"

Jarvis laughed.

I frowned. "Besides, I'll relax plenty when Shiva's been put down."

"A lot of people will."

"So, fill me in. You've apparently been the golden boy on this op. Got yanked off your regular duty to track her, did you?"

"Actually, I've been on special assignment for a few years. Ever since Japan actually."

I looked at him. "You took credit for that hit, didn't you?"

Jarvis shrugged. "You weren't around by the time word filtered back to the Council. What can I say? I would have included you, but you'd just been transferred back and I know being stationed in Boston meant a lot to you. I didn't want to fuck it up for you is all."

"You didn't want to fuck it up for yourself, more likely." I finished the orange juice and crushed the container in my hand. "You're lucky I wasn't sent to some shitville outpost in Des Moines or Boise. Otherwise it'd be your ass right now."

"Okay, okay, message received." He looked away.

"They tell you they sent me after her?"

"Yeah. But she disappeared on you."

"It was supposed to be an interim assignment. A quickie."

"Your phrase or theirs?"

"You know me, Jarvis. I don't assume anything."

"Yeah. But she got away from you."

"The Council yanked me off the case. And they brought you in."

"Yep."

"You having fun?"

"Can't you tell?"

"Oh, sure, it's written all over your face."

"Your new Control fill you in on what she's been doing?"

"Not really. I wanted to hear it straight from you. I prefer firsthand intel to the grapevine."

Jarvis waited for another group of tourists to take a few pictures and move along. "She's killed three agents already."

"What's that make her total now—ten?"

"Almost. Shit, Lawson, we aren't exactly easily replaced. I don't have to tell you the importance of this mission."

"I've met the lady—I know the score." Across the street a homeless man was trying to bum a few bucks off someone for a burger at McDonald's. People with more money than God walked by ignoring him. Typical. "Tell me why she's coming here."

"I picked up her trail in Fiji. You remember Fiji?"

Fiji. According to what the Council had told us,

five Fixers had cornered her in a remote resort villa. "They said the team killed her."

"They lied."

"I heard that earlier. She killed them instead, I take it."

"Yeah. One of the team was a good friend of mine, Lawson. We came up through the training together."

I knew how painful it could be to lose a friend. I'd lost my closest pal not too long ago and it still hurt like a bitch—and not just when it rained. If I hadn't executed the sonofabitch who killed my friend, I'd be a seething mess. And even though he hid it well, I knew Jarvis must have wanted vengeance.

Neither of us spoke for a minute. Maybe it was out of mutual respect for the dead. Then Jarvis cleared his throat. "I almost nailed her in San Jose last week."

"What was she doing out in California?"

"Don't know. Don't care. She caught a flight to St. Louis and then came east to New York and then here. I have no idea what she's up to. But I'm not stupid enough to think I could take her down alone. Especially if I can have a backup shooter like you."

"Flattery?" I grinned. "Damn, she must have you running scared if you'd resort to complimenting me."

"Think of it more as a healthy respect than an outright terror, would ya? I've got a reputation to keep."

"Buddy, the way you run your life, I don't think your rep'll ever be in danger."

"Yeah, you're probably right. Still, she is one formidable chick."

"That's certainly one way to phrase it. Where'd you lose her?"

"The airport actually. I know she was heading here, though. Just can't figure out for the life of me why. I spent the entire flight pondering that question."

In between harassing the flight attendants, most likely. "So, what kind of head start you figure she's got on us?"

"Few hours tops. Still, with that kind of lead, she could be anywhere in the city by now."

"All right, where do we start then?"

Jarvis pulled out a sheaf of papers. "I found these back in California. Haven't been able to make much sense of them. They're coded. They mean anything to you?"

I looked them over, but the weird script covering the pages meant nothing to me. "Probably means zilch to anyone but her."

"Yeah."

"You bring your piece with you?"

"Had to ditch it before the flight." He glanced to his right and exhaled. "Wow, now there's a looker."

I checked. The woman stood about five feet five inches. Tall, but not wispy thin. Good curves. I moved higher, looking at the quality of her eyes. Good eyes on a woman have always won me over.

Bright blue. Almost too bright.

I frowned. There was no softness in them. Only a vague tinge of femininity.

She moved then, drawing her right arm slowly toward her left breast, which was covered with a navy blazer. Beside me, Jarvis grunted.

"Nice . . ."

She smiled, almost milking the moment.

And then she flicked her wrist so casually you would have noticed only if you were staring at her like we were.

I moved, yanking Jarvis with me off the side of the monument where we sat.

We plunged to the ground even as the air above us whispered sharply as the projectiles went zooming toward where our heads had been a second before.

"Shit!"

I pushed Jarvis down and away from me even as I reached under my shirt and grabbed for my gun behind my right hip.

I rolled left, drawing the pistol up from low-ready, searching for a target.

Those people closest to us began screaming when they saw the gun.

Not good.

The woman was gone.

Shiva.

It had to be.

Here I was concerned about how we were going to track her and she was already tracking us.

Jarvis had recovered himself and was busy looking at the soil by the monument's feet. "Fuck."

Seeing that Shiva had vanished for the time being, I put my gun away. Jarvis and I needed to get lost fast. Fanueil Hall sat about a block away from a police station and even the fattest desk sergeant could run that in the space of a minute.

"We gotta fly, dude."

He turned. "Check this shit out."

I looked down into his palm. Three flat pieces of wood about three inches across sat in it, the obviously sharpened edges tainted by dark soil.

I recognized the shape of the plates. "*Shuriken.*"

Jarvis turned around and we started moving. "What's that?"

"Those plates. They're called *shuriken*. Means hand blade in Japanese."

"She's using Japanese weapons?"

"The idea of them anyway." We dodged between two parked cars and hoofed it up toward the State Street Orange Line station. "Traditionally, they're made out of metal. Obviously, Shiva would opt for wood."

"But wood alone wouldn't have killed us."

"Maybe they're explosive."

"The edges are wet."

I took one of them and sniffed it. "Shit."

"What?"

"Smells like turpentine."

"So?"

"So turpentine is distilled from pine tree sap. Distilled tree sap can kill us if it gets into our bloodstreams."

Jarvis sighed. "We almost bought it back there. One of these things had stuck us, we woulda been through."

He was right. Even as much as his proclivity toward hawking women pissed me off, if he hadn't noticed Shiva, we might both be dead. As usual, working with Jarvis was proving at once as dangerous as it was necessary.

The weight of the shuriken surprised me, being heavier than I imagined. But it would have to be in order to fly straight beyond a few yards. I peered closer at it once we were past the subway turnstiles. Behind us, police sirens wailed in the afternoon heat.

"Lignum vitae," I said.

"Huh?"

"Toughest wood known. Makes sense she'd use this. It's tough as hell, can be ground to a fine edge, and has the weight necessary for this kind of weapon."

"You know a lot about these . . . shuriken?"

"Hollywood made 'em popular a few years back during the ninja boom of the 1980's," I said. "It's an authentic weapon, to be sure. Although most ninjutsu students wouldn't say they were designed to kill, more to distract."

"Ninja?" Jarvis chuckled. "Come on, Lawson. You telling me Shiva is a ninja?"

"I'm not saying that at all. I'm saying she's using weapons once used by ninja. Shiva's no ninja, believe me. But she's one helluva dangerous assassin."

"Tell me something I don't know." A train rolled into the station, rushing hot breezes along the platform, flicking newspapers and papers along the gutters. We stepped inside and grabbed seats across from each other so we could better watch the train's interior.

Jarvis leaned across the aisle. "Where to?"

"Let's get you outfitted properly. We can stop by my . . . Control's place." I winced when I said it. Having Niles as a Control made me feel insecure.

And working with Jarvis made me about as happy as a blind pig swimming with piranha.

Four

We grabbed my black Ford Explorer from the parking garage outside Back Bay station, rolled down Berkeley to where it fed into Beacon, and followed that up and out toward Brighton. Ordinarily, the drive to Brighton might take about twenty minutes depending on the flow of traffic.

But past experience has taught me it's better to drive fast when I'm heading somewhere with Jarvis. Thank God traffic was light. Jarvis spent the entire ride extolling the sexual virtues of the Swedish women's volleyball team that he'd met during their promotional tour in Singapore.

Valdeck Street sat in the middle of a typical middle-class neighborhood. As we drove down the two-family homes lining either side of the street, I counted ten children of every race and creed playing in the warm sunshine. None of them seemed to care what color the other was. I admired that.

I found Niles's address and slid the Explorer along the curb. Jarvis leaned over. "This your Control's place?"

"Apparently."

He sniffed. "Kind of a dump."

I looked at him. "When did you find time to join the Martha Stewart fan club?"

"Just making an observation."

"Yeah, well, ease off when you meet this guy. He's a little jumpy."

I rang the doorbell and we waited. Dance music filtered out of the screens, and I tapped my foot in time to the beat. As a rule, I hate nightclubs. But last year, I'd had some interesting times in a few here in town.

When Niles finally opened the door, a sheen of sweat coated him like a newly waxed sports car.

I looked him over. He wore skintight spandex pants that showed just how disadvantaged his genetics were, and a gray sweatshirt with some Latin phrase emblazoned across the chest.

"You, uh, busy?"

He actually panted. "No. Just finishing up a workout."

"What kind?"

"Pilates."

Jarvis smirked. "Rubber bands?"

Niles frowned. "Let me guess. You must be Jarvis."

"That's right."

Niles nodded. "Come in." He backed up and we walked inside.

Hardwood floors and a thin carpet greeted us. A narrow couch sat to one side of the living room, while a few milk crates served as a coffee table. In the corner, a cloth chair sat snuggled against bookshelves.

But if the furniture gave the initial impression that Niles spent a great deal of time Dumpster-diving, I knew it was the kind of high-priced crap so-called artists dig out of trash heaps, blow some environmentally friendly paint over, and then resell for gobs of cash.

Pretentiousness annoys the crap out of me.

In the center of the living room sat the Pilates contraption. It looked a little like some S&M dungeon here in town might be missing one of their torture devices.

Jarvis ran his hand over it. "You really get a workout from this thing?"

"Incredible," said Niles. He plopped down on the couch. "What can I do for you boys?"

I nodded at Jarvis. "The boy . . . needs a weapon."

"A gun?" Niles sat up quickly.

"That's generally what we use, yeah."

"I don't have any guns here," said Niles curtly.

Jarvis looked at me and waggled his eyebrows, which he is wont to do when he is amused and annoyed at the same time. "Can you get me a piece?"

"Controls usually have guns for their agents," I said.

"I don't," said Niles. "You'll have to go to the Council."

"Oh, for crying out loud." I sighed. "You telling me that you're my Control—that you're the Control on this op—and you don't even have any weapons stocked here? I find this very hard to believe. I've never met a Control who didn't know his way around guns."

"I know my way around them just fine," said Niles. "But I told the Council I preferred not to have any dealings with weapons."

Jarvis looked at me again. "Just how desperate were they to find you a replacement?"

"Apparently very much so," I said. "Might have been my fault too. I've been on them something fierce since I killed McKinley."

"Helluva sense of humor on those guys, huh?"

"I'm not exactly dying of laughter here, Jarvis." I looked at Niles again. "All right. So, you don't have any weapons."

"Go to the Council."

I frowned. Going to the Council was probably the last thing I wanted to do. I try to avoid them like the plague. Come to think of it, they try to avoid me as well. We tend to piss each other off.

I try to do my job the way it's supposed to be done, which is to say properly. The Council shoves tons of bureaucratic bullshit in my way and questions everything I do.

We're a match made in heaven.

I had plenty of weapons at my place, but I wasn't altogether thrilled about bringing Jarvis home. For one thing, I don't like a lot of people knowing where I live. Jarvis was the kind of guy who'd roll into town without telling you and then show up drunk at three in the morning on the arm of some cheap slut.

No, thanks.

Plus, my attack cats, Mimi and Phoebe, would probably tear him to shreds. Well, Mimi would. Phoebe would run away, come back, run away again, and finally try to con Jarvis into feeding her.

I looked at him. "You got a place to stay?"

"No."

I cocked an eyebrow. "This isn't your usual style, Jarvis. Normally you got a piece and a place when you come to town."

"Yeah, well, it's been a long time since I was here last. I haven't befriended any of Boston's lovelies. And as for resources—where I can get a gun—well, that's tougher than you'd think nowadays."

"Yeah?"

"Well, especially here in the Northeast. If we were down in Alabama, I could rustle up a gun no sweat."

"If we were down South, you wouldn't last all that long with that cheap cologne you showered with."

"What about you? You got any spare guns at your place?"

"If I loan one to you, am I gonna get it back?"

Jarvis grinned. "Hey, Lawson, who you talking to here? It's me, remember? 'Course you're gonna get the piece back. I promise."

"You need a hotel," I said. No way was this guy going to stay with me at my pad.

He looked hurt. "We aren't bunking together?"

"My criteria for roommates is very strict."

"Yeah?"

I nodded. "You'd need to dump about sixty pounds, lose about five inches of height, and grow a set of boobs."

"Funny guy."

"You aren't the first to mention that."

Jarvis sighed. "I bet I could get the Council to make you take me in."

"And I'll bet I could kill you in your sleep if you do that too."

Behind Jarvis, Niles blanched like I'd just dragged dog crap in on the heel of my shoe. I smiled. "Why not hang out with Niles here? I bet you guys would have a lot in common. Plenty to talk about."

Niles's eyebrows jumped off his forehead. Jarvis grinned. "Hey, not a bad idea. What do you say, Niles?"

"Uh . . . I don't have any room."

"Well, not with this contraption hogging up all

your available space," I said, patting the Pilates machine. "But if you moved it, Jarvis here could slap down a futon or a sleeping bag and be pretty comfy."

Jarvis put a hand to his chin and nodded. "I could at that."

Beads of sweat ran down Niles's forehead. I didn't think they were due to his workout either. He said quietly, "I don't know if that's such a good idea."

"More of a loner, aren't you, Niles?"

"Yes."

Jarvis put his hands on his hips. "Well, that's settled then. Guess I'm gonna have to find me a hotel." He looked at me. "Got one in mind?"

"We can find you one," I said. "That's not a problem. But you need a gun first. I don't like the thought of you going around unarmed. Not with Shiva already tracking us."

Niles perked up. "You saw her? Already?"

"She tried to kill us," I said. "Does that count?"

"So you saw her?"

"We saw a woman. Yes."

"What did she look like?"

"Like a hot babe," said Jarvis.

"Doesn't matter a damned bit," I said breaking in. "Shiva can change herself into anyone she wants. That's her power, Niles. What she looked like earlier today won't be what she looks like later."

"Then how will you track her?"

"Obviously," I said, "looks are out. We'll have to figure something else out. For right now, I don't have a clue. Unless Jarvis here has some new information that might help us."

"Me?" He shook his head. "No idea."

"Then we're screwed until we do. Nothing to do

for now. Let's get you set up and then we can do a game plan."

Jarvis looked at Niles. "Sorry it didn't work out—the roommate thing."

Niles looked worried again. "Oh . . . uh, yeah. Oh, well."

I shook my head and followed Jarvis outside into the sunlight.

Niles was one strange bird.

Jarvis was one dangerous dude.

And Shiva? She just completed the veritable hellish hat trick for me.

Five

Ordinary handguns in Boston are cheap and plentiful, but only if you know where to look. Fixer handguns are not.

Thank God.

The last thing I needed were more kids on the street selling things that could kill me. So, Jarvis and I bypassed the normal bullet-propulsion-device distribution channels and headed back to my least favorite building in town: the Council. After all, I wasn't about to bring Jarvis home and loan him one of mine. The less he knew about me, the better, I felt.

Even if that meant I had to endure the Council.

It was two o'clock when we rolled into the underground parking facility known as the Boston Common garage. I managed to get the Explorer nudged into a space between a Subaru and a Toyota, both of which were improperly parked. What was it about people being unable to drive or park their cars these days?

Ascending the steps brought us out into the warm sunlight of summer in Boston. Most days, it got up to around eighty-five with moderate humidity. In short, it could be real sticky here.

We lucked out today, though. The temperature hovered in the mid-seventies with little stickiness. A cool sea breeze wafted in off Boston Harbor, threaded its way through the underside of Government Center, and blew through Beacon Hill.

The Council building sat in a series of brownstones on Beacon Street. From the outside, the main building looked like any other townhouse that bordered the Common: old and rich, albeit small. On the inside, however, the Council building was linked to the townhouses on either side of it some three deep, making it much larger than you'd think.

Jarvis sniffed as we passed through the wrought-iron gate. "Know how long it's been since I was here last?"

"You betting money I don't know?"

"Nah, casual question only."

"Years?" I was feeling especially precise today.

"Brilliant, Holmes." He half-grinned, half-sneered. "Not since my centennial."

"That long?"

"Yup."

"You aren't going to get all weepy and homesick on me, are you? I don't think I could stomach that."

"Don't you ever get nostalgic?"

I smirked. "Unfortunately, I end up here far too often to ever miss the place."

Jarvis ignored me. "So many years have passed since my last visit."

Vampires age a lot slower than normal humans thanks to the fact that the blood we ingest contains human life force. It tends to slow down our metabolism to the point where years pass a lot slower.

But when we reach one hundred—what we call our centennial—all vampires come before the Council and have their destiny determined. For some, it's just a matter of getting to be an accountant. For others—guys like Jarvis and me—we get to be Fixers.

Actually, "get" is probably the wrong word to use since our role in vampire society seems to be preordained long before we have such a silly illusory thing as choice.

"You haven't been back since?"

"Nope."

"What about when they put you onto Shiva?"

"Orders came through my Control. No need to come back here and waste valuable time when I could be out hunting her down."

"And now . . . here you are."

He sighed. "Yeah."

"Really moving up in the world, huh?"

He looked at me and laughed. I rang the bell.

Two minutes passed before the door opened and Arthur greeted us. A former Fixer, Arthur still looked as alert as ever, despite giving off the appearance that he was anything but. I'd first met him close to a year before when he cornered me with a shotgun after I broke into the building.

He knew how to use it too.

Since that time, we'd gotten to know each other a bit more. I liked him. He was as British as they come and his acerbic wit kept me in smiles whenever I visited.

He looked us both over. He finally settled on me. "Lawson."

I grinned. "Arthur. How ya doing?"

"Be better if I needn't answer the door for a couple of lads like you and Smelly here."

I looked at Jarvis. I'd gotten used to the cologne he wore in the hours we'd been together. Arthur picked up on it right away.

Jarvis stuck out his hand. "I'm Jarvis."

Arthur looked at the hand and then back at Jarvis with narrowed eyes. Then he looked at me. "He with the service?"

"Uh-huh."

He opened the door and let us in. "Interesting."

Jarvis tucked his hand into his pocket and followed me inside. Cool air washed over us. It felt good.

Arthur stood closer to me. "What can I do for you?" He thumbed down a hallway. "They're in meetings if ya come to see 'em."

"I was hoping we could do this without seeing them actually," I said.

"I'll bet," said Arthur with a trace of a smile. He sniffed the air and frowned at Jarvis. "Didn't they teach you about scents back in training?"

Jarvis cocked an eyebrow and looked at me.

"Arthur used to be a Fixer," I said.

"Ah." He looked back at Arthur. "When? Back when Columbus was around?"

Arthur placed a hand over his heart. "Such a wit. Someone help me."

Jarvis frowned. "Times've changed, old man. We can wear cologne."

Arthur started to chuckle. "You working with this one, Lawson?"

"For the moment."

"Be a dead moment, you aren't careful. Guy stinks to high bloody heavens. You got enemies, they'll smell him coming and waste you both before you get a shot off."

"Yeah, we may need to discuss that," I said. "Arthur, he needs a gun."

"Needs a bath, what he needs," said Arthur. "Where's his pistol?"

"Airplanes don't like it when you travel with guns," said Jarvis. "Have you ever seen an airplane, old man?"

Arthur snorted and looked at me. "Really impressed with himself, this one is, eh?" He gestured for us to follow him. "We'll go down to the armory."

I'd been to the armory only a few times before. It lay deep in one of the subbasements in the Council building. We walked through the kitchen and into a large pantry that concealed a hidden door and elevator. We got inside the narrow car, and Arthur pushed a series of buttons in an order I couldn't make out.

The car descended.

Arthur sneezed.

"Damn cologne's cheap too," he muttered.

The car slowed to a stop and the doors slid back. A fresh scent of cordite and oil hung heavy in the air, draping over us like a thick cloak. I noticed a new layer of sound-baffling panels all over the walls.

"What's with th—" I started to ask, but the sound of gunfire coming from the room ahead of us interrupted me.

When it stopped, Arthur grinned. "That's why. We finally got a range built down here."

We came abreast of the doorway. Arthur poked his head inside. "Marty!"

I peered in and saw a woman about my age sighting down a long range with a rifle. She was dressed in jeans and a shooting shirt with reinforced elbow pads. She wore gun shields over her ears and thick glasses. She glanced back at the sound of Arthur's voice and smiled.

"Arto."

I grinned. "Arto?"

Arthur shot me a look filled with spears. "She's the only one who can call me that, Lawson. You'd do well to remember that."

"Understood."

Marty pulled the ear protectors off and they slid down to the base of her neck. I glanced at the rifle.

"That looks like a PSG-9."

She nodded. "Latest generation. You ever shoot one before?"

"Once or twice. I like the MP5 and USP as well."

"Discriminating taste."

"They work when I pull the trigger. That's important."

She grinned and then looked at Arthur. "So, what's up?"

Arthur poked a thumb at Jarvis. "Boy needs a weapon. Can ya outfit him?"

"You a Fixer?" she asked looking at Jarvis.

Jarvis's face took on the look he usually reserved for his sexual conquests. He extended his hand and his greasy charm. "I'm Jarvis."

"Marty. Short for Martina." Marty wrinkled her nose. Most of the time I find that cute on women. But Marty managed to take all the beauty out of it. "That's some cologne you have on there."

I smiled. "He just flew in from California. Couldn't take the gun on the plane."

She nodded. "What's your pleasure, Jarvis?" She went to the wall and slid back a section of it, revealing a long line of weapons. "I got some new Sig Sauers in along with some of the Smith & Wessons.

I just retooled the 9mm's. I'm still doing some work on the 10mm's."

"Uh . . . 9mm'd be fine."

She took one down and handed it to him. "Want to try it?"

Jarvis nodded and moved up to the firing line. We all pulled on the gun shields and glasses that Marty handed out.

Marty handed Jarvis a loaded magazine. He slid it in, chambered a round, sighted, and squeezed off ten shots in pairs at the target downrange. Shells popped out sounding like tinny bells in the close confines of the range.

Fresh smoke issued from the end of the barrel as Jarvis popped the magazine out and worked the slide, making sure the chamber was empty.

"Fires nice."

Marty pushed the retrieval button for the target, and we watched as it came back to the counter. Jarvis's bullets had gone through dead center. His aim was still top-notch.

"No pull. No anticipation of recoil." Marty nodded. "Nice work."

"Nice gun," said Jarvis. "Thanks."

Marty handed him a clipboard. "Gotta sign it out." She plopped three more magazines, a holster, and two boxes of ammunition down in front of him. "This oughta keep you in good measure for a bit."

"Never know," I said. "We might be back for more ammo."

"More?" Marty frowned. "Who are you guys after?"

Jarvis finished signing his name. "We could tell you," he said. "But then we'd have to kill you."

Marty looked at him, her eyebrows already reaching for the heavens. "Are you kidding me with that shitty come-on line? I get better play from the winos lounging around Park Street and Downtown Crossing."

Jarvis recovered quickly. "Sure, just kidding."

"So," said Marty. "Who is it?"

I sighed. "Ever hear of Shiva?"

The looks on Marty's and Arthur's faces told me they'd heard of her before.

They'd heard plenty.

Six

Jarvis and I left the Council building and headed across the street to Boston Common. The early August sky overhead seemed an especially crisp blue. A few green maple leaves fluttered off the trees and wafted toward the ground as we walked along the paved path.

"You still haven't told me why Shiva's here."

"I'm not sure I know," said Jarvis.

I looked at him. "You've got a sheaf of papers there with some kind of coded writing on it. You've been tracking her for months. You probably know her better than anyone else in the service, and you don't have any idea as to why she's here?" I frowned. "I don't like this gig already."

Jarvis sat down on a bench. "All right."

I turned. "What?"

"Sit down, Lawson. I'll fill you in on a few things."

He'd been holding out on me. What a surprise. Jarvis had always held out information. The guy was stingier with intelligence than anyone else I'd ever known.

I sat. "So?"

"Shiva is here to assassinate Belarus."

Oh, Christ. The look on my face must have given it away because Jarvis grinned.

"See? This is why I held out on you. I didn't want to tell you that."

Belarus.

The head of the Council—he insisted the stress on his name pronunciation was nothing like the country of Belarus. He pronounced it Be-LAR-us, as if changing the normal pronunciation would endear him to the populace.

I liked him about as much as I like having my tonsils ripped out with a chain saw. Belarus was one of these fools who saw little use for Fixers. But I'd always felt there was something else to him. Some kind of alternate personality lying under the superficial front he always put on.

And now Shiva was gunning for him. Talk about being torn between saving Belarus and helping his killer. I almost grinned at the thought.

"Why is she after Belarus?"

"That's what I don't know."

I looked at him.

"I don't know. Honest."

I let out a big breath of air and watched a jogger go flying past us, bouncing too heavily on his heels. He'd have serious knee problems within a few years if he didn't already.

"Do we have to protect him?"

As a rule, Fixers aren't used for protection. We've got other fish to fry. In truth, there's not all that much need for protection. We don't normally have assassins gunning for members of our government.

In my world, the government actually manages to get some respect from its citizens. Of course, we don't have elections either.

But if Shiva decided to go after Belarus, that could put a different spin on things.

And the idea of protecting Belarus didn't make me feel all warm and fuzzy inside.

Jarvis shook his head. "No. We aren't protecting him. That make you feel better?"

"Only marginally."

"We're proactive on this one. Our job is to get to Shiva first. Make sure she doesn't get a chance to bring off her plan."

"So, who watches Belarus?"

"Apparently," said Jarvis, "Belarus can take care of himself."

"He tell you that?"

"Yes."

I looked at Jarvis. He didn't look convinced. I wasn't convinced either. The last time I'd seen Belarus after bringing back an Invoker named Jack, I hadn't been impressed with him at all.

"That got you worried?"

He nodded. "Well, sure. I mean, if she's gunning for him, then we should be around him. What chance do we have of getting to her first? She'll be zeroing in on him, not walking around town leaving us all sorts of goodies to follow."

"Belarus is a conceited fool," I said.

Jarvis's face contorted like I'd just suggested he swallow diesel fuel. "Isn't that a little harsh?"

"How long have you known him?"

"Me? Not long, why?"

"Then you don't know shit, pardon me saying so."

"I forgot, you've got something of a past with him, don't you?"

"Who told you that?"

"The grapevine."

I nodded. "Yeah, well, the truth is I don't much care for the way he handles things. Yeah, I know he runs the Council and that's all well and good. And I can separate my duty from my personal inclinations. It's possible to be a patriot and hate your top boss."

"If you say so."

"Plenty of humans manage to do it. Why should they have an exclusive on it?"

"We're discussing human politics now?"

I looked at him. "If Belarus is really in danger, he ought to have some protection."

"He is in danger. But he won't take it," said Jarvis. "I tried to insist."

"When did you do that?"

He looked up. "What?"

"I asked when you did that. You just got to town. You've been chasing Shiva for months. When did you have time to talk to Belarus?"

Jarvis grinned. "You think I went behind your back?"

"I think you'd better explain how exactly you talked to Belarus about protection when you've supposedly been on the road flying from hub to hub."

"You think I came to Boston without notifying you?"

It was standard practice for a Fixer to notify the local Control and Fixer when he'd be in town, even if it was just for a pleasure visit. Being a Fixer, you tend to get nervous when you see another agent on your turf without being told about it.

I glanced back toward Beacon Street. "Did you?"

"No."

"So?"

"What?"

"How'd you talk to Belarus?"

"You ever hear of a phone, Lawson?"

"You're telling me you guys are phone buddies now? Regular Chatty Cathys?"

"I called him from the field, yes. When it became apparent that Shiva was heading to Boston. I knew we'd need to get you involved. I called Belarus. I spoke with him about my concerns, about what we'd need to do to stop her. He agreed about getting you into the case."

"But he disagreed about the protection."

"Yeah."

I sighed. "What fools these vampires be."

"Paraphrasing like that might be considered sacrilege."

"Might be considered appropriate too." I grinned. "Especially by me."

Jarvis stood. "We're wasting time."

"We are?"

"We should be hunting her."

I stood and chuckled. "Okay, Sherlock, why don't you tell me how you plan to do that? I mean, I'm standing here and not seeing shit as far as clues go. So, unless you've held out on me yet again, and happen to have some clues, I'd sure as hell be curious to see what you propose next."

Jarvis ran a hand through his gelled hair and sighed. "I don't have the vaguest idea."

"Tell me something I don't know."

He looked at me. "So, what do we do now?"

I looked at my watch. "Well, it's getting on dinnertime. I propose we adjourn this little strategy session to a nearby restaurant, fortify ourselves with good food, and talk some more about how we put an end to Shiva's illustrious career."

"That's all you've got?"

"You expecting something more?"

"Don't you have a network of contacts we can start shaking up? See if they've seen anything?"

"Oh, sure. That'll be good. I'll just phone them all up and ask, 'Hey, have you seen a woman who can transform herself into anyone she wants? She's part lycanthrope and deadly as all get-out. Oh, and by the way, she uses these wooden shuriken as her main weapon that are lethal to vampires like me.'" I looked at Jarvis. "Don't be stupid. We find Shiva, it's going to be all us and no one else."

"What makes you so sure of that?"

I frowned. "Because Shiva hasn't gotten so good at what she does by relying on other people. She operates alone. She is her own network, her own safety net. She doesn't involve anyone else. That's what makes her so lethal. So damned anonymous. She can slip in and out without even leaving a trace. She doesn't have to worry about being compromised by someone, because there is no one else. It's her alone, operating in the cold. And she likes it in the cold."

"You sound impressed," said Jarvis.

"The woman took out five Fixers, Jarvis. At least. Maybe there's even more. And she's never gone through our training. To be a natural-born killer like that? You bet your ass I'm impressed."

"A little scared?"

"Don't play that macho bullshit with me. I gave up all that pretense a while back. I call it like I see it. And I'd be a damned fool if I wasn't a little scared around Shiva."

We stood there for another minute. Jarvis looked around at nothing in particular. I watched him look around.

Finally, he cleared his throat and turned back to face me. "This restaurant, it any good?"

"You like Chinese food?"

"Who doesn't?"

"I knew a girl once who didn't. I think probably because it mixed with her lithium and gave her one helluvan MSG headache."

"How fascinating."

"You're as sarcastic as I am, you know that?"

"It's been mentioned. I'm getting hungry."

I nodded. "Then let's go. This restaurant is the best damned place you've ever eaten at."

Seven

Why I took Jarvis to dinner is a question that will haunt me for a long time. Well, maybe not. But at the time, it certainly did.

Over the hot and sour soup, he told me about the string of lovers he'd taken while supposedly hunting Shiva. While we ate Peking duck, he recounted a vacation in Bali with three women. And during my favorite spicy beef with red peppers, Jarvis told me about how he'd once licked the hot chocolate off two blondes in Rome.

By the time the bill arrived, I was ready to shoot him and go after Shiva by myself.

I dumped him off at the Four Seasons Hotel and said good night. The fact that he was spending his nights in a five-star hotel didn't rattle me much. In our society, we want very little for money. Jarvis could stay in a palace for all I cared, provided it got him done with his mission and out of my town that much sooner.

After all, I wasn't sure how much longer I could put up with the living incarnation of Penthouse Forum. I pulled out of the Four Seasons and slid back on to Boylston briefly.

Truth was, Jarvis had been telling tall tales of sexual blitzkriegs as long as I'd known him. And that was a helluva lot longer than I wanted to admit.

Most of the time, his stories turned out to be just that. But on rare occasion, he did score. I think somewhere along the line, he started believing in his own prowess. That confidence apparently struck a chord with the ladies.

Me? I'd always lacked a little in the self-confidence area. I could hypnotize and magnetize women with the best of them, but using just my natural charm sometimes backfired in a bad way.

Made me wonder why someone like Talya had fallen for me.

And that made me miss her a whole lot all of a sudden.

A lot of cars tagged along behind me—I noticed and made some mental notes. Like I always do.

I slid up Boylston to Tremont and banged a right, heading into the Theater District. From there, the shot back to Jamaica Plain was pretty simple.

I wove in and out of traffic watching the flow behind me do the same. Up and around the New England Medical Center, I lost most of the cars behind me.

Except for one.

The same headlights that I'd picked up just after I left the hotel.

I made a mental note to stop hanging around the Four Seasons. My track record for good things happening around that place has not been a good one.

Picking out a tail at night is tough. Darkness limits the ability to see colors and definite makes and models of cars. Instead of trying to make any of those details out, you stick with what you can see: headlights, front grillwork, and extra lights.

An expert tail won't get close enough for you to

see his or her face. For that matter, a professional will work with at least three other cars. They'll run patterns around the target; sometimes driving parallels, sometimes driving a box, and sometimes other techniques even more obscure.

But if you're alone and you're forced to tail someone, your choices are limited. You've got to keep the target car in sight, and stay far enough back that you don't get burned.

I broke out of the Chinatown neighborhood and onto Tremont Street again in the South End. Traffic on this road was two lanes. That made options tougher.

What I took to be my tail had nestled itself in about three cars back. Close. They must have been frustrated, but traffic just wasn't heavy.

I crossed over Massachusetts Avenue and further on behind Northeastern University, I turned left and caught Columbus Avenue. Columbus gave both the tail and me more options. This part of Columbus held four lanes that seeped out of the South End, skirted Roxbury, and ran into Jamaica Plain.

The tail tucked itself back about five cars.

I slid into the right lane and slowed my speed. I checked my rearview mirror.

The tail was already in the right lane. Obviously, they'd guessed my move.

I turned right near the Roxbury Crossing T stop, and slid up to take a left on Parker Hill Road. It was a one-lane one-way street that wound its way up and over Mission Hill. It was a good way of verifying if you had a tail or not.

I shot up the street, adding some gas, trying to use the curves to my advantage. Nothing appeared in my rearview mirror.

Maybe I'd imagined it.

I shook my head. I don't imagine things. Not when you've got as many years in the service as I have. In fact, the only time I usually ran into trouble was when I second-guessed my instincts.

I'd made a mental note a long time ago to stop doing that. If I could keep my logical mind at bay, I'd be okay.

That's easier said than done.

I dropped down on the other side of Mission Hill and circled the rotary at the base, zipping back out to Columbus Avenue and turning right to head back toward Jackson Square. At Centre Street, I turned right, consciously checking my rearview mirror every twenty seconds.

Nothing.

I breathed out, releasing some tension. Whoever'd been behind me had obviously figured out they'd been spotted. That was almost as good as them not being there at all.

Almost.

At Lamartine Street I turned left and shot down going a good clip. I like to drive fast. Always have. In my experience, it's not the people who drive fast that are the problem. It's the ones who drive as if they're terrified of every little thing in front of them. Indecision and cowardice kill more often than not.

Lamartine dumped me out on Green and I jumped Centre further on from there. I slowed down going past JP Licks, briefly considering heading in for a coffee Oreo ice cream. Then I remembered what ice cream does to me after a hearty meal. I kept driving.

At the Civil War monument I eased right and

continued down Centre Street. Still, I kept a close watch on my rearview mirror.

And still, nothing.

Good.

If there'd been someone back there, the last thing I would have done was drive straight home.

Techniques for dumping tails are as varied as the techniques you can use to tail someone. Long, winding roads are good. So are streets full of alleyways, driveways, and cul de sacs.

So is just stopping the car and shooting the sonofabitch.

One of my favorite techniques involves a stretch of road out in Cambridge. It's got a nice straightaway and plenty of intersecting streets. I dumped a tail there once by accelerating very quickly, throwing a handbrake one-eighty, and speeding in the opposite direction and then disappearing quickly down one of several side streets. That part of Cambridge has so many small intersecting streets that unless you know the area as well as I do, you'll get hopelessly lost and confused.

And I disappear.

Technically, you can do the same thing in Jamaica Plain. But I don't like tearing down streets around here since my neighbors know what kind of car I drive.

The last thing I wanted was one of them traipsing over to my place, ringing the bell, and standing there with a self-righteous expression as they told me to stop speeding along the streets. The Jamaica Plain I grew up in was a different place from what's it's become now. Nowadays, there are far too many Earthy-crunchy folks whose parents must have done mucho drugs back in the 60's. Bumper stickers espousing love and peace and tolerance plaster a lot of JP's cars. And that's cool. But sometimes the emphasis is a little misdirected. Some of these folks need a lot more common sense in their lives.

I smiled at the thought of what they'd do if they knew what I really was.

So much for remaining anonymous.

I followed the Arborway up toward Jamaica Pond and rolled clear around it one more time, just in case my tail was too far back for me to see, or running without their lights.

Coming back on Parkman Drive, I still had no cars behind me. I headed up the backside of Moss Hill anyway, turned left onto Rockwood Street, and followed that over to Pond Street and back down to the Arborway.

If it sounds extremely circuitous, it was. But that's how you make sure your six is clean before you head home to the roost.

At least, that's one way you do it.

The other way involves phoning up several friends, planning a rendezvous, and leading the tail into an ambush. You then confront the tail, interrogate him or her, and then do whatever else is necessary.

Unfortunately, I don't have many friends so that option is rarely a viable one. I'm not sure it'd work that well anyway.

On a whim, I peered out through my windshield. I doubted it, but nowadays, technology's pretty cheap. An industrious soul can purchase a homing device and a receiver pretty easily. They could put a chopper over me, tail me from a height I couldn't even see them at, and I'd never be the wiser.

I didn't see anything.

I slid my window down.

I didn't hear anything either.

I yawned.

Hell with this. Time to head home.

I reached behind my right hip and unsnapped the restraining clasp on my holster, just in case.

I rolled down my street.

I live about halfway down on the left. It's an old Victorian about a hundred years old. My ancestors built it when they came over from Germany. It's been with me for a long time.

Usually, parking on my street fluctuates from no spaces at all to completely empty. When it's crowded, everyone seems to park in front of my house. Maybe I should practice martial arts and target shooting on my lawn. Maybe that way they'd stop parking there.

I reconsidered. Knowing these people, they were so oblivious, they wouldn't notice an asteroid if it hit them on the ass.

I slid the Volvo into the space in front of my house, partially amazed I could. I threw another glance into my rearview mirror.

Nothing.

I sighed. Good.

I got out of my car.

Turned.

A car I hadn't seen before was parked across the street from my house. And it had the same front grille and headlight build I'd seen tailing me.

I forgot to mention a particularly neat tailing trick. If you know where your target lives, or is headed, you can simply break off the surveillance and pick them up later on.

When they reach their destination.

That way, they get lulled into a false sense of security and start blathering on about their oblivious neighbors.

I started to reach back for my gun.

I started to.

But I stopped.

When I heard the voice.

"I wouldn't do that, Lawson."

I stopped; not because of what the voice said. I could have cared less about that.

I stopped because I recognized the voice.

I hadn't heard it in almost a year.

Had it been that long?

I turned.

Already smiling.

Sitting on my front steps, hidden in the shadows.

Talya.

Eight

Surprise is something I try to limit in my life. You don't stay alive very long as a Fixer if you jump at every unexpected thing that comes your way. And it's impossible, by and large, to be shot at as many times as I have and not develop some instincts about things.

But sometimes the instincts fail.

Sometimes the unexpected still throws you a serious curveball.

And sometimes you swing so hard at that curveball, you almost knock yourself over like a brand-new rookie on his first day of spring training.

But you swing anyway.

Talya.

God. It had almost been a year since I'd last seen her. The final image I had was her walking away from me. Almost running. Damned if I didn't love her, but she chose to leave, concerned about what might happen to us.

All because of the damned Council.

Falling in love with a human is one of those things that is absolutely forbidden in vampire society. Sex is okay. Hell, it's necessary. You need a little flesh-play sometimes just to get some juice off someone.

But love—no dice. The Council made it very clear

what would happen if I continued my affair with her. Talya chose to leave. Even though she loved me too.

She sat on my steps looking as beautiful in the darkness as the last time I saw her. Her hair was shorter now, cut to frame her sculpted eyebrows. She'd pass easily as a fashion model. But she'd be the deadliest thing on any runway she walked.

Her eyes glistened, half almonds paying tribute to her part-Russian, part-Chinese heritage.

And the lethality she emanated came off her in waves.

Controlled.

Disciplined.

Complete.

Talya'd been a professional hitter almost as long as I was. She'd worked for the KGB during the latter part of the Cold War, assigned to wet squads engaged in assassination work. Once the Berlin Wall came down and Communism waved farewell to Mother Russia, she went freelance. By her own admission, she'd done jobs for everyone from the Israeli Mossad to the Colombian cartels and assorted rogues in between.

I walked toward my steps and she came off of them in one fluid motion that reminded me of a jungle cat. Her lips glistened. I swept her up and into my arms, breathing deep of her scent. She smelled like a fresh shower of rose petals. That surprised me because she usually had a very slight scent only.

Her voice was velvet in my ear. "Lawson."

I kissed her on the neck, aware of the warm throb pulsing beneath her skin.

She pulled away with a smile. "Don't you even think about it, mister. I'll have to shoot you dead and that would spoil the evening."

"It's shameless the way you flirt with me."

She sighed and held me close again. "It's been too long. Far too long."

"Almost a year," I said pressing back into her. Her curves melded with mine. A perfect fit. "Where have you been?"

"Where haven't I been might be the better question. The market picked up suddenly. I had jobs to do. Places to go—"

"—people to kill."

She nodded. "People to kill. Yes."

I glanced up the street, still checking for lights. I turned back to her. "You the one following me around town?"

"You know anyone else who could do it as well as I can?"

"I tagged you pretty quick, sweetheart. You must be getting rusty."

She laughed. "You wish. You tagged me because I wanted you to."

That was probably very true. Talya'd been in the business long enough to know every trick in the book and then rewrite the stupid thing. I couldn't discount her skills. I didn't want to anyway. She was a pro in every sense of the word. And having gone through the wringer with her just twelve short months ago, I knew she could operate under the gun.

I respected her immensely.

"How'd you find out where I live?"

"How many Lawsons do you think live in this town?"

"Don't know. I'm unlisted."

"Unlisted." She laughed.

"You've got contacts obviously."

"So would you if you were in a strange town."

"You think Boston's a strange town?"

"I don't call it home."

I grinned. If it had been anyone else but Talya, I'd be pissed off. I take my privacy very seriously. Given what I do, it's essential. You don't stay alive as long as I have by giving out your number and address to every new friend you make.

But it was Talya.

I hugged her again. "I've missed you so damned much."

She pressed into me again. "Let's get inside. I don't much feel like putting on a show for your neighbors."

"Be the most action the lot of them have seen in ages anyway."

But we got inside anyway. As I unlocked the upstairs door, Mimi and Phoebe came tumbling down the steps. Phoebe took one look at Talya and ran away. She'd be back later when I cracked the can of Iams cat food open.

But Mimi, social butterfly that she was, promptly introduced herself to Talya. Talya stooped and rubbed Mimi's back. Mimi arched it and stuck her tail straight up to twelve o'clock. Mimi's ancestral line included some Coon cat. They must have been some damned sociable big cats.

Mimi licked Talya's hand and chirped appreciatively. I looked at Talya. She looked at me.

"What—you've never known a woman who had a way with felines?"

"I've never had a woman over here."

"You're joking."

"Well, aside from my neighbor."

"Oh?"

"She looks after the girls when I'm off on assignment."

"You mean when you're off killing people."

"Touché."

Talya smiled again. "You're lucky to have such friendly cats."

"Mimi's friendly. Phoebe is too. But she's kind of schizophrenic."

"I've known many who were."

"Many cats?"

"Many cats. Many people. In the end, does it really matter?"

"Probably not."

"We've had similar lives, Lawson. You know that?"

"I knew it a long time ago."

"Seems like years now, doesn't it?"

"Yeah."

Her lips glistened. "Did you really miss me, Lawson?"

"More than you know."

"More than you can show?"

"I don't know about that."

I kissed her then, pressed my lips to hers, tight, seeking. Wanton. She pressed back into me, melding every curve of her mouth and body to mine. A perfect union of two souls.

I tasted her. She tasted me. Our juices swirled and we moaned collectively, breaking the seal only to take a breath of air.

She leaned back against the counter. "I see you can still kiss with the best of them."

I wiped my mouth. She never used to salivate so much when we kissed. I chalked it up to time apart. "You're still pretty good yourself."

"Only pretty good?"

"Maybe too much tongue."

"Is there such a thing?"

"I think so."

She frowned. "You don't like the way I kiss."

"I didn't say that."

"Sounded like you did."

I pulled her to me again. I closed my eyes and sighed, hugging her close. Mimi pulled herself up on my leg, chirping. I looked down.

"Cat's hungry."

Talya nodded and slid away from me. Every movement she made was as economical as I've ever seen. She wasted no motion. Just enough. Each time.

I walked to the cabinet and pulled down a can of Iams Ocean Fish. I hate the smell, but my girls love it.

I cracked the can and heard Phoebe jump down from wherever she'd stowed herself and come tumbling ass-over-teakettle downstairs from the third floor.

She ran into the kitchen, ignoring Talya and heading straight to the dish. I plopped the contents into the ceramic bowl and stood back, watching them both attack it.

I chuckled and dumped the can in the trash. "Just give me a second to wash my hands."

"I'm not going anywhere."

I looked at her. "Thank God."

I walked down the hallway and ran some hot water, soaped up with the antibacterial soap, and scrubbed for a minute, remembering to sing "Happy Birthday" to myself to ensure the bacteria was destroyed.

I toweled off and strolled back down the hall.

Talya.

Here.

In my house.

I sighed. My day had been far too shitty, far too long, and far to just-not-what-I-wanted-it-to-be. I was completely thrilled that Talya was here.

I walked into the kitchen. Mimi and Phoebe were still gulping down cat food like they'd been starved for years.

Talya had disappeared.

I frowned and walked out of the kitchen.

"Talya?"

"Upstairs."

I grinned.

This was getting better by the minute. She'd already beaten me to the punch. My mind filled with images of the last time our bodies had joined. Back then, we'd been in a hotel over in Harvard Square. Things had been . . . stressed. We'd been hunting maniacs.

But the sex was still amazing.

I wondered if she had on nice underwear.

I'm a sucker for nice matching underwear.

Maybe tomorrow, it would be my turn to piss Jarvis off with some of my own sexual-escapade stories. Nah, I don't usually kiss and tell.

I walked upstairs. The lights were off. No matter. I can see very well in the darkness. I moved down the hall as quietly as I knew how. Moving quietly in my house is tough to do since the wooden floors were designed to creak if you apply weight to them. In Japan, they call them "nightingale floors" because they squeak.

I know a few techniques that enable me to bypass the squeaking.

My bedroom sat at the end of the hallway, the giant king-sized bed off to the right.

I framed the doorway. I could just make out her form on my bed.

"Lawson?"

"Yes."

"Come to me."

I moved toward the bed. I took a deep breath.

And stopped.

The scent—it had changed.

What the fuck?

I backed up, reaching for the light switch. My hand found it and flipped it on.

Light flooded the room, making me blink several times to get my vision straight.

The images registered like stills in an old movie:

Woman.

On bed.

Curled up.

Gun in hand.

Not Talya.

God, no.

Shiva.

Nine

"Try not to look so surprised, Lawson. You'll give me a big ego."

I sighed, feeling all the desire go flooding out of my body. Anger rushed in, filling the void. "Shiva. What a wonderful treat."

"You're a horrible liar." She gestured with the gun. "Sit down over there. We need to talk."

"Before you kill me?"

"If I have to, I will. Don't think I won't."

"Oh, no worries there. I know all too well about what you did to those other Fixers. I wouldn't doubt your resolve for a second."

"Good. Glad to hear it. Now sit down and shut up."

I sat in the corner chair. Mimi came into the room, chirping. She stopped, sniffed the air, realized something was wrong, and then hissed at Shiva. I smiled. Good cat.

Shiva sniffed. "I even fooled your cats, Lawson. I'm pretty convincing as your girlfriend, wouldn't you say?"

"My cats never met Talya. So, don't go patting yourself on your back just yet."

"What about you?"

"What about me? I can be fooled. I'd say you demonstrated that admirably."

"It wasn't exactly a challenge."

"What's this all about? Why not just finish me off right now?"

She chewed her lower lip. "I don't want to kill you, Lawson. Not unless I have to."

"Lucky me. Tell me something. How'd you know what Talya looks like?"

"Video."

"What video?"

"Last year when you were both very much the item. The Council had a team on you, shooting video and audio. I'd say they did a very good job since you two never noticed them."

But Talya had suspected it. I might have also if I wasn't so in love with her. "Where were they?"

"I believe it was right after you reported into the Council. The day after you killed Cosgrove. You and Talya were in the Public Gardens, I think. On one of those benches. The video was a little grainy, as they always are. But I managed."

"Where'd you dig up information on her background?"

"It's in the files that your old Control dug up. All of which, including the video, is stored on the Council's computers."

I shook my head. "You hacked into them?"

She shrugged. "Just another skill. You should know. Didn't you hack them yourself a few months back?"

"I don't know what you're talking about."

"Of course you don't." She smiled. "Perhaps we'll get to that later. How to cover electronic footprints and all that. You definitely need a refresher course."

Later was a good sign. I decided to go at her straight on. "Why are you here in Boston?"

"To kill Belarus."

At least Jarvis had gotten that part right. I was surprised Shiva would tell me something like that so openly. I said as much.

She shrugged. "Why bother keeping it from you? I need you, Lawson. As such, you need to know exactly what the nature of all of this is about."

That'd be a change from how I normally operated: completely in the dark. "So?"

"Do you know what I am, Lawson?"

"Aside from a trained killer?"

"Obviously."

"You can shape-change. You've got lycanthrope blood in your genes. I was told it was a small amount. But enough to give you the ability to change."

She nodded. "It's true: I am part lycanthrope. I have the ability to morph into anyone I can visualize. It's a trait that has served me well, as you can imagine."

"Sure I can. You disappeared right in front of me the last time I hunted you. You did it again this afternoon."

"I wouldn't be able to do that if I only had a little lycanthrope blood in my veins."

"What are you talking about?"

"The amount in my blood is far greater than you were told. I am, by birth, fully half lycanthrope."

Lycanthropes were like vampires. Another branch of evolution some would say went awry aeons ago. I had no idea how lycanthropes were able to change themselves. I wasn't really interested either. But since Shiva'd become a part of my life, at least right now, I made a mental to find out when I had more time.

If Shiva was half lycanthrope, it meant one of her parents was fully lycanthrope and one was fully vampire. Such a marriage would have been odd by anyone's standards.

Not to mention it was frowned upon by society.

"I'm not the only half-and-half walking around these parts, Lawson."

Part of me had been afraid she'd say something like that. And a bigger part of me even knew what was coming next. "Let me guess: Belarus."

She smiled. "You are a smart one."

"Thanks for the boost."

"Belarus is also a half-and-half."

"Seems impossible, given his position, though."

"Why so? As half lycanthrope he can easily disguise himself. And he is half vampire anyway. The disguise would work well enough to fool any of your kind."

"My kind makes up fifty percent of you, Shiva."

She sighed. "Not really. There are a lot of others like me, Lawson. Like Belarus. We rather consider ourselves our own people."

"I'm not much interested in debating semantics with you, Shiva. Tell me why you want to kill Belarus."

She shifted on my bed, finally sitting up. "Belarus has been engaged in a systematic extermination of the half-breeds. It's genocide on a whole new scale."

"He's killing off his own people?"

"To preserve his place at the top of the power structure in vampire society. Belarus has never liked being half lycanthrope. Sure, he'll use what he can to get what he needs, but he knows if there's greater acceptance of half-breeds in either lycanthrope or vampire society, it could be disastrous for him."

"How so?"

"Belarus is known in the half-breed community. He wasn't always in your community. We know of him from a long time ago. Before he left us. Before he came to you."

"How many of you are there?"

"A few hundred."

"Half-breeds?"

"Yes."

I sighed. "It'd take him years to kill you all by himself. How can you be so sure?"

"He's not killing us by himself. He's got allies. He's got squads of half-breeds that think like him. They want to take over both societies and rule them as one."

That would never happen. As long as I'd known about lycanthropes, they'd never been very welcome openly in our society. Nor had we been welcome in theirs.

I don't know if it was racism or not. I think it had more to do with what we each needed to live. Vampires drank blood, what I like to call juice. Lycanthropes needed human flesh.

A lot of vampires considered the act barbaric. Almost bordering on virtual cannibalism. Their naïve thought processes elevated the act of drinking blood to a higher level than it deserved.

Trust me, the act of taking blood is just as primal as ripping flesh off someone.

Lycanthropes were like us in that they didn't need much to sustain themselves. Sometimes they'd only need a hangnail. During the full moon, however, the desire became greater. Lycanthropes needed more. For that reason, lycanthrope communities tended to spring up around war zones where bodies littered the ground in abundance.

Dead or alive, it didn't much matter. Provided the corpses weren't too decomposed. Fresh kills worked best, I was told.

"Belarus always did strike me as ambitious," I said.

"He's more than ambitious, Lawson. He's flat out dangerous. If he's allowed to continue killing half-breeds, he'll be better poised to infiltrate both societies." She stopped. "Well, he's already infiltrated yours fairly well, hasn't he?"

As head of the Council, he sure had. But I wasn't so ready to believe her. "Why should I take you at your word? You could be lying."

"Why would I lie?"

"To get my help."

She laughed. "I don't need your help, Lawson. I've never needed the help of a vampire. I am more than capable of carrying out my mission on my own."

"If that's true, why am I still alive?"

"Because I don't like killing unless it's necessary."

"You took out five Fixers before. Was that necessary?"

"They weren't Fixers. They were a half-breed extermination squad dispatched by Belarus to find and kill me."

"Well, they didn't succeed."

"They certainly did not."

I leaned back against the wall. Mimi reappeared and circled my feet like a shark. "I'm supposed to be hunting you, you know that?"

"Of course. That's why we're having this little chat."

"You nearly killed me today."

She shook her head. "No. I nearly killed the man with you."

"Jarvis?"

She smiled. "Yes."

"But he's a Fixer like me."

"No, Lawson. He's a half-breed like me. He's also in league with Belarus. You were enlisted to help them. You're being used." She sighed. "Yet again."

I frowned. I'd been used so much I felt like the epitome of a limp wet condom littering the urine-soaked streets of Chinatown after some john had paid for a twenty-minute bang in the back of his Buick.

"Jarvis is a half-breed?"

"Sorry to have to be the one to tell you, dear. But it's the truth."

"He told me he's been on to you since shortly after he left Japan. Is that true?"

"More like I've been on to him. We lose each other in the fray. Both of us having the ability to transform makes it a little difficult to keep tabs on one another."

"I'll bet." I wished I had the ability to transform myself into pretty much anything other than what I was at that moment.

"If Jarvis is a half-breed, how did he make it past the Council during his centennial and get into Fixer training?"

"I don't know. Maybe he assumed the identity of another vampire."

I didn't know about that. Having your profession chosen for you by virtue of a test the Council puts you through seemed pretty full proof to me. But then again, I didn't know jack shit about everything.

"And you're telling me he's in league with Belarus?"

"Oh, yes. They are quite the inseparable pair, I assure you."

"How'd they get to be so close?"

"They're both half-breeds. They both know what it's like to have to live a lie. And they're both dedicated to exterminating the rest of the half-breeds. In their minds, it's better to be pure lycanthrope or pure vampire. One or the other. No mixing of the two."

"How the hell do they reconcile such an antiquated attitude with their own identity?"

"As far as I know, they're living in a world of denial."

"And you're here to stop them."

Shiva nodded. "I was dispatched to stop them both. The killing of my people must stop. We've done nothing to warrant such actions. Belarus must be stopped. Jarvis too."

"And you're quite prepared to kill them."

"That's the only alternative I see."

"And what do you want me to do?"

"Stay out of my way, Lawson. That's all I can ask. I wouldn't dream of requesting that you not do your job. I've read too much about you to know that you'd never do that. You're far too honorbound. But if you can just give me some breathing room . . ."

I frowned. I wasn't really in a position to say no right then. Not with a gun being aimed at my heart. I could be a man of principle any time I wanted to. Now, however, was one of those times when prudence was quickly beating the crap out of my principles.

"Tell you what. Let me do some checking around on my own. See if what you told me holds water. If it does, you can have at those two for all I care."

She nodded. "I can do that. You've got forty-eight hours."

"Forty-eight hours? That's not nearly enough time to do the digging I'll need to do."

She smiled and slid off the bed in one smooth motion. "Forty-eight hours, Lawson. After that, I move. With or without your support."

She thumbed the magazine release and the clip fell out of the gun. Then she racked the slide and I watched the round in the chamber vault onto the bed. Shiva walked over to me, handed me my pistol, and leaned close. "You might want this back. It's yours."

I started to feel behind my right hip. She'd taken it off me when we'd hugged or kissed. At least she'd gotten that talent of Talya's right.

"Forty-eight hours."

Her voice sounded just like Talya's too. I closed my eyes and fought back the pain in my heart.

When I opened them again, Shiva was gone.

But the pain remained.

Ten

The next morning arrived a helluva lot sooner than I would have liked. I'd slept like shit. Having Shiva show up impersonating the one woman I happened to love and then lay a mountain of crap on me just wasn't my ideal prescription for a good night's sleep.

I made a mental note to write strong letters to the authors of the various meditation books on my shelf. Counting breaths, visualizing white light flooding my body, and paying attention to my bowels might work for the fruit loops of society already baked on soy milk and garbanzo beans, but it did zilch for me. As far as I was concerned, their techniques sucked.

I downed a glass of juice and followed that up with a solid breakfast. I decided against doing any exercise this morning since it would have sapped my energy even more.

As I drove over to pick up Jarvis, I felt about as anxious as a virgin in a whorehouse. Not knowing which way was up was an aspect of my career I've accepted for a long time.

That doesn't mean it ever gets any easier. It just means it comes with the territory. And damn, was I sick of traveling through the same territory again.

The morning sky promised rain, but here and

there bright sunlight pierced the gray clouds with beams that spoke of more warm weather. That was fine with me. I could use a little sunshine in my life.

Jarvis was downstairs waiting for me when I rolled in. He hopped into the car, way too bright and way too cheery for me to stand it for very long.

"What happened to you?" I asked. "You eat a smile for breakfast and then have it repeat on you?"

"I got laid last night."

"She must have obviously had sinus problems if she could stand that damned cologne you insist on wearing."

"You're just jealous."

I frowned. Again with the kiss-and-tell stuff. No matter if you didn't want to hear it. Jarvis would tell you anyway. In fact, he'd parade around like some peacock strutting his stuff and belaboring the fact that he'd gotten his rocks off the previous night.

If I remembered correctly, and I wasn't sure I did, Jarvis claimed to have bagged at least twelve women during our mission over in Japan.

I'd bagged none. But that's just me. When it's time to go to work, that's what I do. When work time is over, then I can decompress.

A little.

The sole exception to that rule had been Talya last year.

And it had been one damned fine exception.

Not that I'd tell anyone about it. Although apparently the Council knew plenty.

Jarvis was still smiling as I pulled out of the parking lot and spun around to head back down Beacon Street toward Kenmore Square.

"Where are we going?" Jarvis's smile didn't waver. Not for a second. I felt nauseous.

"I thought we'd head on over and visit our good friend Belarus. Maybe he can shed some light on why Shiva wants to kill him."

The smile vanished. "Is that really necessary?"

"You don't think it is?"

"I didn't say that. It's just that Belarus is already quite upset with Shiva even being here. And now we're going to go and bother him? I just don't know if that's such a good idea."

"What do you think we should do then?"

"We should be looking for Shiva."

I wanted to look at him and tell him I'd already found her. Well, she'd found me, but I wouldn't tell Jarvis that. I wanted to watch his smile plummet. I wanted to watch his jaw drop into his lap and maybe stay there for an hour.

Then I wanted to ask him some hard questions and watch his physical reaction to them. He could say anything he wanted but I wouldn't be listening. I'd be watching his pupils. I'd be watching the pulse in his neck. I'd be looking for body cues that would tell me he was lying.

But I didn't say anything about Shiva's nocturnal visit. Now wasn't the time. Not yet.

Instead I cleared my throat. "Look, Jarvis, you told me yourself you've got no real clues to work with. So, how the hell are we supposed to find her?"

"I've got these papers." He pulled out that same sheaf I'd seen him with yesterday.

"So what? They still look like they're covered in hieroglyphics to me."

"It must mean something," said Jarvis. "If we could find out what, maybe they'd give us a trail to follow."

I kept an eye on the road and reached for the papers. "Let me see them."

We slowed down at a red light by the Common. I glanced down. The writing was some sort of script. It looked alien to me. Maybe it was some kind of lycanthropic language or something. I mentioned this to Jarvis.

"Could be. I don't know."

I frowned. If Shiva was right about Jarvis and Belarus, then I was being lied to. I hate being lied to.

The light changed and I gunned us down and up onto Beacon Hill. I'd have to show these papers to someone who could decipher them or at least give me an idea on where to head with them.

And the only person I knew who knew anything about pretty much everything was Wirek.

Wirek was a recovering drunk. Moreover, he was an Elder. In vampire society, the Elders preserved our traditions. They knew Taluk, our language, and they knew all about the mystical aspects of our society.

Wirek knew even more.

Years back, he'd grown disillusioned with the politics of vampire society and withdrawn, seeking solace in alcohol. Sounds pretty weird talking about a mystical Elder sucking down tequila, but that was Wirek.

Earlier this year, he'd done a complete one-eighty and cleaned himself up. He'd helped me out on an earlier case that involved us going to Nepal and the Himalayas, of all places, to track down a young kid with some pretty amazing supernatural skills.

Wirek had come through all that shit with flying colors.

As far as I knew, he still lived above the convenience store I'd found him in a year back—when he was still tainted and tempted by the fermented spirits.

I parked the car on Charles Street and looked at Jarvis. "Get out."

He looked relieved to see we weren't heading to the Council after all. Well, fuck him. We'd go later on. Depending, of course, on what Wirek had to say.

In the close confines of the hallway in Wirek's building, Jarvis's cologne became nearly unbearable. I tried not to sneeze and failed. I leaned on Wirek's buzzer.

"Yeah?"

"It's Lawson."

The door clicked and we went up. The building still looked like a sty. Old circulars and newspapers clogged the stairway. The dank smell of urine cloyed at us as we climbed the three flights.

I heard the door open above us. Wirek called down. "Who you got with you, Lawson?"

I grinned. Behind me, Jarvis whispered, "Who the hell is this guy?"

"Tell that guy you're with that he stinks," Wirek called.

"I already did," I called back. "Didn't do much good."

Wirek snorted further up. We crested the third floor and he stood there.

His head gleamed. Wirek had gone bald. Deliberately, by the look of it. His scalp glistened in the heat of the apartment. He looked taut too. I think he might have actually been exercising. The wonder of it all.

"Nice cue ball." I shook his hand. "You look good, pal."

He rubbed his head. "You like? Drives the ladies nuts."

I laughed. Wirek always had combined an earthy ribald sense of humor with an unyielding respect for the old ways. The mixture always produced interesting conversations.

I nodded back at Jarvis. "This is Jarvis."

Wirek's eyes narrowed. "Not a Fixer."

"Yeah. He is."

Wirek's eyes narrowed some more. "Interesting."

Jarvis tried to reach a hand over to shake Wirek's. He didn't quite make it and almost fell over us in the process.

Wirek shot me a look and we followed him inside. He closed the door behind us. "Time was, Lawson, I wouldn't have let you in here unless you had a bottle of the good stuff."

"Time was."

He grinned. "It's good to see you, pal."

"Likewise. Wish this was a social call."

"If it was, you wouldn't have dragged the walking perfume display with you." He nodded at the open door. "Come inside."

Wirek's apartment was completely different. New furniture lined the living area. A cushiony chair had replaced his banged-up recliner. And he'd installed more bookshelves. They still overflowed with books and notes.

"What can I do you for?"

I turned. "Jarvis here is tracking an assassin—"

"With Lawson's help," said Jarvis cutting in. "I couldn't handle it alone, so I came to him for backup."

Great, now he was trying to be modest. I sighed. "Anyway. He's got these papers with some kind of script on 'em. I can't make heads or tails out of it, so I figured we'd try you. You mind taking a quick look?"

Wirek grinned. "I got anything else to do?"

"I don't know. Do you?"

He glanced at his watch. "Not for a few hours yet. And she'll wait if necessary."

"There you go then."

We sat down. I sank two feet into the couch. "Jesus."

"Comfy, huh?"

I tried to extract myself. "Thing's like quicksand."

"Real comfy for the ladies, though."

I shook my head. Wirek was a gigolo now. Great. I had two of them in my life and it wasn't even lunchtime.

Jarvis looked uncertain. I frowned. "Give him the papers."

He did so reluctantly. Wirek had to grab them out of his hand, and that resulted in him shooting me another look. I shot back. I couldn't answer for the guy's actions. Truth was they annoyed me too.

Wirek took out a pair of glasses and slid them halfway up his nose. He peered over the rims and unfolded the papers.

His eyebrows shot up immediately.

He glanced at Jarvis.

And then he looked at me. "Where'd you get these?"

I pointed at Jarvis. "Ask him. He came to town bearing gifts yesterday."

Wirek looked back at Jarvis. "Well?"

"I found them."

"Great, sonny, you wanna tell me a little bit more about them?"

"I think our target left them behind in California. I found them at one of the locations she'd used as a hiding spot."

Wirek's eyes narrowed again. "Really."

"Yeah."

Wirek looked at him a second longer and then nodded. "Okay, well, you've got yourself some interesting things here."

I tried to lean forward, but found that difficult with the cushions sucking my backside into the sofa. I gave up trying and settled back. "Like what?"

"This is Geralach."

The last part of what Wirek said sounded like he was clearing his nose and spitting a giant hunk of snot at something. I shook my head. "What?"

"Geralach." He wiped his mouth. "I can't even pronounce it properly. It's the language of the lycanthropes. The old language, though. Not what they might speak nowadays."

"Like an earlier version of Taluk," I said.

He nodded. "Yes. But this script is old. These are notes that haven't been rewritten. These are actual notes written probably a thousand years ago."

Jarvis sniffed. "Ridiculous. That paper wouldn't have lasted two hundred years, let alone a thousand. You're mistaken."

Wirek's eyebrows shot off his head as he turned slowly toward Jarvis. "Sonny, I got a bad feeling about you. And I trust my feelings. But since you're with Lawson here, I'll overlook your stupidity this one time. But allow me to impart this small tidbit for your own edification: You don't know shit."

I needed to redirect this. The last thing I needed was a fistfight in Wirek's place. Wirek would probably kill Jarvis anyway. "Tell me about the notes, Wirek."

"Just to clarify: This paper is about a thousand years old. The preservation methods of lycanthropes are very interesting. This, for example"—he held up the paper—"has been coated in a resin that would preserve the notes."

"What kind of resin?"

"Resin might be the wrong word," said Wirek. "Lycanthropes of old tended to use their own saliva to coat important papers."

"So you're holding thousand-year spittle there?"

He shook his head. "Make light of it if you want, Lawson. But this wouldn't have been coated like this unless it was incredibly important."

"Wait," said Jarvis. "Saliva helps break things down. Now you're telling us they used it to preserve things? That doesn't make any sense."

"The saliva is treated with a mixture of herbs that nullifies its acidity and gives it a sort of bonding power. I don't know the formula they used. It went out of style hundreds of years ago."

I nodded. "Okay, okay. So what's the big deal with it? They a journal of some sort?"

Jarvis was trying hard to feign indifference to the conversation, but it wasn't working. I could tell he was listening closely.

"Not a journal," said Wirek. "More like a road map."

"A map? To what?"

Wirek unfolded another piece of paper and studied it for a minute. Finally, he looked up again. "These are directions for finding what the lycanthropes call the 'Cha-ga-kal.'"

"The Chaka-Khan? What?" I shook my head. "Give it to me in English, would you?"

"We would call it the Lunaspe. It's an ancient amulet that allows lycanthropes to harness untold powers."

I sank back further into the couch. Great. On top of some kind of supposed genocidal conspiracy, now there were ancient artifacts involved. Past experience has taught me when the stuff of yore gets involved, it generally means my life is gonna get worse.

A whole lot worse.

Eleven

"Where'd you dig that guy up anyway?" Jarvis asked.

"Why? You pissed off about him riding you about the cologne thing?"

Jarvis grunted.

Well, I knew how he felt. I'd been there before. Wirek could rub you the wrong way. But I was also kind of protective about the guy. Wirek and I had come through some serious business only a few months before. And you can't go through what we went through and not bond.

"He happens to be an Elder. And he seems to know a lot more about what we might be dealing with than you do. You might show the guy a little respect."

"I give respect to people who respect me first."

I wheeled the car down Charles Street. "That attitude must win you a lot of friends."

"People don't like it, they can kiss my ass."

"Ah, tact too."

"Fuck tact. Tact is for jackasses who seek the approval of everyone else. I'm my own man. I do things my way. People don't like it—"

"Yeah, I heard you the first time." I sighed. "Jarvis, I've really missed you."

"You don't know how lucky you are that I'm here."

"Lucky doesn't figure into my life. You sitting there is proof enough of that."

"You're still as sarcastic as ever. What's your excuse?"

"Having to put up with insipid commentary from the vast majority of people I come across."

He stayed quiet for a moment. "That include me?"

I didn't answer. Better to let him stew a while. "We need some information on the Lunaspe thing."

"The amulet Shiva's supposedly after?"

"According to Wirek, there's no supposedly about it. That's what was written on those pages you found."

"And you believe him?"

"You're not giving me any reasons not to. For that matter, neither has Wirek."

"So where do we go for information?"

"The Council."

Jarvis slumped back into the seat. "You sure your friend back there wouldn't have that information?"

I shook my head. "He did, he would have told us. You heard him, he said the Council library has it."

"Maybe he's lying. Maybe we should go back and have a stronger conversation with him."

I pulled the car over to the right side of the street and parked it in a loading zone. I switched the engine off and turned to look at Jarvis.

"Let me tell you something. That man back there has proven himself to me in the freezing wilds of the Himalayas. You, despite all appearances, have not. I know of you. I know of your reputation. And we've even had a mission together.

"But I have not seen you in combat. I don't know what you're capable of when the shit hits the fan. Wirek has my respect. More importantly, he respects me enough to fill me in on what he has and what he doesn't have. If he says he doesn't have the information, he doesn't have it."

I turned the engine back on. "Now, until I do see for myself exactly what you're made of, you will be a doubt in my mind. Wirek will not be." I looked at him. "You've got your work cut out for you . . . old friend of mine."

Jarvis's jaw clamped shut. I could see the strain of his neck muscles. He'd either take the dressing-down in silence, or he'd pop and we'd be beating each other up in the front seat of my car.

"You saw me in action in Tokyo."

"No, I did not." I shook my head. "We got separated. I had my hands full and you disappeared. All I know is you came back alive." I pulled back out in the slipstream of cars. "That doesn't tell me a damned thing except you made it out alive. You could have paid those bad guys off and I'd be none the wiser."

Jarvis sat quietly for another minute. "I can handle myself, Lawson. Belarus wouldn't have assigned me this mission if he didn't feel confident in my abilities."

"Belarus's opinion about you matters to me about as much as the welfare of the Mediterranean fruit fly."

"He might be pissed if he heard that."

I glanced at him, trying not to laugh in his face. "Is that a threat? You think something like that is going to make me cower in a corner somewhere? Don't waste your breath. Belarus knows I hate his guts. I've never tried to hide that fact. I'm a straight shooter. If I don't like you, I'll let you know. Or I'll treat you like my best buddy . . . right up until the time I kill you."

I pulled us around Beacon onto Arlington and then back onto Boylston. We'd made a complete circle cutting around the Public Gardens back toward Beacon Hill. Sometimes I thought Boston's street designs might have been inspired by a bad bout with hallucinatory drug use. Then again, back when they'd laid out the city, most of it was swampy landfill anyway, carted in from outlying portions of town.

At the Boston Common parking garage, we slid down two levels and parked near the stairway leading up. Every time I parked in this garage, it was for the same reason: visiting the Council building.

And I never liked it any better.

Jarvis hoofed the stairs two at a time leaving me behind. I wasn't taking the steps in any particular hurry. Today promised a lot of heat and humidity. I'm not a big fan of either.

Sure enough, at the top, Jarvis was already perspiring. He'd need a drink of water soon.

We headed across Beacon and pushed our way through the iron gate at the building entrance. I rang the buzzer and waited.

Arthur appeared moments later. He cracked the door, smiled at me, and then rolled his eyes when he saw Jarvis.

"Brung Smelly back with you, I see."

I grinned. "We need to use the library, Arthur."

"Library? What for then?"

Jarvis frowned. "Research, old man. What else?"

I looked at him. "Way to work on improving your tact, partner."

Arthur eyed him again and then stepped back. "Hurry up and come in, you'll let out the cold air."

We stepped into the dark cool interior. Instantly, I felt better. The thermostats in the building kept the temperature at a mild sixty-five degrees. Vampires prefer dry, cool weather. Well, most do. I know some Fixers who work down in South America and Africa who love the sun.

Arthur stood back and pinched his nose to show his dislike of Jarvis's cologne. He pointed up the main staircase, his voice now a nasal twang. "Two flights up, down the hall, and third door in. You can't miss it. It's got all the books inside."

I nodded. "Thanks, Arthur."

He walked away. "No dramas."

Jarvis started up the steps. I followed. My feet pressed into the dense red carpeting silencing our footfalls. The dark mahogany railing felt firm and solid under my hand.

We walked the two flights and then banked down the hallway, at last finding the door. A large crystal doorknob, the kind they used in homes around Boston at the start of the twentieth century, marked the library entrance.

Jarvis turned the door handle. I heard the click and we went in. Bookcases and shelves towered over us and sprawled on all sides. I saw titles in almost every language known to man, and a few not known yet. I recognized some Taluk script running down the bindings of the books. But other scripts, I had no idea what they were about.

Part of me wished Wirek had come along with us. We could have used his help on this jaunt. But Wirek had an abnormally intense hatred of this building. I'd dragged him here earlier this year and the Council had soundly walked all over the poor guy.

I'd even lobbied for the Council to elect Wirek to the Council itself, following an unforeseen vacancy that had sprung up as a result of our actions.

They'd almost laughed me out of the damned building right along with Wirek.

Some people never learn.

Jarvis immediately moved to the right. "I'll grab this side."

It was the most he'd said to me since the garage. Fine with me. He could clam up for the rest of this case and I'd be a happy little camper. I knew he wouldn't, however. I knew he'd eventually want to talk so bad, he'd burst. And then for maybe thirty minutes he'd babble nonstop.

I looked forward to that occurrence about as much as I would having my teeth pulled out by a blind dentist suffering from Parkinson's disease.

I moved left, running my hands along the shelves. I looked at my fingertips, but no dust clung to them. Arthur kept this place spotless.

Zero, my old friend and mentor, once told me that the number of legends surrounding Arthur's days in the service bordered on unbelievable. Arthur had been out on operations that seemed bloodier and more violent than any in recent memory. And when he'd done his time, he'd volunteered to come and work at the Council in Boston. No more legends, just a humble man content with the relative peace of his work.

He reminded me a bit of Cincinnatus, the farmer who came to the aid of Rome when his country needed him, only to return once more to his humble roots when he was no longer necessary.

Arthur had outlived many other Fixers. Including my friend Zero. That was something Arthur and I both still grieved. Zero'd been dead less than a year, but the wound still felt as fresh to the touch as if it had happened yesterday.

I pulled out a book and opened it up, hearing the old leather crack as I did. Inside, pictures and text blossomed before my eyes. For a minute, I thought I'd picked up the book I was looking for. Then I realized it was a pictorial essay of vampire architecture.

I slid it back on the shelf and glanced across the room at Jarvis. He must have gotten lost in the stacks.

In fact, I couldn't even hear him.

I frowned. "Jarvis?"

No answer.

The hair on the back of my neck stood up. Shiva couldn't be here, could she? She'd said she wouldn't move for forty-eight hours. She'd honor that agreement, wouldn't she?

I slid further down left and then maneuvered my way through two aisles of stacks. The library seemed bigger inside than from the outside, but that was the nature of the Council building itself. Everything seemed larger inside than from the exterior.

I could smell the musty old pages. I could feel the vague draft that circulated among the stacks.

But I couldn't sense Jarvis anywhere.

Shiva's words came back to me. Jarvis was a half-breed. As such, he could transform into anyone. Maybe he could transform into a shelf of books. I didn't know. This whole lycanthropy business didn't sit all that well with me. I had a hard enough time dealing with errant vampires, let alone lycanthropes that could alter their form at will.

I completed the circuit of the room and began

moving toward Jarvis's side. I didn't think he'd left. We'd closed the door behind us when we'd entered.

Maybe he was hiding. Trying to show what an accomplished Fixer he was.

"Jarvis, cut the shit and come out. We've got work to do."

No answer.

I frowned. I patted behind my right hip and felt my pistol. I've lost count of how many times I've done that over the years. Just feeling that hard reassurance packed into a lethal frame can do wonders for your spirit.

I rounded another bookcase and slid down another aisle. Still, I couldn't feel a damned thing.

I'd been working a lot on sensing intention lately. The ability to sense the premonition of danger is one of those skills humans have long since tucked away in the furthest reaches of their subconscious. For vampires, particularly Fixers, the ability to sense danger needs to be as heightened as possible. Our survival depends on us not walking into ambushes.

And right now, I felt like I was heading in that direction.

I stopped.

Waited.

Felt what I thought was a breeze about the break on the back of my neck. Moved and knelt in that same instant.

Jarvis's body went flying over mine. He screeched, and went crashing into a bookshelf. Books tumbled out of the case and thundered down on his head. He lay there sprawled akimbo as papers drifted down from above.

I got to my feet and shook my head. "That was stupid."

"How'd you do that?"

"Do what?"

"Get out of the way like that. You couldn't have heard me."

"I didn't."

"So?"

"So what? I just felt a need to move."

"I was going to tackle you from behind. Put you down and show you how good I was at being stealthy."

"You're good," I said. "No doubt about it."

"Not good enough to get you, though."

I smiled. "No. Apparently not."

Arthur came exploding through the door. "—the bloody hell is going on here? Sounds like a minging cock-up!" He glanced over at Jarvis and then back at me. "Lawson, you've gone and bunged the whole spot up, haven't ye?"

I'd noticed that Arthur's proper British accent went to Cockney slang when he was pissed off. I kind of liked it better when he talked like that.

I looked from Arthur to Jarvis and then back to Arthur. "Jarvis here just lost his footing and fell down."

"That a fact?"

I looked at Jarvis. Jarvis picked himself off the floor and brushed himself off. "Yeah. That's what happened."

Arthur pursed his lips. He didn't buy it for a second. "Don't muck about in here, Lawson. Get what you need and then get gone. Don't want none of them downstairs types getting their shit in an uproar cuz you lot have fucked up the library."

"Will do."

Arthur left. I looked at Jarvis. "Playtime over?"

He looked sheepish. The Don-Juan-stud-boy façade was gone. "Yeah."

"Good. Let's get to work."

Twelve

We didn't come up with much. The reference books that the Council library had didn't give us very much information about the Lunaspe. I was trying my damnedest not to grab Jarvis by his lapels and wring the truth out of him. If what Shiva had told me was true, there was a good chance Jarvis already knew about the Lunaspe.

At the same time, I still had plenty of doubts about whether Shiva had lied to me or not. She'd proven in the past she could be incredibly cunning. Maybe she'd spread some disinformation to distract me from the real goal of her mission.

Then again, why bother doing that when she could have easily killed me last night?

We finished scanning the volumes about two hours later. In-depth research wasn't really an option at this point. We needed information and hard data as quickly as possible.

I looked up, suddenly tired. I hadn't had much juice in a long time. I needed some.

Jarvis still had his nose buried in some book. I cleared my throat. "I need a drink. You okay here for a minute?"

He nodded.

I shrugged and left the library. Outside, my footfalls stayed silent, sound sucked into the depths of the plush carpeting. I wound my way down the stairway and toward the back of the building. To the kitchen.

I like the kitchen. That's where Arthur hangs out a lot. And not many members of the Council ever go back there.

Which is just fine with me.

I stepped through the door and saw Arthur peering into a large pot simmering on the stove. "Whatcha got cooking?"

He glanced up and grinned. "Stew. For dinner tonight. You hungry?"

I frowned. "Need some juice actually. Got any on hand?"

He chuckled. "Oh, yeah, sure, I think I could scare up a drop or two for ya, mate." He looked around me. "What'd you do with Smelly?"

"Still upstairs in the library."

"You should leave him there. The wanker." Arthur shook his head. "Something not right with that boy. You watch out for him, Lawson, you hear me?"

I nodded. That was the second time today someone I respected had told me to watch my back around Jarvis. And it was three if you counted Shiva. I wasn't really ready to count her yet, but what the hell. I'd consider it a hat trick.

Arthur poured me a glass of juice and I drank it deep. I've never had much luck convincing myself that I actually enjoy drinking blood. But I need it to survive, so personal inclinations be damned, it was going down the hatch.

I downed the drink fast. I never like drinking slow. I slid the glass back on the counter just as the door opened.

Shit.

Belarus walked into the kitchen.

Arthur nearly fell off his stool. "Yes, sir? What can I do for you?"

Belarus surveyed the kitchen with a look of mock contempt. God, I hated his guts. Pomposity in any form always turns my stomach.

He finally brought his eyes to rest on me, almost as if I was some unimportant speck of dust. "Lawson." He sighed audibly. "What a surprise."

I'll bet. I tried to grin. "Belarus."

"What brings you here to the building?"

"Research."

"Oh?"

"Your boy Jarvis found some interesting paperwork while he was tracking Shiva. We're here trying to figure out some more details about it."

"'My boy'?"

I shrugged. "You dispatched him to find and kill her."

"Yes. Only after you failed to do the same thing."

"I think what you meant to say was only after the Council failed to let me continue to pursue her."

"Why should we have let you do that? You'd already proven she was too much for you."

"She might just be too much for anyone."

"What's that supposed to mean?"

"Maybe there isn't a Fixer good enough to stop her. You know, from completing her task here in Boston."

Belarus's face began to change color. Maybe it had suddenly occurred to him that insulting one of his potential protectors wasn't the best course of action.

I shook my head. "Well, lucky for you now you've got both Jarvis and me on the case."

"Only time will tell if it's lucky or not, I suppose,"

said Belarus. He glanced at the counter and saw my glass. He frowned and looked at Arthur. "Are we supplying Fixers with blood now?"

Arthur cleared his throat. "The lad was parched, sir. I didn't think anything of it."

"Start thinking then," said Belarus. "We're not running a concession stand here." He glanced at me. "I would have thought you would have made time to replenish yourself before beginning work today."

I smiled. Enough of this. "Yeah, well, I've been awful busy trying to make sure a top-notch assassin doesn't manage to hunt you down and kill you."

Belarus licked his lips. "Ah, Lawson, how I so wish you were close to retirement."

"Are you kidding? I've got so much incentive to stay active."

Belarus sniffed. "If only to annoy me, I suppose."

I nodded. "If only that. Yes."

"I should have had your job six months ago."

"You couldn't handle my job."

"I meant I should have fired you."

"Good thing you didn't."

"How do you figure that?"

"Well, if you had, you'd only have Jarvis to track Shiva down. And she'd smell him coming from a mile away. Then she'd kill him. And then she'd come here to the building and plug your heart full of so much wood you'd die a hundred times over." I leaned back against the counter. "Say what you want, you need me and you know it."

Belarus smacked his lips together. "For now, Lawson. For now. There will come a time, perhaps in the not-too-distant future, when you are expendable."

"I'm expendable now, Belarus. That's the nature of my profession."

"It's unfortunate all of you don't try harder to be so."

Arthur frowned. "Something you needed, sir? Something I can get for you so you can be on your way?"

Belarus turned back to him. "I stopped in here to see what you had planned for tomorrow's luncheon with the visiting governors."

Arthur cocked an eyebrow. "I believe Liv the cook would be in her office planning that out, sir. Best you'd go and see her to find out."

Belarus nodded. "I will." He looked at me again. "I'll be watching you, Lawson."

"Just let me know which angle you prefer."

"What?"

I turned around. "My front or my back? I've been told I've got a nice ass, but then some folks think that—"

Belarus turned and disappeared out of the door with a stomp. Arthur shook his head and glanced at me. "Bollocks, Lawson."

"What's that?"

"You've got bollocks. Head of the Council comes in here and you stick it to him like a pincushion. He's not the healthiest enemy to make, you know?"

"Fuck him."

Arthur nodded. "Aye, fuck him. He's a wanker, all right. Insulting Fixers when he knows straightaway that I used to be one." He shook his head. "But you watch your back, Lawson. You're needed in this town, even if the Council's too damned foolish to realize it."

"Thanks for the support."

"Just make sure you live long enough to be useful."

"Yeah, I will."

"You find what you needed upstairs?"

"Not really."

"Want to tell an old man about it?"

"We've got some kind of map that tells the location of a lycanthrope artifact. We can't decipher the directions. Wirek said it was written in Geralach and very old at that."

"If it's Geralach, it'd have to be, wouldn't it?"

"You know about it too?"

Arthur shrugged. "I been around some in my time, Lawson, you know that. You see things, learn things, you stay alive that way. I heard some things."

"Got any ideas?"

"You need translation done, why not go to an expert?"

"I would if I knew one."

"You don't know any lycanthropes?"

"Not really. Never had much occasion to."

"Now you do, though, eh?"

"Yeah."

"You think this artifact is part of the reason Shiva's here in Boston?"

"Might be. But then again, she might just be here to kill Belarus."

"I don't think either of us believe in coincidences, Lawson. Do we?"

"Nope."

Arthur swiped the glass away from in front of me faster than I'd ever seen him move. The guy might have been old, but his reflexes were lightning-fast.

"You go on up to Maine and see a woman I know up there."

"Maine? Whereabouts?"

"Mount Desert Island. You know it?"

"Sure. It's only eight hours away, though, by car."

"You can drive it in six if you keep a good speed on. Or you can fly into Bangor and drive on down from there. Either way, that's the way to get your document deciphered."

"Who's the woman?"

"Name's Belladonna. She's what we'd call an Elder."

"Lycanthropes have Elders too?"

"Sure enough. Someone's got to preserve the old ways. Belladonna's old and withered away by now. Last I heard she was going on four hundred, which for one of them is a damned sight old. She lives in a small cottage overlooking the ocean just outside of Southwest Harbor."

"And what—we just show up and ask her to translate the papers?"

Arthur shook his head. "No. You show up. Alone. You leave the walking cologne dispenser behind. Here in Boston. You let me keep a tab on that bugger. You go see Belladonna and see what she's got to say about the papers. Then come on back."

"How are you going to watch Jarvis while I'm gone? You've got your own job to do here."

Arthur smirked. "If what I believe is true, it won't be any great stretch of my time and effort to keep the bastard under wraps. Just go do what you've got to do and get on back here soon as you can."

"All right." I slid off the bar stool. "Thanks for the drink."

Arthur nodded. "Look for the pale-blue cottage overlooking the ocean. Not the harbor, but the ocean. Belladonna lives on the cliffs. She likes to watch the waves pound the rocks below. It's about two hundred feet of sheer rock face up from the ocean below."

"No address?"

"You won't need one. You find that cottage, the next thing you'll see are the cats. Belladonna loves her cats. Things'll swarm all over you. That's how you'll know it's the right place."

"Okay."

"You tell her Arthur sends his regards."

"You two go way back?"

Arthur's eyes gleamed. "Aye. There was a time. A long time ago at that. But there was a time."

I smiled. "You telling me you romped around with a lycanthrope?"

Arthur shrugged. "Some men, they like vampires. Some men"—he eyed me—"they like humans. Me? I happen to like the lycanthropes."

"Fair enough."

Arthur stirred the pot of stew on the stove top and began whistling. I walked out of the kitchen, leaving him to the fond memories swirling through his head.

Thirteen

I could have flown.

Maybe I should have, but I chose driving instead. Sometimes, there's nothing like getting out on the open road to help clear away the cobwebs. I wasn't really looking for a great deal of introspection. I didn't think I was anywhere close to needing it . . . yet.

Plus traveling by air means I don't have access to my pistol.

I didn't know Belladonna. And I didn't know when Arthur had seen her last. Maybe she'd be friendly, maybe she wouldn't be. But visiting a complete stranger, let alone a lycanthrope, without the benefit of my gun, wasn't a good idea.

In truth, my gun wouldn't do much to a lycanthrope. Frangible wooden-tipped bullets don't affect them.

But I felt better with the gun.

The drive took the better part of six hours. Five to reach Bangor and then another hour to cut back southeast finally arriving on Mount Desert Island.

Most folks, they hear Mount Desert Island and immediately think of Bar Harbor. But the island itself has a bunch of cozy little towns and villages nestled away from the congested expanse of Bar Harbor.

Not to say I don't love Bar Harbor, because I do. Some of the best filet mignon I've ever had was in a classy joint called Galen's overlooking the harbor at sunset.

But Belladonna didn't live anywhere near Galen's. Damned shame about that too.

Southwest Harbor lay on a tiny finger of land jutting straight out into the cold Atlantic Ocean. Fleets of small wooden sailboats, expensive yachts, and fishing trawlers littered the harbor waters. As I drove down the main street, I passed a sandwich shop I'd visited a few years back. They served a damned fine breakfast in there. Toasted apple muffins dripping with fresh butter and fresh-squeezed orange juice have a way of making me want to hang around. I made a mental note to take in a meal there before I left.

Summertime this far north meant a lot of tourists. Cars littered the side streets. Fortunately, I knew a few hidden spots, and lucked out on one just as a minivan pulled out. I slid my Explorer into the spot and parked it.

Outside, a warm breeze jumped in off the harbor, keeping the humidity down to a tolerable level. My understated Hawaiian shirt covered my pistol in the small of my back. Normally, I like wearing it just off my right hip. But loose shirts usually necessitate a small-of-the-back position. At least for me.

I paused by an antiques shop where I'd seen a home-improvement celebrity a few years previously. She had some giant house up here and presumed to go around telling local antiques dealers how to run their business. I remember walking the street and seeing people whispering as she passed. Whatever.

If gawking at pretentious celebrities excites you, well and good, but it never has done much for me.

Unless they happen to be beautiful women.

Up here, they aren't.

I rounded the main street and tucked down a side avenue. A bakery advertised fresh corn muffins. Next door, a small bookshop hawked the latest vampire novel on a sandwich board. I grinned and wondered what people would think if they ever knew the truth.

Probably better they didn't, I decided.

I crossed the street and slid over to the other side. I walked aimlessly. I didn't want to head toward Belladonna's first. Not yet.

Back in Boston, ditching Jarvis had been almost too easy. I wouldn't have thought the guy so ready to accept my excuses. I'd told him I had to go out of town and research something and that it shouldn't take me longer than a day. He'd just nodded.

Accepting.

That didn't make much sense. Not after how he'd been acting.

So, my roundabout walk through town had a purpose even if I tried hard not to make it seem so. I needed to know if I was truly alone.

Throngs of people surged around me. I recognized the lilt and accents of at least a dozen states. Live long enough and you develop an ear for them. I ticked off Maryland, Wisconsin, New York, and California as I strolled past the tobacco store. I caught an earful of South Carolina, Texas, and Kansas as I hit the crosswalk to walk up a one-way street.

Tailing someone who is walking is tough work. If you have enough people, you can do it easily enough, but I wanted to flush any tails out of their cars by walking up one-way streets where they couldn't easily navigate. Plus, given the close confines of the streets in Southwest Harbor, I was banking on the fact that any tails would have to be what a Fixer pal of mine over in London calls "foxtrot," or on foot.

So I walked.

And walked.

A real pro won't ever let himself be spotted. But it can be tough. It's a helluva lot easier in some giant city like New York. You can lose yourself in crowds, cross streets, flag down cabs, and even sit outside. All of it looks natural, and all of it makes it a lot harder to determine if you're being followed.

But in Southwest Harbor it was a different story.

I kept moving.

By the time fifteen minutes had passed, I'd made a big loop around on my own route and begun following it again. One of the oldest commandments about ambushes says that if you think you're being followed, you make a winding circuit and come around again on your own path. That way you come up behind the people following you and, in theory, ambush them.

I didn't necessarily want to ambush anyone. I just needed to see if I was "clean."

I wasn't.

I was dirty.

I caught sight of her as I rounded a corner. She'd positioned herself neatly on an intersection that gave her a wide-angle view of the road I'd recently walked up, while at the same time she could see the route I was coming back along. As far as observation posts go, she'd chosen well. If I'd been in her shoes, I might have picked the same.

But it's tough to look natural standing out in the open for too long, which is what she was doing. It's how I spotted her. Everything else seemed very natural. I wasn't sure if she was a Fixer or not, but someone had obviously shown her how to do surveillance.

At least to about a high school level of competency.

Was it Shiva?

I didn't think so. Shiva didn't have much reason to go tailing me around. And I was still within my forty-eight-hour grace period she'd generously supplied me with.

I didn't think she was the local Fixer. Women are rare in the service. Not because they aren't capable, but simply because they aren't normally predestined for this work. I'm not sure why.

But the local Fixer could have employed her.

Standard operating rules dictate that you contact the local Fixer when you're on their ground. That was one reason Jarvis's appearance in Boston and my subsequent realization he'd been there before without my knowledge had pissed me off so much.

But I hadn't done the courtesy call because it would have meant they'd be interested in my business. I didn't think my involvement with a lycanthrope elder like Belladonna would make for cheery coffee talk down at the Council.

Besides, the closest Fixer was in Bangor. And he was a new recruit only recently back from his overseas apprenticeship. He'd have plenty of other things to worry about settling in than considering my boring mission to this town.

I considered my options as I waited for the light to change. I could continue walking around aimlessly and hope to lose the tail. But there was no guarantee I would. If they knew my car, and there was a fair chance they did, all they'd have to do was stake it out and wait for me to return.

The light changed.

I crossed the street.

Hell with it. One of my old basic training instructors used to advise us that when we were in doubt, the best thing to do was attack. In the years since then, I'd sometimes followed that advice. Most of the time it ended up almost costing me my life.

But sometimes. . . .

I stepped onto the sidewalk and headed right for her, staring at her with enough intention to scare the pants off of anyone standing close by.

She looked up, locked eyes with me for a brief instant, and then looked away.

That wasn't good. You never look away. It reveals your position. If you look up and see your target looking at you, simply keep staring at them for a few seconds and then go back to what you were doing. You'll come across as someone simply attuned to their environment. You'll be thought of as someone merely checking things out and then resuming your activities once you're satisfied everything's cool.

But glancing away means you don't want that eye contact. It means you've got something to hide.

Which is why as I came parallel to her, I grabbed her around the triceps with my left hand and lifted her up slightly, steering her back down a side alleyway.

She didn't protest. Another bad sign. If she'd been an innocent or a highly skilled operative, she would have either made a huge scene or immediately gone into a counteroffensive.

I put a wall of bricks between us and the street and shoved her toward the wall. I jerked my gun out—holding it on her at a distance of ten feet.

She whirled, fumbling under her own shirt.

"Uh-uh-uh . . ."

She stopped, saw my gun, and slumped back into the wall with a sigh.

"Who are you?" I asked.

She chewed her lip. "They told me you were good."

"Listen, honey, buttering me up with compliments doesn't mean a damned thing to me. Answer my questions quickly and succinctly and there's a good chance you'll walk out of here."

"A good chance?"

"I'm not promising anything. After all, it was a long drive."

"Lucky me."

"Not right now, you're not." I gestured with my gun. "Now, do I need to ask you again?"

"I was told you were coming up here. I was told to keep an eye on you."

"Okay, well, you did that."

"Not very well."

"Your words not mine. Who put you on to me?"

"I don't know his name."

"His?"

"Yes."

I looked at her. She must have been around twenty-eight in human years. She kept her blond hair short. Loose jeans and a baggy shirt probably concealed a pistol. She wore sneakers.

All in all, a sound choice for tailing someone.

Comfortable clothes and shoes are often underestimated in importance, but I've been on enough tails and stakeouts to know their real value. The woman in front of me was dressed for a long job.

"And what were you supposed to do if you spotted me?"

"Keep tabs on you. See where you went. See that you didn't cause any trouble."

I grinned. Didn't cause any trouble? Me? Jeez. Whoever had put her on to me must have been a real comedian.

But I had work to do. And I didn't need intrusions right now by less-than-stellar operatives working for some shadow figure.

She was looking at me as if I'd pull the trigger at any moment. That was another sign she was an amateur. A pro would have known I wouldn't shoot unless I absolutely had to. The noise would have brought everyone running.

"Well, we've got ourselves a little dilemma here."

She frowned. "You're going to kill me?"

"I don't want to do that." I sighed. "But I've got some things I need to do. Some things I need to do *alone*. I can't afford to have you tagging along behind me like some mistimed shadow."

"How did you spot me so easily?"

"You picked an obvious observation point."

"I needed to be able to see multiple lines of sight, though. It was textbook."

I nodded. "Yeah. Yeah, it was. Which is exactly why I was able to spot you so damned easily. In the future, if you have a future, pick a spot that offers the same angles but is a bit more hidden."

"There was nothing there."

"There was a café ten yards behind you with outdoor seating. You could have used that. Even that wasn't perfect, but it was better than standing out in the open on a corner."

She nodded. "Thanks."

"Who taught you how to tail people anyway?"

"The same person who taught me how to ambush people like you."

What the hell was she babbling about? "And that would be?"

She smiled. "The woman standing behind you."

I whirled, but as I did, I felt a vague whisper of a touch brush across the skin of my neck. I felt pressure exerted on a point I recognized briefly as a vital point.

The pressure increased.

My consciousness began blacking out.

I slipped, dropped, fell toward the ground.

And everything went dark.

Fourteen

I awoke to the sound of soft meowing and what felt like five cold, wet noses nudging my face. For a split second I thought it was my cat Phoebe, who always enjoys waking me up that way whenever it gets ten seconds past feeding time.

But then I remembered the drive up to Southwest Harbor.

And knew it wasn't Phoebe nudging me awake.

I cracked an eye and saw two yellow ones staring back at me. In the background, furry faces with long whiskers peered at me intently.

Cats.

Hadn't Arthur told me that Belladonna had a lot of them wandering around her house?

I sat up too fast and was rewarded with a burst of intense pain in my head. I felt a solid hand on my chest pushing me back down. I couldn't resist and fell back down onto a fluffy pillow that cradled my head and neck.

After a few seconds, I opened my eyes again. This time, another set of eyes like my own peered back at me.

"How are you feeling, Lawson?"

Her face looked young, but it was her voice that sounded old. Very old. I squinted. The bright light hurt my eyes.

"Where am I?"

She smiled. "You're at my house, of course." She leaned back. "I am Belladonna."

"Who nailed me from behind?"

She chuckled. "That was me, of course."

"You?"

"Most assuredly."

"But Arthur mentioned you were old."

"I am old. But I'm not so old that I can't slip up behind an unsuspecting Fixer and knock him out with a quick zap of my hand."

"You and that girl . . . you ambushed me."

"Yes. We most definitely did."

I tried sitting up again and succeeded. I glanced around. Corner lamps lit up the room, showing bookcases and thin patterned rugs. I lay on what felt like a long sofa. Belladonna sat in an armchair opposite me. Cats swarmed around the base of the sofa, purring like motorboats.

I must have been out for a while. The sun had disappeared. I glanced at the window and could make out the moon rising over the ocean. From outside, I could hear the crashing surf against the rocks that must have been a few hundred feet below.

Belladonna offered me a steaming cup of something. "It's tea. Drink it slow. You need some fluids in you."

Tea wasn't the kind of fluids I needed. But somehow, asking for a glass of human blood seemed rude. And I doubted if she had any in stock. I took the tea.

"You're good, you know," she said. "As skilled they come."

"If I was good, I wouldn't have fallen for that ambush."

Belladonna grinned. "She's perfect for that role, don't you think? She looks naïve. Perfect."

"Yeah. Great."

"Don't be too hard on yourself. Every Fixer who has ever come to town has fallen for that trick."

"You got a lot of Fixers wandering through here?"

"You're only the second one."

"Great. That does wonders for my self-esteem."

"Awfully self-critical, aren't you?"

"I have to be. It's part of who and what I am."

"That's exactly what Arthur told me you'd say."

I paused and set the cup down on a small wooden side table. "What do you mean Arthur told you?"

"He called us. Told us you'd be making your way up here."

"So you were waiting for me?"

"Naturally. You'd have done the same in our situation. After all, a vampire—let alone someone as potentially dangerous as a Fixer, of all things—isn't normally the kind of visitor we get in these parts."

I heard footfalls somewhere off in the house. "Who's that?"

Belladonna smiled. "That's Monk."

"Monk?"

"The woman you met earlier today. The one who led you into our neat little arrangement."

"You knew I'd tag her, is that it?"

"We suspected you would. I'm well familiar with the rules governing covert operations. I knew what your options would be. And thanks to Arthur, I knew what your response would likely be."

I frowned. "I'll have to remember to thank Arthur when I get back to Boston."

"Now, now, I wouldn't go fretting about Arthur.

He probably didn't see the harm in it. If anything, he might have been concerned about you traveling up here alone."

"Why would he be?"

"Well, from what he mentioned to me earlier, you have reason to be concerned."

I wasn't about to confirm anything. I've found it's usually best to keep quiet in these situations. If Belladonna wanted to keep talking, that was fine with me.

She smiled and pointed at the cup. "Drink the tea, dear. Then we can talk."

I took a few more gulps, feeling the warm liquid heat my insides up. Surprisingly, I felt a lot better. It must have showed because Belladonna smiled.

"The tea is a strong curative. I don't have any blood in the house here, so I'm afraid you'll either have to do without or else go hunting in town later when you get some strength back."

"I think I can probably manage without it for tonight."

"You'll be hungry tomorrow morning, though. Possibly very weak."

"I've got a pretty good constitution."

She nodded. "I noticed it took a little extra effort to subdue you earlier. Which reminds me." She reached behind her and pulled out my pistol. "You'll be wanting this back, I'm sure."

I took the gun, popped the magazine, and checked the chamber. Everything was as it should have been. I felt the reassurance of its weight in my hand. I tucked it behind my hip and finished off the tea. "Did Arthur tell you why I was coming up to see you?"

"He mentioned something to do with an old

lycanthrope legend. He said you had some material you needed translated."

I nodded. "I was told the papers are written in Geralach."

She smiled. "You have excellent pronunciation for our language."

"I took a guess and hoped it was right."

She nodded and held out her hand. "You have the papers with you?"

"Yeah." I pulled them out of my pocket. "I'm told they point the way to finding something called the Lunaspe."

Belladonna took the papers with reverence and slid a small pair of glasses onto the tip of her nose. She peered down at the papers and her eyes narrowed for a few minutes.

I let my hand down toward some of the cats. Belladonna had black cats in abundance, although a calico here and there interrupted the ebon monotony. As soon as I let my hand down, the cats all crowded around me, getting a whiff and nuzzling me. I smiled.

Belladonna slid her glasses off. She looked at me. "Where did you get this?"

"From someone I'm working with."

She frowned. "Not a vampire."

I shrugged. "I'm not totally sure about that myself. He claims to be."

She shook her head. "No. There's no way he could be. No vampire would ever come into possession of these papers."

"They were in my possession until two minutes ago, Belladonna. And I'm one-hundred-percent vampire. I know that for a fact."

"Don't make light of the situation here, Lawson.

These are ancient lycanthrope documents. They do indeed show how to recover one of our most ancient and most powerful artifacts. What you called the Lunaspe."

Why would Shiva have those papers? She didn't seem very interested in recovering an artifact, only hunting down and killing Belarus.

"The person you got these from," said Belladonna, "it is very likely that he would be at least half lycanthrope."

That's what Shiva had told me as well. "Why so?"

"Whoever finds the Lunaspe will be able to draw down what we refer to as the power of the waxing moon. Each month, at the full moon, the gravitational pull of the moon increases substantially. Humans have thought for years that it affects moods and emotional states. That's true to a small extent. But for lycanthropes, the moon is like our sun. When its power is magnified, we become immensely powerful. And our ability to draw that power is facilitated by the Lunaspe."

"What exactly is it?"

"A medallion or amulet, if you will. It is made of a large chunk of iron with ancient Geralach script running around the outside edges. The script is the incantation that must be spoken to begin the process."

"And a lycanthrope with this Lunaspe would be able to do what exactly—become more powerful?"

Belladonna nodded. "Yes, but not just over humans, but also vampires, and even other lycanthropes. The power would be difficult for anyone to resist."

"How long does it last?"

"That depends on the moon, the month, the

time of year, the season even, and of course, the person attempting to wield the amulet."

"Give me the worst-case scenario."

"If the lycanthrope was powerful enough before using the amulet, it would increase their power by a magnitude of at least fifty times."

"Potent stuff."

"That's an understatement," said Belladonna. "Worse is the fact that if the lycanthrope is not stopped and recites the incantation on the opposite side of the amulet, the power shift is virtually irreversible."

"So, we'd be talking about one immensely powerful lycanthrope walking around."

"We would indeed."

"Great."

She leaned forward. "Lawson, I don't need to tell you that such a lycanthrope would prove not only dangerous to the human population, but to your kind as well."

"Yeah, I got that."

"You Fixers place a great deal of faith in something you like to call the Balance. Isn't that right?"

Of course it was. The Balance was our Bushido, our code, it was what we died protecting—the secret coexistence of humans and vampires.

I nodded at Belladonna. "Yes."

"Then you must know that if this amulet falls into the wrong hands, your precious Balance—indeed, our version of the Balance—would be swayed to a cataclysmic scale. Everything we've all worked so hard for would be brought to ruin."

I pointed at the papers. "Those things say where this amulet can be found?"

"They do."

I leaned back. "So, what should I do? Try and find this thing first? Destroy it or something?"

"You could try, but it wouldn't work."

"Why not?"

"You're a vampire. The Lunaspe will not allow itself to be found, let alone touched, by someone who is not at least half lycanthrope."

"Wonderful."

"If you had a guide, however, who could help you locate it, a guide who was lycanthrope, that might make matters easier for you."

I shook my head. "I'm supposed to be working on tracking down a killer and now I'm getting wrapped up in a chase for some forgotten relic."

"Did you ever think the two might be entwined?"

"They usually are," I said with a half grin.

Belladonna smiled again. "Arthur said you had a wry sense of humor."

"I got so much wry I could make a sandwich. Doesn't really help me now."

"You need a guide," said Belladonna. "And I have just the person for you."

"Not you?"

She laughed. "Heavens, no, I'm far too old to be traipsing around on such an errand." She called out once, a harsh sound that almost sounded like a bark. I guessed it was the language of lycanthropes.

We waited.

The door opened.

Belladonna smiled at me. "I believe you remember Monk."

The woman in front of me smiled, and I suddenly felt a whole lot less sure about things. "Yeah. I remember her."

"Excellent. She'll make a good guide for your journey."

I looked at Belladonna. "Is she any good?"

"I fooled you, didn't I?" said Monk from across the room.

Belladonna held up her hand, quieting her, and then looked at me. "Monk is young by our standards. I have trained her in a great many things. But she is not tested in your terms. She would no doubt benefit immensely from your experience. And at the same time, you might benefit from some of hers."

I sighed. The last thing I wanted or even needed was another partner. Let alone an untested lycanthrope.

But if what Belladonna had told me was true, then I needed to sort out this Lunaspe thing. I needed to find it, figure out if Shiva wanted anything to do with it, and if she didn't—who did?

And in order to do that, I was going to need Monk.

I looked at her standing there in the dim light of the room. A thin smile slid across her face as she saw the resignation on my own mug.

I nodded. "Okay."

Fifteen

I drove fast on the way back to Boston.

I didn't like being away from my town with Jarvis, Belarus, and Shiva all doing God knows what to destroy what I've fought long and hard to keep safe. The side trip to Maine, while apparently necessary, made me nervous about what I'd potentially left behind.

Beside me, Monk looked out of the window. She seemed absorbed in the Maine highway system, but I knew better. Either she was nervous about being alone with a vampire, or she was simply being quiet so she wouldn't be tempted to laugh out loud at me for having been forced into this situation.

In the darkness, she seemed much more vulpine than I'd noticed earlier. I had to keep reminding myself that lycanthropes could change themselves into pretty much whatever they wanted. It wasn't simply the wolf-creatures of human legend. Lycanthropes could choose their state of transformation with unerring accuracy.

Accuracy I'd seen demonstrated by Shiva.

Lucky me.

Monk stood a little over five feet tall. I would have guessed five one and a half. She carried about a 115 pounds on her frame. Lithe but not waifishly thin. I could tell there was sheer muscle under her skin. Her forearms alone looked like twisted metal cords.

Her short blond hair framed her cheekbones, and I thought I could see some streaks of auburn highlights throughout.

She turned and caught me appraising her. "Yes?"

I looked back at the road. "Just wondering if you were ever going to say anything."

"It takes two to tango."

I hate that expression. I always have. People who say it usually don't even know how to tango anyway.

"Have you got any kind of weapon with you?"

Monk's eyes narrowed. "Why would I need one? My assignment is to simply guide you to the location of the Lunaspe. That's it."

"Yeah, but see, there are other people involved here who also want the Lunaspe. And they may not be the nicest folks in the world. In fact, they might like nothing better than to rip you apart limb from limb."

"You don't hang out with very nice people."

"Story of my life." I checked the gas gauge. We still had enough to make the trip. "So you see, when I ask if you've got a weapon, I am referring to it with the idea that you just might need it for self-defense."

"Oh. Well, in that case, yeah. I've got a weapon."

I sighed. "What is it—a gun?"

Monk laughed. "No. We don't like guns so much. They make you lazy."

"What?"

"What I mean is they enable you to kill from a distance. You lose your edge that way."

"Not if the person you're trying to kill also has a gun."

"Maybe it's a cultural thing."

"Don't go crying racism here, Monk. That's not the best way to start off a working relationship with me."

"I'm not. All I'm saying is that vampires have customarily been more interested in a lack of physicality is all. Lycanthropes indulge in the fleshy arena. We're much more tactile in that sense. So, naturally, our defensive instruments are much more physical as well."

"Who told you vampires shy away from the physical?"

"Everyone in the lycanthrope community thinks that."

"Everyone?"

"At least in my area."

"I don't think Belladonna would agree with that."

"Why not?"

I thought of Arthur. "Just a hunch."

"Well, if not her, at least everyone else."

I didn't agree with her assessment and told her so. After all, I love the scent of warm human flesh. Preferably the neck, the back of the thigh, and the crook of an elbow. Even if I don't much care for drinking blood, I can appreciate the fruits of flesh.

"So, what kind of weapon do you use?"

Monk slipped her hand into the waistband of her slacks and produced what looked like six spikes about the length of a large pen. She took one and slid it into my hand.

The weight surprised me. "Throwing spikes?"

"They're silver-tipped, designed to inject silver nitrate upon impact."

I nodded. "Nice."

"I guess I don't have to explain that silver in our

blood does.the same thing that wood introduced into your blood does."

"I'd heard that, yeah." I handed the spike back to her. "You usually throw them?"

"Depends on the distance." She slid the spikes back into what must have been her holster. "Sometimes, I fight in close with them."

"How many times has that been?"

"What?"

"Fighting in close."

"Not many."

"What's 'not many'?"

"Twice."

I sucked my lower lip. "What about throwing them?"

"At someone?"

"Uh . . . yeah."

"Once."

"Nifty."

Monk wasn't just untested. She was pretty much as green as they come. Belladonna had glossed over that somewhat. Well, it was too late now to bitch much about it. I needed Monk and she knew it.

"Lawson, you can count on me."

"You say that like you've never said it before, Monk."

"What do you mean?"

"Most people don't understand what that simple phrase means. In my work, another Fixer says that to me, I get nervous. Because true professionals never really say that. It's implied. It's something we sort of emanate. You can tell a good operator just from the way he carries himself. You don't get to do what I do unless you are very, very, very good at this stuff. I go into the shit with another Fixer, I know my back is covered."

We passed a blue Suburban on the right. As we drew abreast, I glanced over and saw Monk's frown.

"But people who've never experienced real combat before say that expression not knowing what it really means to be in the thick of it. It ends up being almost an empty thought, you know?"

"I won't let you down."

"And then they follow up with that." I almost laughed. My situation was becoming comical. Not to mention rife with deadly liabilities. I'd be lucky to get this wrapped up still alive.

"Well, what do you want me to say then? All I want to do is my job. Then I want to go home. Is that so wrong?"

"Nope. That's the best thing you've said so far, in fact."

She quieted down for a minute. My subconscious was flagging me down. I ignored it.

"What do you do for the lycanthropes anyway?"

"What do you mean?"

"Well, in vampire society, our roles are generally determined when we reach our centennial. We visit the Council and they tell us or have us take some tests."

"Is that how you got to be a Fixer?"

"Yeah."

"Was it a tough test?"

"Not really. I think it was more along the lines of determining if I'd really been predestined for it or not."

"And you were."

"Apparently."

She nodded. "Lycanthropes are different. We

rely much more on our instinct. Although, honestly, there aren't as many of us as there are of you. We live in smaller pockets."

"Nature once again playing out her dominant role."

"What do you mean?"

"Everything's in a Balance, you know? If there were too many lycanthropes walking around and eating human flesh, then things would fall out of whack pretty quick."

"What about you guys drinking blood?"

"We don't require all that much. We don't kill our hosts."

"Neither do we. Just a bit of flesh here and there—"

"More around the full moon."

"True." She looked back out the window. "But I've heard stories about vampires draining all their victims and leaving their bodies like husks on the street."

I nodded. "Yep. Been more than a few of those. That's when I get a phone call."

"You kill them?"

"Yes."

In my rearview mirror, I could make out the Suburban's lights. They'd switched lanes. The Suburban was jockeying for the left lane now. I was in the middle.

Ahead of us, only a few cars spotted the road. We were on a straightaway. The closest car in front was about a mile and a half up. On the opposite side of the road, there were no cars.

I switched the air conditioner off and cracked the window.

Monk looked at me. "Why'd you do that?"

"Be quiet."

"Don't tell me—"

"Monk! Shut up! Listen!"

I could hear it then. The Suburban's engine began torquing up. They were pouring on gas. I stepped on the gas as well. I knew the Suburban could catch us, it had more horses under the trunk. But I'd make them work.

I glanced at Monk. She looked worried. Good. She should have been.

I certainly was.

"What's going on?"

"The blue Suburban we passed a minute ago seems to be taking an interest in us."

"What kind of interest?"

"I'm not sure."

"How did they find us?"

"They might have been with us the entire time. I don't really know. It doesn't really matter now anyway."

We closed some of the distance down between us and the cars about a mile ahead. The Suburban kept gaining.

They'd chosen the ambush spot well. A straightaway offered little cover in the event that we were stopped and drew weapons. Light traffic at night. Almost no residential homes nearby.

I kept one hand on the wheel and reached behind my right hip, unsnapping my holster. They were going to have to ram us. I knew it and they knew it.

I edged the pedal down to the floor trying to gain speed. It didn't work. The Suburban simply chopped it down again.

I looked at Monk. "You ready?"

Her face looked green in the darkness, a mixture of nausea and abject terror. But she nodded.

"All right, I'm going to try something."

"I trust you."

Great. In the space of five minutes, Monk had become master of the trite expression. "Thanks."

I eased my foot off the gas pedal.

"What the hell are you doing?"

I tried to grin. "Relax, I know what I'm doing."

And just before the Suburban slammed into us, I thought: Now who's the trite one?

Sixteen

They hit us hard.

The Suburban came in from behind and nudged us on the left rear side of the Explorer. It's a common tactic police use to stop a speeding suspect. The effect is that the car spins to the left and comes to a stop.

But I know the maneuver since I've used it a few times in the past. So, even as the Suburban made contact and we spun to a stop, I was already pulling out my pistol, unlocking the doors, and then shoving Monk out on her side to the highway.

The Suburban sat ten meters away from us, its lights blinding us. I dragged Monk over behind the engine block and we used that as cover. Bullets have a tendency to find their way through every other part of the car. But short of a .50-caliber sniper rifle, I didn't think there'd be much chance of them penetrating the engine.

In the darkness, I could hear Monk's fast breathing. I heard my own shallow but longer rhythm. I knew adrenaline would be flooding my bloodstream.

"What are they waiting for?" Monk's voice sounded quiet next to me.

As if in response, the doors to the Suburban opened and I thought I saw a shadow spill out, heading for the tree line. They were going to try and flank us.

I knew the situation they were in: On an open road, with the chance of traffic coming, they had to put us down fast and then disappear or risk discovery by the authorities.

A gunshot rang out and I heard the zip of the bullet streak over my head. I ducked slightly by reflex. I hadn't seen a muzzle blast.

The combination of the headlights and the darkness made it tough for my vision to penetrate the area. Normally, I see great in the dark. But in this fifty-fifty environment, it was like trying to make out vague shapes and images.

The only problem was, these fuzzy shapes could kill me.

And trying to get a bead on someone was even tougher.

I fired a round off toward the left. The Suburban's engine remained on.

I heard another door open. The driver?

On a Suburban, it could have been the passenger doors, though. The truck holds upwards of eight people easily. I sincerely hoped there weren't eight members on this team, or my working relationship with Monk would be extinct before it even got started.

Monk squatted next to me, her hand wrapped around one of her spikes. I hoped the hell she knew how to throw those things—accurately.

A thought occurred to me about the same time as a series of gunshots flew over the engine block. I ducked. I had no idea of knowing what kind of kill team this was. Were they vampires? Lycanthropes? Half-breeds? It raised several disturbing questions.

Most importantly, if they were lycanthropes and I was firing wooden-tipped bullets at them, it wouldn't do a damn bit of good. Lycanthropes can be pierced by wood without any ill effects.

But if they were vampires, then Monk's spikes wouldn't do any good either. Vampires have no fear of silver at all.

Our best bet was if the team was comprised of half-breeds. At least then the playing field would be about as level as we'd be able to get it.

For the first time, I was actually glad I had Monk next to me. I didn't think I'd be glad for long, though.

I fired another round to our left. Another round came singing back at us.

For a hit, the team wasn't exerting very much effort.

I'd expected a full thunderstorm of hell upon us stopping.

And more, if this hit had been better planned, there would have been another team to hit us from one of the other sides. We'd be caught in a funnel of crossfire and dead in a very short span of time.

Instead, things seemed very lukewarm. I saw no other hit teams around us. I looked at Monk. Her eyes scanned the darkness to our left.

"You see anything?"

"No." She frowned. "I thought I saw someone jump out of the car and go running there."

"Yeah, I thought they were going to flank us."

"Now I'm not so sure," said Monk.

Neither was I. And that didn't make me feel any better.

Monk nudged me. "Look."

And then I saw it, behind us, about three miles

down the road on the opposite side of the highway, two sets of headlights.

I gripped my gun a little tighter. I hoped to hell it wasn't reinforcements. If the team had been ordered to stop us and then wait, this whole situation could go south very fast.

I took immediate stock. My gun still had a dozen rounds. I had two magazines as backup. Monk had six of her silver spikes.

The odds weren't good.

Then again, they never are where my life is concerned.

Another shot rang out. I couldn't even tell what they were aiming at.

The headlights drew closer. Traveling at sixty miles would mean they'd get here in under three minutes. But since most folks drove faster than the speed limit, I knew they'd be here even sooner.

One set of headlights looked lower than the other. That meant it was probably a car and not another truck or sport utility vehicle. That made me feel a little better.

I felt even better a second later when I heard some kind of shout from the Suburban, caught another glimpse of someone running in from the woods and two doors shutting. The Suburban's engine gunned, drove in reverse about fifty meters, and then swung around, cut across the highway divider, and took off back the way we'd just traveled.

Monk sighed.

No time to rest, though, not with that traffic headed our way. I pushed Monk back into the Explorer and hopped in on my side. I swung into action, jerked us to the right, and drove on.

What the hell kind of botched job had that been?

And what kind of yell had come from the truck?

I asked Monk about that, but she only shook her head. "I've never heard anything like that."

"Never?"

"Nope. It's not a lycanthrope dialect as far as I know."

"Well, it sure as hell wasn't Taluk either."

"Maybe it was some kind of half-breed tongue."

"There such a thing?"

"I don't know," said Monk. "But judging from what we saw just now, I guess I wouldn't doubt it."

"Yeah."

Monk stayed quiet for another minute. Then she cleared her throat. "I have to go to the bathroom."

I could have used one too. As many scrapes as I've been in, there's nothing that ever stops the natural course of action. Adrenaline drips into your blood, everything constricts, and suddenly, you have to take a leak. It's just the way the body works—human or vampire or, apparently, lycanthrope. Even combat-hardened vets will tell you the urge to piss always stays with you no matter how many years in the field you've got.

But right now I wanted to get as far away from our encounter as possible. I thought I could hold out for another hour or so. But one look at Monk told me she wouldn't be able to.

That was to be expected. After my first run-in with someone shooting at me, I'd pissed my pants and nearly changed their color to brown as well.

All things considered, Monk had held up pretty well.

She pointed. "There's a sign for a rest stop."

"You can't wait?"

She looked at me wide-eyed. "You nuts? It's all I can do to sit here and not move. We need to stop."

"All right, but keep your spikes handy. I don't want that Suburban coming after us. If they figure out we've stopped, we'll be dead for sure."

"We ought to be dead now, shouldn't we?"

I sighed. "Yeah. I suppose we oughta be."

"But we're not."

"Nope."

"Why?"

I shook my head. "I look like the answer man here, Monk? Hell if I know. They had us in a pretty bad spot back there. If they'd pressed the attack— yeah, we probably would have died."

"This ever happen to you before?"

"What—that kind of botched hit?"

"Yeah."

I saw the blue sign up ahead and fought the urge to flick on my turn signal. I wouldn't be using that tonight. The red light was visible for miles behind me.

I followed the signs for cars, and we slid into a neon-harsh rest stop complete with a McDonald's. I could use a burger. I sighed. I could use some juice even more.

"We need to get home as soon as possible," I said. "So make sure you tie a knot in it when you're done."

She sat there looking at me. "You didn't answer my question."

I looked at her. "I thought you had to go to the bathroom."

"I do."

"Just not until I answer your question, though, huh?"

"You got it."

I sighed. "Okay, yeah. It's happened to me once before. What should have been a clean kill on me didn't work out that way. They held back."

"Did you ever find out why?"

"Yeah, I did."

"So?"

"It was a setup."

"A setup?"

"Jeez, Monk, it was designed to look like a hit in order to get me to do one thing. In reality, it wasn't supposed to be a hit at all. I should have done the exact opposite of what I did. But I got suckered. I fell for the trap."

"Did you get hurt?"

I looked away. Sometimes, at night, in the darkness, the memories of past events and places seem so real you think you're back there. You see the faces, hear the screams, feel the fear all over again.

And then it's gone.

I glanced at Monk. "I didn't get hurt."

"That's good then."

"No," I said. "It's not."

"Why?"

"Because someone died as a result of my actions. Someone who ought to be alive still. Someone who ought to be breathing, getting married, and having little vampires." I looked away. "But instead, they're dead."

Monk's touch felt light on my arm. "You did your best, though. Right?"

I tried to smile. I didn't succeed. "You're going to find out, Monk, that sometimes, even your best won't stop people from dying. And when that happens, it's just about the worst goddamned feeling in the world."

She took her hand away, stayed still another minute, and then walked off toward the bathroom.

I watched her go.

And then felt very old.

Seventeen

We reached Boston just after four in the morning in large part because I ignored the speed limit. As we drove into the city, it suddenly dawned on me that I had no clue where I was going to stash Monk. I mentioned this to her, and the look on her face told me she hadn't given it much thought either.

"Can't I just stay with you?"

"Monk . . ."

"Jeez, Lawson, it's not like I want to sleep with you or anything. I just need a place to crash, get some sleep, and a shower. Later on, we can go get started on the search, that's all. Okay?"

It wasn't okay.

It wasn't the fact that Monk was a woman that had me so reluctant. The fact is, my house is sacred to me. My ancestors who came over from Germany a few hundred years back built it. Over the years, that house has become my refuge.

I don't like mixing work with my home.

It's happened in the past, and each time it does, I make new vows never to let it happen again. Never seems to work, though, as my present situation demonstrated. Add to that Shiva's little trickery a few nights back, and the idea of opening my home up again didn't sit well with me at all.

But Monk had to stay somewhere.

"All right."

She smiled. "See? That wasn't so hard."

"Hope you're not allergic to cats."

"You have cats?"

"Two."

"I love cats. Belladonna's house is simply crawling with them."

"You don't eat them, do you?"

"What?"

"Just checking."

"Lawson, I'm a lycanthrope. That means I enjoy human flesh." She sighed. "Besides, cats make poor meals. They're too small."

I looked at her and she broke into a toothy grin. "I'm kidding. It was a joke."

"Good."

"You're awfully uptight, Lawson. You know that?"

"I'm uptight because I'm being paired with a lot of people I don't normally work with. One of them is probably a traitor at the very least. I've got a certifiable professional killer loose in Boston whose aims may or may not be counter to my own. I've been getting more partners than I ever wanted. I'm going to look for a relic that's part of a culture I don't even understand. I have no idea what's really going on. And to top it off, I've got to open my house—no offense—to a complete stranger." I looked at her. "So, yes. I am uptight."

Monk stayed quiet for a minute. I'd noticed she was big on pauses. "We're not complete strangers, Lawson."

I sighed. "You know what I mean."

"If it makes you that unhappy, I can go crash at a hotel."

"Forget it. You won't be comfortable. You can stay with me. Really."

"You sure?"

"Yeah."

"Okay then." She stared out of the window as we wound our way down Storrow Drive. We exited at the Kenmore Square off-ramp, slid down into Kenmore, out onto Beacon, and then took a left that eventually put us onto the Riverway and then the Jamaicaway.

I kept checking my rearview mirror for headlights. This early in the morning, some commuters were already on the road heading into their cramped four-by-four cubicles for another nine-hour stint in Corporate Slavery America.

But no one drove behind us. For the first time in the last few hours, I actually breathed a little easier.

My energy was shot.

I hadn't had any juice since I'd left Arthur's warm kitchen almost twenty-four hours ago. I needed a hit of the stuff bad. If anything went wrong now, I'd be in miserable shape to ward it off.

At last we cruised toward Jamaica Pond and my home. I rolled the Explorer into the spot in front of my house, relieved that none of the post-college frat idiots had taken it.

Monk looked up at my house. "Wow."

It has that effect on a lot of people. You simply don't see the kind of craftsmanship in houses built nowadays. My German ancestors were all master carpenters. The molding and intricate woodwork is testament to their level of skill. It's a skill I wish I possessed. I have all their tools. I have the desire.

But I've got little time to indulge that particular passion.

Maybe someday, though . . .

I walked up the steps and unlocked the hall door. My mail lay inside, scattered about. I could already smell the perfume samples stuck into the department store catalogs. I'd dump those immediately. There's nothing worse than tickling scents that cling to your skin after you flip through a flyer. They reminded me of Jarvis and his awful cologne.

Monk stayed quiet behind me as we crested the steps. I heard a thundering tumble down the stairs and I knew Phoebe was coming. The cat is tiny, but sounds exactly like a bag of bricks falling down the stairs.

Mimi's a lot quieter and materializes out of nowhere with little fanfare.

Phoebe skidded to a stop when she saw Monk. This was the second time in the last few nights a stranger had shown up. Phoebe would need some lithium before this week was out.

Monk knelt down and held out her hand. Mimi appeared out of nowhere and took an instant liking to her. Mimi does that with everyone. Sometimes I get jealous.

Phoebe banged into my leg, seeking reassurance. And probably a can of Iams.

I clucked for them both, and got some dinner squared away in their bowls. I opened the refrigerator and poured myself a tall glass of juice.

Monk stood in the doorway of the kitchen watching me suck it down in a few gulps.

"God."

I put the glass down. "What?"

She frowned. "Nothing. I've just never seen that done before."

"What—a vampire drinking blood?"

"Yeah."

"Makes you feel any better," I said, "I've never seen a lycanthrope tear into human flesh and chow down on it."

"You've been deprived."

I smirked. "That is doubtful." I nodded to the hallway. "Come on, I'll show you where you can sleep."

She followed me upstairs to the third floor. I gave her the bedroom next to mine. "Bathroom's down the hall. There are fresh sheets on the bed." Well, they were fresh to me. I'd put them on about three months back, but since no one had used them yet, I figured they were still good.

The early morning air dripped with humidity. I'd perspired in the short time we'd been in the house. It might have also been the hit of energy I got from the juice.

"There's a window fan in there that'll give you a good breeze. Plus, you're on the cool side of the house. Sorry, I can't offer you any air-conditioning."

"I don't mind the heat," said Monk. She wiped the back of her hand on her forehead. It came away wet.

I tasted the remnants of the juice in my mouth. "Right. Well, we both need some sack time. Otherwise we won't be in any shape to do any searching this afternoon."

"How long do we have to sleep?"

I thought about Shiva and her forty-eight-hour deadline. I didn't want to waste any time, but sleep was a necessity. Shiva wouldn't move probably for another day. I hoped.

It was just after four-thirty. "Why don't we plan on getting started around noon? That'll give us almost eight hours to sleep. We can get a lot done this afternoon and evening."

Monk nodded. "That sounds good."

"Okay. Good night then."

I turned.

"Lawson."

"Yeah?"

Monk smiled at me. "It's morning now."

"Yeah. Sorry about that."

I closed my bedroom door and stripped down. I flipped the AC unit on and felt the cool breeze come out. It felt great hitting my hot skin.

I slid under the sheets. I've always loved sleeping in the cold. There's nothing like bundling under a pile of blankets, feeling all warm and snug.

Mimi materialized on top of the bed. She must have snuck in while I was talking to Monk. She settled herself at the end of the bed and launched into her aerobic cleaning routine. Mimi's a longhair and feels a need to clean herself religiously at least two dozen times each day. For her never-faltering discipline, I'm rewarded with messy hairballs on the average of two each month—no matter how much hairball-formula cat food I buy.

I leaned back and felt the pillow embrace my head. It felt good to be home. I don't like being on the road. Even for a few hours.

I thought about the situation. Sometimes I do my best thinking in bed. I can sort through stuff. Try to make sense of it.

If Jarvis and Belarus were in league, what were they after? The Lunaspe? Why would Jarvis have shown me the paperwork then? Why risk exposing that secret? Maybe he and Belarus couldn't decipher it. Maybe they needed it translated. Maybe they'd set up the ambush on the Maine highway to confuse me.

I needed to keep Monk a secret for now. The less anyone knew about her, the better. If Jarvis and Belarus were after the Lunaspe, they'd kill Monk and me to get at it.

But once they had it, what did they plan to do then? I didn't like considering the implications of half-breeds running around with powerful artifacts.

I turned slightly.

Monk.

The kid was green. No doubt.

Still, she hadn't gone to hell when we'd been ambushed. She might have even been able to hold her own if they'd come on strong for us.

I still wasn't convinced.

I tend to be a real skeptical sonofabitch when it comes to matters of experience. I've seen far too many examples of incompetence getting people killed. I'd even heard about some insecure loser who set himself up as an anti-terrorist expert in the wake of the September 11th terrorist attacks.

From what I knew about him, the guy had about as much anti-terror experience as I do selling Avon products door to door. But he didn't care. He didn't care that what he was showing to people could get them killed. All he wanted was the ego-stroke and the paycheck.

Nowadays, everyone wants to be a teacher. But they don't want the responsibility—the serious responsibility—that goes along with it.

In my opinion, it's the teachers who have years of experience and yet still maintain a humble attitude that are the best—no matter what the field. The so-called experts who parade around casting dispersions and harsh judgments on everything under the sun are the fools to be avoided.

So I tend to harp on experience.

I turned at that moment.

And saw my door handle turning.

I sat up.

Mimi cocked her head.

The door opened.

Monk stood in my doorway.

Naked.

I could see the lithe, taut muscles all over her body. The firm abdominals, the ample bosom, the curve of her hips, the tilt of her neck, erect nipples.

She oozed sex.

I could smell the pheromones leaping off her like jumpers off a bridge.

I cleared my throat. "Yeah?"

"It's too hot in my room."

"I thought you said you didn't mind the heat."

She took a step in and leaned against the doorjamb. My head felt a little light as the blood cells abandoned my cerebellum and plunged south.

Traitors.

"I just thought that maybe I could sleep in here with you." She smiled and let her eyelids dip half-closed. Sultry.

Humidity bled into the room. I could feel the contrasting air fronts battling each other. Hot. Cold. I felt like I was in some bungalow in Belize waiting for Maria the bar girl to deliver a coconut drink and a happy hop in the sack.

My head felt even lighter. I needed to lie down, but if I did, there wouldn't be much chance of concealing my growing proclivity to taking Monk up on her offer. Damn the good genes I was blessed with.

"Go to sleep, Monk."

She frowned. "Really?"

"Yes, really. Go back to your bedroom. Get some sleep. We need to be sharp later on. There's no time for this now."

She came over to the bed and leaned over me, her breasts dangling just a few inches from my mouth. I licked my lips subconsciously.

Monk reached down and squeezed me through the sheets. Her eyes widened. "So . . . I do have an effect on you."

I took her hand away, as much as I wanted it to stay there. "Monk, I like women. And naked women especially. So yes, you do have an effect on me. But like I said—"

She put a finger to my lips. "We could be dead later today, Lawson. Don't you at least want to experience me before that happens?"

I took her hand away again. "Go to bed, Monk. If you're with me, you won't die. And neither will I."

I patted her on her butt and nudged her off the bed. "I need sleep and so do you."

She sighed and shook her head. "Just trying to be friendly. Good night."

I watched the door close and took a deep gulp of air. I hadn't had sex in almost a year. Not since Talya. For a sex-crazed guy like me, a year felt like a millennium.

My groin felt hot. I was still swollen like a bad lymph node on steroids.

Monk looked even better with her clothes off.

I didn't get to sleep for a while.

Eighteen

Monk kept to herself when we woke up. I showered and dressed quickly, and then she did the same. I left some dry food for Mimi and Phoebe and then we took off.

In my Explorer at the end of my street, she suddenly turned to me. "Thank you."

I looked at her. "For what?"

"For not . . . you know."

"Forget it. It's not a problem."

"I think the ambush on the highway freaked me out. I think maybe I was reacting to it in an unusual way."

"It happens. Is that the first time you've ever had someone try to kill you?"

"Yes."

I wheeled us onto the Arborway and began driving toward the city. "I thought it was my unmistakable sex appeal that drove you to that."

She laughed. That was a good sign. "You're a handsome man, Lawson. No doubt. But I don't usually come on that strong."

My ego sufficiently stroked, I smiled. "You hungry?"

"Starving."

"Human food okay?"

"I suppose it will have to do for now." She sighed. "The moon is waxing though."

"Which means?"

"The closer it gets to full, the more desire I'll have for human flesh. It can't be helped. I need the flesh or I'll die."

"I'll see what I can do."

"It's not really your concern. If the opportunity presents itself, I'll take care of the craving on my own."

"Just don't leave any bodies lying around, okay?"

She looked at me. "How do you guys manage anyway? I mean, I don't see you out stalking humans for their blood. Hell, you've got a container of it chilling in your fridge."

"Being a Fixer has some fringe benefits. Damned few, in fact, but there are some. I get a supply of blood delivered to my house by some vampires who work for a blood bank in town."

"Convenient."

"Sure is. Most of the time, I don't have a second to spare to go hunting. The Council recognized that early on in our history. Ever since, they've taken care of us."

"And the rest of vampire society?"

"Our society has created some creative techniques for ensuring we always have as much as we need. Some of the vampires hang out in strange night clubs where letting some blood flow isn't deemed weird. Some work in the medical field and can acquire blood for others. And some still like the thrill of the hunt. As long as no one notices us, there's no problem."

"I see."

"Why? How do things work for lycanthropes?"

"We're on our own for the most part. Once a year there's a large feast where the local community comes together in celebration. Usually the main course is a recently deceased cadaver. One time we managed to talk a heroin addict on the brink of suicide into letting us have him instead."

"You ate him while he was still alive?"

Monk smiled. "It's not as awful as it sounds. My people have a thorough knowledge of herbology. He drank a potion that anesthetized him before we began. We bled him then. He died as if he was going to sleep. Then we ate him."

Suddenly I wasn't so hungry anymore. The thought of chewing on a human being for dinner made my stomach do somersaults. I cleared my throat. "Well."

"Yes," said Monk, "I wouldn't expect you to fully appreciate what my kind do."

"Nor would I expect you to understand how vampires operate."

"Okay."

We rolled back down the Jamaicaway and over toward Fenway Park. Normally, I would have headed right for my favorite Chinese restaurant. I can eat there every day and not get tired of their amazing hot and sour soup, dry noodles, and spicy beef.

But today, for some reason, I opted otherwise.

"Where are we going?" said Monk.

"You like Italian?"

"Sure."

I drove up Beacon, past the Chinese restaurant, and kept going through Coolidge Corner, past Washington Square. I stopped three blocks up. Right in front of Vinny Testa's.

"Here we go."

Monk hopped out. I walked in and we got seated. Monk ordered the veal parmigiana. I stuck with spaghetti and meatballs.

I broke some focaccia bread and dipped it in the olive oil and basil. "So, where do we start with this search anyway?"

"Good question. How about letting me see the papers?"

I pulled out the sheaf of them and suddenly remembered Jarvis. Cripes, he'd be going out of his mind right about now. Not to mention the possibility that Shiva might be getting ready to move.

I needed some way to contact Shiva.

But how? Our last discussion hadn't entailed contact information.

And I still wasn't sure that Jarvis was the bad guy she said he was. After all, I had the sheaf of papers showing the location of the Lunaspe. If Jarvis and Belarus were trying so hard to find this artifact, why would Jarvis have given me the papers?

I sighed. Monk looked up. "What's wrong?"

"I gotta make a phone call." I stood and walked to the rest rooms. I picked up the phone and dialed Niles at home.

He answered out of breath. "Lawson?"

Jeez. Was everybody else a psychic but me? "Yeah."

"Where in God's name have you been? Do you know there are people looking for you?"

"You don't know the half of it, Niles." I stopped. "Wait—who's looking for me?"

"Uh, well, only this guy Jarvis and, oh, yeah—the head of the goddamned Council, Belarus."

Why was Belarus looking for me? "I told them I had business out of state to attend to."

"Yes, well, Jarvis says you've got something that

belongs to him. And Belarus is apparently quite upset that you've left Jarvis alone in the event that Shiva comes calling. They're both quite distressed, I can tell you that."

"What about you?"

"What about me?"

"Are you distressed too?"

He paused. "Well. No. Not really. I mean, I read your jacket, Lawson. I know what you're capable of. I know how you operate. I like to think you've got things pretty well handled."

I actually smiled. "Well, I appreciate the vote of confidence, Niles. That means a lot to me."

"Not that everyone else doesn't think I'm an absolute fool for trusting you like this. They're already talking about sending me someplace else; they're saying I can't control you."

"Don't worry about what they say. We'll deal with them when the time comes. For now, just keep them off my back."

"Are you local again?"

"Yeah, just having some lunch."

"You'd better hook up with Jarvis as soon as possible."

"Can you relay a message to him for me?"

"Why don't you call him yourself?"

"I'd rather have lunch undisturbed. Jarvis is liable to trace the call and show up here."

"Uh . . . okay. What's the message?"

"Tell him I'll meet him at the Council building at five this evening, okay? I'll bring the papers he had."

"What about Belarus?"

"All you need to do is tell him I'm back in Boston and working the case again. Tell him his ass is safe."

Niles paused. "I don't think I'll phrase it like that."

"Probably better not to, yeah."

"Five p.m.?"

"Yes."

"Okay."

I hung up and walked back to the table. Monk was knee-deep in veal. My spaghetti was getting cold. I twirled some strands around my fork and plopped it into my mouth.

"What'd you figure out there, Monk?"

She chewed slowly. I could tell she was savoring the veal. Hell, she probably wished it was human flesh.

"We need to go to the Blue Hills."

"The Blue Hills?"

She nodded. "The artifact is buried there, unless I'm mistaken."

"Are you often mistaken?"

"No."

I nodded. "How'd you learn this stuff anyway?"

"I apprenticed under Belladonna."

"For how long?"

She smiled. "I'm still learning."

That was refreshing. Nowadays, most people take a quick course and think they're a master of anything. I knew people who took a weekend course in a martial arts system and came out thinking they were Bruce friggin' Lee. At least Monk knew she'd been learning for a long time.

"We can't go to the Blue Hills yet."

She frowned. "Why not?"

"Because I've got to see some people in a few hours."

"But, Lawson—"

"Look, Monk, I want to get this all done as much as you do. But I can't cut out on seeing these people. Too many flags will go up. Something is going on here, and I need to make sure my ass is covered as best as it possibly can be before I go digging up some forest looking for some ancient relic."

"Okay. What do you want me to do in the meantime?"

I shrugged. "Honestly? I don't know. I don't have to be there for about three hours."

Monk grinned. "We could go back to your place and kill some time."

"I thought you said all that seduction jazz was due to the ambush."

She shrugged. "Maybe not all about the ambush."

I smiled. "Right. How about I take you to see a friend of mine instead. Maybe you can spend a few hours copying the notes from those papers. I've got to give them back to their owner."

"Okay. We can do that. What are you going to do in the meantime?"

"Oh, I've got something in mind."

Although the thought of trying to attract Shiva's attention was the last thing I wanted to do.

Nineteen

A balmy breeze blew over Boston Common by the time I arrived there an hour later. I'd dropped Monk off at Wirek's apartment. Wirek took one look at Monk and shot me an upraised eyebrow. At first I thought maybe it was the first good-looking woman Wirek had had over to his place in years. Then I remembered what he'd said to me a few days earlier about chicks loving his bald head.

I wondered if Monk's virtue would be safe.

After Monk made a copy of the notes, I took the originals and headed back down toward Beacon Street. I parked back at the Boston Common garage and eased out of the stairway on the Common. I tried waving my arms around to ditch the smell of carbon monoxide and exhaust that seemed to cloy at the interior stairwells of the garage.

The maple and linden trees on the Common swayed in the slight breeze making my Hawaiian shirt ruffle. Outside, I kept my arms down making sure the breeze didn't suddenly expose my gun.

I had no idea how to contact Shiva.

Supposedly, she was here to kill Belarus. The truth of the matter was, she could have just as easily been here for that damned amulet as well. But even if that was true, she'd need to dispose of the other players involved. So that meant killing Belarus.

If I'd wanted to kill the head of the Council, my mission would dictate a lot of reconnaissance.

That meant Shiva would have to stake out the Council building.

There were only so many vantage points that afforded a decent view of the building's entrance. Of course, Shiva could easily have staked out the back of the building, thinking Belarus would possibly come and go through there.

But if she knew what an egotistical bastard Belarus was, she'd know he'd stick with the front door.

And from what I knew about Shiva, she took the time and was precise enough in her work to know the habits of her targets.

I strolled the paths with the idea that I'd surveil the people on benches facing the building. I'd narrow down the choices and try some eye contact. I'd see if anything developed.

I soon realized the better option would be to simply make myself visible. After all, there were a lot of benches. And sunny late summer afternoons on Boston Common mean a lot of people.

I made a circuit twice.

No one moved in the time it took me to walk around the park.

Lady Luck had once again flipped me the bird.

I sat down on one bench and leaned into the new plastic pseudo-wood they used in bench repair. Supposedly it lasted longer, being made of recycled materials, and all that jazz. Part of me longed for the honest feeling of solid wood instead.

I closed my eyes halfway and checked my watch. I had just over an hour before I was due to meet Jarvis and hand over his precious treasure map.

A heavyset man wearing shorts that creased his

crotch like a sandwich bag attempting to contain a blue whale waddled by with a small Pekinese dog. The dog sniffed at my shoe and began yapping uncontrollably.

Dogs have never liked me.

Come to think of it, I have much the same problem with a lot of people.

A woman in a short skirt walked toward my bench. I'd left space to my right. She sat down and crossed her legs. I smiled. I love the summer.

She caught me looking at her and smiled, showing brilliant white teeth. "See something you like?"

Aggressive too. I inclined my head. "Just admiring your genes."

"I'm not wearing jeans."

"And thank God for that."

She laughed. "You're funny."

I looked away and couldn't help the smile that crept over my face. Something about a beautiful woman just made me all warm and fuzzy on the inside.

I glanced back. "My name's—"

"Lawson."

Oh, shit.

"Goddamnit." I shook my head. "I should have known it was you . . . Shiva."

"You always this much of a sucker for good-looking women?"

"Uh . . . yeah. Usually."

"Least you're honest."

"How long have you been watching me?"

She shrugged and recrossed her legs. She showed an ample amount of thigh. I had a tough time remembering she probably didn't look a thing like that. Then I remembered I'd never even known what she looked like in her natural state. All the surveillance photos the Council had on her were taken while she was transformed. All the times I'd seen her, she was disguised.

"Long enough," she said. "I had to make sure no one was on you."

"Am I clean?"

"Dirty as hell. That's what I hear about you."

"I meant do I have any tails?"

"No."

That was a relief. I didn't think I'd had any, but confirmation from another source is always nice.

"My forty-eight hours is up."

She nodded. "I kept my word."

"Yes. You did. And as much as it pains me to say this—thank you."

She inclined her head. "Least I could do for the world-famous Fixer."

"Last time you and I tangled, I didn't think either of us was going to walk away."

She smiled. "It was a knee in the crotch, wasn't it?"

I nodded, remembering how we'd closed to a grapple and then I felt the sudden bowel-dropping sensation of her kneecap exploding into my groin. It still hurt.

"Yeah. You got me good."

"It was a desperate move."

"You don't have to be kind to me, Shiva. It was a good move. You know it. I know it. Sometimes the simplest techniques work best."

"You're a modest man, Lawson. You had the upper hand for most of that fight."

"We going to debate this all afternoon?"

"No." She smiled. "Have you confirmed what I

told you about Jarvis and Belarus? Do you understand why they have to die?"

"That's one reason I wanted to talk with you. The
only thing I've discovered is that this thing is a
whole lot messier than at first glance."

"How so?"

"You want to tell me about the Lunaspe?"

"The what?"

My mind struggled to recall what Wirek had
called it in Geralach. All I could come up with was
"Chaka-Khan."

Shiva laughed. "Ah, yes. Okay, I know what you
mean now."

"Well?"

She swiveled so her back was to me a bit more.
We had to be careful. If someone from the Council
building spotted me talking to her, they might
piece it together and interrupt our conversation.

"The Lunaspe is the one relic that has been
hunted more than any other in the lycanthrope
society."

"Christ, there are others?"

"Yes, but none so desired as the Lunaspe."

"Because of its power."

"Yes. It is a very powerful artifact. Not only for a
lycanthrope to possess, but also for a half-breed,
or even a vampire."

"But we don't get power from the moon."

She looked at me. "Is that what you were told?
That all it does is give the wielder power from the
moon?" She sniffed. "The . . . Lunaspe, as you
called it, is incredibly potent. Yes, it draws its power
from the moon, but it also bestows on the wielder
additional attributes. Some of them I don't even
know about."

"And you're looking for this amulet?"

"Me? No. Not at all, actually. But Jarvis and Belarus are."

"You told me they were looking to exterminate the half-breeds."

"They are."

"Okay, but they want the amulet as well?"

"They need the amulet to complete their extermination plans."

"You telling me this thing is some kind of incredible weapon?"

"I'm telling you the Lunaspe is more powerful than most people realize."

I thought about what Belladonna had told me about the relic. She'd warned that its falling into the wrong hands could be disastrous for all races, not just the lycanthropes.

I decided to take a chance. "Jarvis had some kind of map to find the Lunaspe."

Shiva nodded. "I know. I had hoped to get it away from him."

"Would it do you any good? Can you read it?"

She looked at me. "You've seen it?"

"He showed it to me, yeah."

"Did you understand it?"

"Nope. It was in that language lycanthropes use. Geralach."

She nodded, still watching me. "I need to find that relic first."

"Or at least kill Jarvis and Belarus."

"Or that," she said. "But preferably both."

"What would you do with the Lunaspe if you had it in your possession?"

"Destroy it if possible. It is too powerful for any one person to possess."

"Do you think that's your right, to destroy it?"

She smiled. "Lawson, you really have no idea of the exact ramifications the Lunaspe has for not just lycanthrope society, but your society as well. This isn't some simple charm we're talking about here."

"It's that powerful?"

"Anyone who tells you otherwise is lying to you."

Great. Just what I needed to hear. I looked at my watch. It was getting late. "I have to head across the street soon."

"You're seeing them?"

"Jarvis, yes."

She nodded. "I suppose I shouldn't suggest you lead him out here where I can finish him off then?"

I shrugged. "Depends. You could suggest it. I might say okay. Or I might not listen to you at all."

Another grin crossed her face. "Oh, Lawson, you know you remind me a lot of myself."

"Is that so?"

"Yes. We both do things our own way. We both live a life dictated by honor, even at the expense of everyone else." She slid closer. "It's a lonely life sometimes, isn't it?"

"It's lonely realizing there aren't many like us. If that's what you mean."

"That wasn't exactly what I meant."

I nodded. "Yeah, I kinda figured that."

"We could be great together."

"No." I shook my head. "We'd kill each other within a week. You know it as well as I do. We're too much alike, to use your phrasing."

"Be fun while it lasted," said Shiva.

Somehow I doubted that. I stood. "I've got to go."

"Enjoy your meeting." She glanced down at her fingernails. "But Lawson?"

I looked at her. "What?"

"Like I said before: The forty-eight hours is up. You're out of time. I have to move on them—with or without your involvement."

"Thanks for the reminder."

"If you're there, I won't like it. But you know I'll do what I have to."

"Yeah. I know it. But just so we understand each other: I'll do what I have to do too."

She smiled at me once more.

I turned and walked away.

Twenty

Jarvis couldn't decide if he was happy to see me or just plain pissed off. I met him coming in the main entrance at the Council Building. Arthur hung in the background, an amused expression splayed all over his face.

"Lawson," said Jarvis, "where the hell have you been?"

"Out of town. I told you I had some things to do."

Jarvis licked his lips. "Did you, uh, forget what we got going on here? Did you forget that Shiva is trying to kill Belarus?"

"Nope. But I had some things I needed to run down."

"Jesus Christ, I've been looking for you everywhere. I even paid a visit to that old coot Wirek over on the Hill. Then I tried calling your very ineffectual Control."

"What'd he tell you?"

"In so many words? That where you were was none of my business."

Chalk up another point for Niles. I liked a Control who wasn't afraid to tell someone like Jarvis to kiss off. "Well, that was nice of him."

"It's bullshit, Lawson. That's what it is."

"I've been gone for one day. Keep your skivvies on."

"I don't wear any." Jarvis shook his head. "What the hell did you do with those papers we were supposed to be researching? I don't have to remind you that's pretty important information. Information that shouldn't have left my possession."

Arthur raised his eyebrows at me and then slipped away toward the kitchen.

I brought the sheaf of papers out of my pocket and held them up. "You mean these papers?"

Jarvis grabbed at them, but I snatched them back. "Want to tell me what this is all about?"

"What are you talking about? Give those to me."

"Did you find anything out?"

"Of course not. Aside from what the guy Wirek told us, I haven't found anything out."

"So, what you're telling me then is that these papers are pretty useless."

"What? I'm not saying that at all!"

"I could almost toss these into the garbage and it wouldn't make one bit of difference."

Jarvis stopped hopping around. "Lawson. Stop dicking around. Give me those papers."

"Didn't you even make a copy of them beforehand?"

Jarvis dropped his eyes to the floor. "No."

If what Shiva had said was the truth, then Belarus had probably torn Jarvis a new asshole for letting the papers out of his sight.

I held the papers out. "Here."

He grabbed them away. As an afterthought he looked at me. "Did you find anything out?"

I shrugged. "Some."

"Want to share?"

"Sure. I was ambushed last night on a highway in Maine."

"An ambush?"

"Yeah, except it wasn't a particularly effective one. They rammed my car, but then they backed off after they fired a few rounds at me." I deliberately kept Monk's name out of it. I didn't want anyone but Wirek knowing about her.

"You got any idea who'd do that?"

"Well, it sure as hell wasn't Shiva's style. The only thing I can figure is that someone somewhere was getting a little antsy about me not being in Boston. Or maybe they were upset that I had something important. You know, something like those papers."

"Who would—Jesus, you don't think I had anything to do with that, do you?"

"I don't know. Should I have any reason to suspect you?"

"Of course not. Lawson, we're on the same team here. Do I have to remind you of how much action we've seen together?"

"I think you'd better, considering I've never really seen you handle your own before."

Jarvis's jaw dropped, but then he closed his mouth. "So, that's it, huh?"

I shrugged.

Jarvis kept talking. "Work with a guy, get his back, and this is the thanks you get. I get it now."

I shook my head. "I don't think you do, Jarvis. See, the truth is, I don't know what the hell is going on here. And I like operating in the dark about as much as I like having my teeth yanked out of my head. I'm being lied to on a number of fronts. I've got people all over me, telling me things that make no sense, and I've got other people telling me other things at the same time. All I know is this: I am watching out for myself and trusting no one. Not even you, pal. You got it?"

Jarvis looked at me. "Yeah. Yeah, I got it, Lawson."

"Good. Because I don't much like having these kinds of conversations." I grinned. "Now. What did you find out?"

"Not much."

"You have any idea where Shiva is?"

"None."

"So she could strike at any time and we wouldn't know jack shit."

"Correct."

"What about security precautions for Belarus?"

"I've been close to him ever since you left. I figured that'd be the best way to cover him in the interim."

"Okay. What's next then?"

"I've got an errand to run tomorrow that will take me out of town," said Jarvis.

I frowned. "You kidding? I go out of town and get reamed out by the likes of you, but now you turn around and tell me you're headed out too? Nice double standard there, pal."

"I don't intend on disappearing for days on end. Nor will I be taking some important evidence with me."

"Great."

"Can you cover Belarus while I'm gone?"

"Oh, there's nothing I'd like better than to spend some quality time with Belarus." I eyed Jarvis. "He know you're going out of town?"

"Yes."

"And he knows I'll be watching him?"

"Yes."

"Is he excited?"

"About as much as you are."

"Tomorrow should be a great day."

"Be here at nine if you can, Lawson," said Jarvis.

I turned around and walked back out into the evening air. The humidity had retreated in the few minutes I'd been inside. That was one of the best parts about living in Boston. If you don't like the weather, just wait a minute and it'll change.

Now a strong breeze blew in from the northeast, tinging the air with a slight chill off the ocean. The dry air made everything sound crisp. Cars slid down Beacon Street, homeward bound from the government buildings on top of Beacon Hill.

I crossed over to the Boston Common again and headed toward the staircase and my Explorer.

Couples wound their way along the path, some of them still dressed in their corporate garb. I saw more dogs out now, crisscrossing the grass in search of an adequate dumping site. By the corner, a pretzel vendor scented the air with warm and salty bread dough and mustard.

And in that postcard-esque setting, something didn't seem right.

I frowned and closed on the small house that served as an entrance to the stairway. I paused at the door, making believe it was tough to open. I used the glass to check my background, looking for a familiar face in the crowd.

I saw nothing.

It didn't make sense for Shiva to be stalking me. I didn't think she'd waste any time on the likes of me. She was after bigger fish.

So who was it?

Or was I even being tailed at all?

My paranoia level had understandably risen since

the ambush attempt on the Maine highway last night.

Maybe I was simply imagining things.

I frowned. Every time I tried convincing myself of that, something truly bad happened that reminded me I don't imagine things.

I stepped into the house and started down the stairs. At my level I exited the stairway and paused. Listening.

Down in the cool garage interior, I could smell the fuel and exhaust. Motor oil stains scarred the pavement. Lines of cars beckoned.

But I didn't hear much.

I frowned again. This time of day, there should have been more activity down here.

It didn't make sense. Especially since most of this level was still full.

I started walking, listening to my own footfalls echo across the garage. Even wearing rubber soles doesn't mean you don't make noise. Sometimes the damned things are even louder than other shoes.

I kept walking, keeping my right hand close by my shirt in the event I needed to draw my gun fast.

The good news was there was plenty of cover down here. Plenty of places to hide.

And plenty of places to ambush someone too.

I sighed.

And hoped I wasn't being set up again.

Trying to figure out who was playing what cards this hand was really making my head spin like a washing machine stuck in the spin cycle.

I hadn't lied to Jarvis when I told him there were people involved who were playing me for a fool. I don't like being played for a fool. I like getting an assignment, going out and doing the job, then going home and playing with my cats.

Lately, that seemed to be a real pipe dream.

I reached my Explorer and spent another minute examining where the Suburban had rammed into me. The body was going to need some work. Probably almost a thousand bucks worth. That meant the accounting department at the Council Building was going to get an expense voucher.

Cripes, I hate bureaucracies.

I'd take the car to Tony down in Roxbury and have him work the dents out. Tony did work for both the local gangbangers and cops alike. He did good work. You do the kind of work Tony did and you attract customers from all walks of life. Tony stayed in the middle doing his job and he got treated with respect.

I thought about how many times I'd tried to stay in the middle, and remembered that I'd almost gotten squashed the same amount of times for my effort.

I opened the door to the Explorer and slid inside, still glancing around.

The new-car smell had weakened considerably.

I closed the door and slid the key toward the ignition, popped it in, and started to turn—

—at exactly the same moment I caught a whiff of marzipan.

I ripped the door open.

Ran.

And flattened myself behind a row of cars.

Just as the explosion ripped up through my driver's seat.

Pieces of my beloved truck went caroming off the cement ceiling, bouncing over other cars and trucks.

Glass shards sprayed the air. The Explorer's gas tank caught and exploded a second later. I smelled the acrid smoke, and kept my head down as the sprinkler system kicked in.

I risked a look.

Flames engulfed my Explorer, charring the hulk of burning metal, scorching the surrounding cars in the process. Glass and metal littered the entire area.

My ears rang.

The smell of marzipan. A dead giveaway for plastic explosive like the kind they used to use in antitank mines.

If the smell hadn't registered—if I had turned the key sooner and completed the circuit—if my instincts hadn't taken over . . .

I'd be dead now.

Someone wanted me dead. It had happened before.

I was obviously becoming a liability. I'd done that before too.

And like all the other times, I'd follow the same procedure I always did when it became apparent I was overstaying my welcome.

I'd go on the offensive.

Twenty-one

In the wake of the explosion, I hauled ass. It doesn't do much good hanging around while human police and fire officials converge on a scene. After all, they ask questions.

And I'm allergic to questions from humans.

So, I dragged myself back across the street to the Council Building. Arthur answered the door with his ever-present shotgun at ready.

"Holy shit."

"That's about how I feel."

"Inside." He rushed me into the kitchen. "Are ya hurt, lad?"

"A few dings and scrapes. Nothing serious."

"What happened?"

I filled him in on the bomb. He frowned as he dressed some of my lacerations. "Probably had some wooden fragmentary device atop the explosive, eh?"

"Yeah." I felt like shit. Getting caught close to a bomb blast is not a fun experience. My ears were still ringing.

Arthur finished dressing my injuries. He stepped back and pronounced me seaworthy again. Then he snapped his fingers. "Hang on a sec."

He disappeared out of the kitchen, and came back a second later carrying two glasses of what looked like thick cherry and brown liquid. He handed one glass to me.

"What the hell is this?"

"A family recipe I refined a few years ago. I call it the 'boomshanka.'"

"What is it?"

"Blood mixed with a fine single-malt whiskey. Drink it down. It'll put you to right in no time."

I hefted the glass. "Cheers."

I tilted it back to my lips and felt the drink slide down my throat. It hit with a wallop. I coughed, sputtered, and gasped. A thin line of sweat broke out on my forehead.

"Damn!"

Arthor downed his. "Yeah, she hits like a freight train, don't she?" He chuckled to himself.

I tried to catch my breath. I had to admit the stuff worked. I felt like a fresh wind of strength had fluffed my sails. "A phone. I need a phone."

I called Niles next.

I base a lot of my judgments about people on first impressions. I rely heavily on how I feel when I meet them. Sometimes, it's good. Sometimes, it's bad.

And sometimes, my first impression is wrong.

Take Niles, for example. When I met him, he looked about as competent at being my Control as a eunuch at a nymphomaniacs' convention. I would have guessed the guy couldn't handle any degree of stress. After all, I'd stopped trusting the Council's assessment of personnel skills a long time ago.

But I had to admit that Niles's stock kept rising in my respect portfolio.

Especially now.

From his apartment in Brighton, Niles quickly got a cleanup crew dispatched, and set about making sure any paperwork on the matter subsequently disappeared down some bureaucratic back alley where it would never be found again.

How do I know he was successful?

Because yours truly wouldn't be dusting the business end of a chair in some crummy cop station with my glorious butt any time soon.

Niles did his job well.

And he didn't even whine the way some of my other Controls had in the past.

He was concerned, however. But more along the lines of who might have been behind the bombing.

"I wish I had something to tell you, but I don't," I said.

"Be careful, Lawson. Whatever this Shiva thing has mixed you up in, it's obvious someone doesn't like you."

"Lucky me."

"You need to disappear."

"Excuse me?"

"You heard me. Get out. Someone wants you dead, let them think you're dead."

"That's going to be tough."

"Why? Where are you?"

I told him.

"It's after hours, Lawson. No one's there but that caretaker friend of yours and you."

"True."

"So, disappear. You've got resources I don't need to mention."

Presumably, he meant Wirek. "Okay. But I'm supposed to be protecting Belarus here tomorrow morning."

"You can't very well do that if you're dead, Lawson."

"What if they check out the police report? There'll be no mention of a body."

"There will be."

That surprised me too. "Can you get a rundown on the explosive?"

"Shouldn't be a problem. Did you recognize it?"

"Could have been old Eastern Bloc plastic. Smelled like marzipan."

"What about how it blew?"

"Confined space of the garage would have messed up my judgment."

"Okay." I could hear him making some notes. Another plus. Provided he flushed them ASAP. "I'm guessing there would have been a shaped fragmentation charge in there as well."

"Yeah," I said. "Probably enough lumber to build a house inside my chest cavity."

"Time's wasting, Lawson. Get gone. I'll let you know when you can surface again."

"How?"

"Your friend there. You call him every forty-eight hours. He'll let you know. I'll leave it to you guys to decide what the message will be. I don't want to know."

I grinned. Surprised in spite of myself. "Thanks, Niles."

"No problem, Lawson. This is what Controls are for."

"It's been a damned long time since I heard that."

"I know." He hung up.

I looked at Arthur. "I'm leaving."

"Going to ground?"

"Yeah."

"Good plan."

"Niles will call you every few days and let you know if the coast is clear."

"All right then."

"We need a message that you can use to let me know one way or the other if things are cool or not."

Arthur nodded and washed the two glasses that had held our boomshankas. "How 'bout if it's all rosy, I'll tell ya so."

I smiled. Arthur didn't go in much for spy-movie dramatics. "And if it's not?"

"Then I'll tell you it's a bag of shite."

"Plan like that," I said, "no way we can lose."

Arthur smiled. "You can't lose anyway, Lawson."

"Don't I know it."

I made it over to Wirek's place an hour later. I had to backtrack on myself about four times, using the quiet secluded streets of Beacon Hill to make sure I didn't have any surveillance on me. I didn't think there'd be much, but I try not to assume at all if I can remember not to.

Whoever'd ambushed me and planted that explosive would most likely be spending a fair amount of time trying to figure out if I'd been killed or not.

Hopefully, Niles could convince them I had been.

Wirek buzzed me up once I whispered into his intercom system. I heard the door open above me, and I took the steps three at a time to make the landing sooner than I would have otherwise.

He stood there dressed in dark sweat pants and sweatshirt.

"Where the hell have you been?" he said.

"Long story. Let's get inside."

I closed the door behind us and made sure it was locked. Not that locks ever seemed to stop people determined to get in here. A few months back, a snatch team had simply blown the door off the hinges and stormed the place. Wirek had opted not to improve security procedures.

Monk lay on Wirek's couch. I knew that thing could be damned cozy. I could use some sack time myself.

"She okay?"

"Tired." Wirek looked me over and sniffed. "Something blow up around you?"

I grinned. "My fucking truck."

"The Explorer? You just got that."

"Yeah. I know."

"Who—?"

"Don't know. Niles is running a subterfuge routine now to try to throw them off the trail. He thought it'd be better if I went to ground."

"Good plan and all, but I hope you aren't staying here all that long."

"No. They'd look here first."

He smiled. "And I just got that door replaced."

"Wouldn't want 'em blasting it off again, huh?"

"Pissed off my neighbors the last time," said Wirek. "Don't want old Mrs. Henshaw down in 2G getting her petticoats in an uproar."

I pointed at Monk. "She make any progress?"

"On what? Not much to do. She knows where the map leads. She knows what to do when she finds it. Only thing left to do is actually go and get it now."

"Maybe not now. Maybe daylight."

"You wouldn't find it in the dark anyway."

"No?"

"The Lunaspe can only be found by the light of day."

"This thing is for real then, huh?"

"Real enough that a lot of people seem to be willing to kill you over it."

I cracked a grin. "People have wanted to kill me for a lot less a lot of times before."

"Yeah, and you usually have the bad taste to drag your friends in with you."

I nodded at Monk. "She's been here with you the entire time today?"

"Nah. She went out for a walk earlier."

"A walk?"

"Said she was hungry. The moon thing. You know how it is with lycanthropes."

"How long was she gone for?"

"Not very. Maybe twenty minutes."

Not long enough to rig up the bomb that had decimated my Explorer. "Did she find something to eat?"

"No. She came up empty."

Damn. "She out of sight any other time while I was gone?"

Wirek sighed. "Lawson, I took a bath for about fifteen minutes earlier this evening. That was the only time she was out of my sight. It seemed a little rude to ask her to come in and watch me soap up my crotch."

"What time was that?"

"About an hour ago."

"Okay. Let's get some rest and head out first

thing tomorrow morning." I looked at him. "I could use your help on this one, pal."

He nodded. "I know you could, but how's it going to look if I'm not here? They'll sniff something up."

"We don't even know who 'they' is yet."

"Seems obvious that Belarus and that Jarvis puke you brought round here are dirty."

"And Jarvis would think to look here for me if he thought I'd survived."

"Sure would."

"I hate leaving you out of the game."

Wirek chuckled. "Lawson, sometimes I think I'm too old for this game."

"I hate it when you talk like that."

He nodded at Monk. "You and her, you two are the next generation."

"She's a lycanthrope, Wirek. An untested lycanthrope at that."

Wirek smiled. "Oh, I don't know about that."

"Huh?"

He shook his head. "Never mind. Listen, you just make sure you get that amulet before the bad guys do. And be quick about it. There's a full moon tomorrow night and if you don't succeed, they'll be able to wreak havoc with it, okay?"

"Okay." I turned and headed for the bathroom.

Wirek stopped me. "Lawson, one more thing: You need to get the little lady there back to her home soon. She hasn't had much to eat in terms of what lycanthropes like to eat. She's getting weak. She needs food."

I frowned. "Yeah."

"And since tomorrow night is the full moon . . ." His voice trailed off.

I nodded. Tomorrow's full moon would mean that Monk would be especially hungry. She'd need to eat a lot more than a simple hangnail.

Combined with the quest for the Lunaspe, tomorrow was looking to be one helluva day.

I just hoped I lived through it.

Twenty-two

Driving initially looked like it would be a major problem the next morning. After all, some very callous folks had left my Explorer blown to smithereens in the Boston Common garage. For a brief second, I thought perhaps Monk and I would need to rent a car.

Until Wirek tossed me a set of keys.

"You bring her back with so much as a scratch and we'll have a big problem."

I looked at the keys. They looked like they'd fit a European car. The piece of leather dangling from the ring read, "Sully's Newbury Street Garage."

"Lot 242," said Wirek. He eyed me. "I mean it—that car means the world to me. You get to be my age, you don't have many other things. She's my girl."

"Relax, I'll make sure she gets back safe and sound."

"This from a guy who gets his car blown up." Wirek walked away muttering obscenities. I watched him go and smiled.

Monk and I set off; taking the fire escape down to the alley that ran behind most of this section of lower Charles Street. We skirted Dumpsters and smelly trash and puddles of human excrement until we emerged near the good part of Charles Street close to the Boston Public Gardens.

Across the street we vanished into the park, and then reappeared on Newbury. Sully's sat half a block down. Deep in the blue-blood-Boston richness section.

But Sully himself was anything but blue blood. A squat balding hulk of an Irishman with a Scully cap dangling off his head and a stub of cigar stuck to his lower lip, Sully looked more like a leg-breaker for the Winter Hill gang that ran Charlestown. He frowned when I handed him the keys. "You ain't Wirek."

"That's right. I'm a friend of his. He's loaning me his car."

"Wirek don't lend that car to nobody, pal. Now get outa here before I get the cops on ya."

"Call him if you don't believe me."

"I call him and nobody answers, you and me is gonna have problems." He disappeared into the booth and yanked the phone off the wall. He watched me the entire time, the frown still stuck in place.

After a minute of talking, he came out. "Okay, Wirek says you're cool. But he also told me if the car comes back with so much as a scratch, I get to tear you a new asshole."

"You flirting with me, Sully?"

A glimmer of a smile cracked the frown's exterior. "Fuckin' comedians." He thumbed over his shoulder. "I'll go get her. You stay here."

He vanished again. I could see Monk outside leaning against the building. Her curves seemed to meld into the walls without effort.

I heard the elevator behind me. The heavy steel

shutter doors slid back revealing one of the most beautiful cars I'd ever seen in my life. Sully drove the Mercedes out and as soon as the sunlight caught the wax, it gleamed.

Sully slid out of the driver's seat, leaving the engine running.

I just looked at the car. "Holy shit."

Sully chuckled. "Yep. See now why Wirek doesn't go loaning this baby out that much?"

"Uh-huh."

"You're the first, pal. Bring her back like she is now . . . mint."

I dropped into the kid-leather driver's seat and felt the cushion give way for my back. The support was incredible. The dashboard was state of the art, with a multi-CD system in dash and a navigational computer further down. I felt like I was in a part-capsule, part-space ship.

The gearshift felt wonderful in my hand. I dropped it into drive and rolled out to Monk.

She whistled. "Some ride."

"That doesn't even begin to describe it."

The car must have set Wirek back untold gobs of cash. It seemed completely out of character for the guy considering what I knew about his past.

Even more, Wirek was an Elder. Most vampires—including myself until recently—think Elders are weird old guys who make sure the old ways get passed on and preserved for the next generation to discover.

That might be so, but Wirek was also a bit of an oddball. When I first met him almost a year ago, he'd been a stone drunk who could barely speak in short sentences. Then he'd cleaned himself up.

And now he drove a Mercedes.

Maybe he'd had it all along. I didn't know. What I did know was that the car rode like a dream. The automatic transmission purred as it ticked up into the next gear, clung to curves like a horny teenager lusting after a lingerie model, and accelerated like a gunshot.

My kind of car.

Monk approved too. She let the window glide down, and leaned her head out the window until she almost looked like a small dog with its head in the wind.

I thought about telling her so, but then decided otherwise. The reference might come across like an insult.

She'd been quiet this morning, and I wasn't sure why. I wanted to ask. But something inside me held me back. And since I'd been trying—really trying lately—to pay attention to my instincts, I kept my mouth shut.

We slid into Mattapan, and then out toward Hyde Park and Milton, getting stares the entire way. The car was nice, to be sure, but for covert work, it stuck out like a fat guy down in South Beach.

The Blue Hills rise out of the horizon to the southwest of Boston, blue silhouettes of pines and maples left over from the last ice age. Nowadays, they're a mass of nature trails, ski slopes, private residences, and some dead-end drop-offs. There's a lot of wildlife poking its way through the foliage, especially near the end of summer. Rumor has it there are even rattlesnakes up there, though I've never seen one. Soon enough we wound our way through the curving road that cut through the hills.

Around us, high walls of forest sprung up on

either side of the road. I looked at Monk. "Where am I headed?"

"Just keep driving," she said. She almost looked like she was asleep.

"You okay?"

"Shhh."

Great. Now she was telling me to shut up. I shook my head. Some field trip this was turning out to be.

She looked at me then. "Tonight is a full moon."

"Yes. I heard that."

"Wirek tell you?"

"Uh-huh."

She nodded. "He explain what that means?"

"With regard to you or the Lunaspe?"

"Both."

"He told me the artifact gains its greatest power during this time. He also said you were starting to get weak from lack of food—that your appetite would increase during the moon's waxing."

"Increase?" She laughed. "Lawson, it's going to fucking explode."

"Okay."

She turned her head back out the window. "You know what it's like?"

"What?"

"Eating a human?"

"Uh . . . no."

"It's disgusting. It's the most vile and revolting thing I can think of doing. To look down and realize that what you're feasting on once walked and talked and laughed and cried. And you just sit there, looking at it, tasting the blood, chewing the fat, yanking sinews and tendons out of your mouth in search of the meaty muscles."

I wrinkled my face. She was right. It didn't sound all that appetizing.

"And I have no choice," she said. "No damned choice at all. If I don't eat, I die."

"What it's worth," I said, "I'm not a big fan about drinking human blood either."

She smiled. "No?"

"I call it juice, you know? Makes me feel better, I guess. Maybe it gives that distance I need."

"What do you hate the most?"

"I guess the knowledge that it once coursed through the veins and arteries of someone else."

"Do you prefer it cold or warm?"

"Neither," I said. And I meant it. If I could have had my way, I'd never drink the stuff again. But like Monk, I didn't have any choice.

"That's not an answer."

"All right, warm, I guess. I have to keep it in the fridge so it doesn't spoil, but I don't like it. I had it really cold one time a few months back when Wirek and I were overseas. It had coagulated somewhat during the flight. It dripped down my throat like coppery molasses. It was all I could do not to puke it up."

She eyed me. "You really don't like it, do you?"

"No."

"I thought maybe you were just trying to butter up to me."

"Why would I do that?"

She smiled. "I don't know. Maybe you thought I was mad at you for refusing my advances before."

"I thought we were over that."

"We are. We are." She smiled anyway, and I knew we weren't.

I looked out the windshield. "You sure you'll know when we get there?"

"The directions were very specific," she said. "Plus there are some other attributes at my disposal you don't know about."

"What's that supposed to mean?"

She smiled. "Don't worry, Lawson. Everything's cool."

Monk had dressed in simple jeans and a loose cotton top with hiking boots. I doubted she needed them. She could probably steal through the forest as silent as a ghost if she needed to.

"Say, Monk?"

"Yes?"

"Lycanthropes can morph into whatever kind of human they want, right?"

"Yes."

"What about animals?"

"What about 'em?"

"Well, it's just that human legends have always maintained you guys can change into wolves, rats, that kind of jazz. I've never really had the opportunity to ask a real lycanthrope about that."

"That so?"

"Yeah. You're here now, so I figured what the hell."

"Get all your questions answered, eh?"

"Yeah."

"How about a quid pro quo?"

"Sure."

"Yes, lycanthropes can change into animals. My turn."

"Shoot."

"Can you guys turn into bats?"

"No. At least not any vampires I've ever met. What kind of animals do you guys change into?"

"Depends. Mostly it has to be an animal that's a member of the cat or dog family."

"Yeah?"

"Yes. What about the ethereal mist thing? Can vampires do that?"

"Nope. Not as far as I know."

She nodded. "Wow. I'm learning a lot here."

I chuckled. "Where'd you get your knowledge about us?"

"Twisted lycanthrope schools, of course. They skewer everything. What's your excuse?"

"Same damned one."

"Uh-huh. Your turn."

"Anything other than silver kill you guys?"

"Not really. We're just like you in that regard. If silver enters our bloodstream and pools at our heart, it's over. For you guys, it's wood." She smiled again. "Nature's way of keeping the scales in balance, huh?"

"So what about half-breeds?"

"Not your turn, Lawson."

"Sorry."

She was quiet for a second. "Forget it, I can't think of any more. Half-breeds, as far as I know, can be killed with either wood or silver."

"Kind of puts 'em at a disadvantage, huh?"

"Depends on how you look at it, I guess."

"Meaning?"

"Well, a half-breed has the advantages of both vampires and lycanthropes. So it stands to reason they'd have the drawbacks as well."

"Good point."

"Glad you approve."

The sun burned bright overhead, beaming through the windshield onto the chestnut-brown leather seats. Monk pulled her legs up under her with a fluid motion I could never manage. She sniffed the air.

"Slow down."

I slowed the car. In the rearview mirror, only open empty road lay behind us.

Monk had her eyes closed. "There will be a path coming up on the right-hand side. There's parking ahead. Pull us in there."

I smirked. How the hell could she know that? Sure, she had a map, but she didn't know this area. We could be anywhere. We could be—

I sighed. We'd come around a bend and sure enough, a pull-off on the right beckoned us. I slid the Mercedes in and parked the car.

I turned to Monk. "How'd you do that?"

She smiled. "We're all through playing quid pro quo, Lawson. It's time we got started finding that amulet."

She opened the door and got out.

"You want me to leave this car *here?*"

Monk smiled. "Do we have a choice?"

We didn't. And as much as I hated having to leave the comfort and safety of the Mercedes, I followed.

Twenty-three

An Audubon trail map had been tacked to a wooden bulletin board, but the edges fluttered in the wind. I wondered why it wasn't behind a layer of heavy-duty plastic, until I saw the plastic lying a few feet further along the gravel and dirt trail. Obviously, some vandals had torn the cover off.

Monk didn't even glance at the board or the map.

In the sunlight, the late summer sun felt hot on my arms. But as we passed through the archway of thin birch tree trunks and creeping vines, the air changed to a cooler, drier atmosphere.

The trail swept up, rising at a gradual angle for about fifty yards before leveling off and leading down toward what looked like a fork.

Monk stayed on point, which worried me somewhat, especially when I saw that she seemed to have her eyes closed. I hoped the Lunaspe was courteous enough to lay hidden along a trail. I wasn't much in the mood for bushwhacking.

Monk's feet seemed to roll along the ground with a confidence I've never seen in people who walk with their eyes closed. Obviously, this was one of those other assets she'd mentioned.

I looked up and saw beams of sunlight filtering through the tall branches of a stand of oak trees, cutting through leaves with a searing intensity.

At the fork, Monk swung right and the path abruptly began a steep climb. I watched as she simply shifted her body positioning and leaned into the trail the same way I'd been taught so many years ago.

Monk might have been young and green, but she knew how to walk in the woods. I had to keep reminding myself that she was a lycanthrope and this stuff came naturally to them.

A line of sweat began forming along my forehead and down the small of my back. The air felt thicker as we climbed in altitude. I looked down and saw I was leaving a lot of sign in my wake.

I altered how heavily I walked, and watched my tracks get lighter until they seemed to vanish.

I could imagine the trail we were on becoming a muddy funnel for rains during the early spring. Large stones and boulders jutted out of the ground, obelisks of volcanic antiquity that made us skirt and climb over them as we walked.

But Monk simply kept moving.

She stayed unaffected by the uneven and jagged nature of the path. Her body simply flowed over the route like water over stones. There seemed little effort in her movements, just a simple economy of motion.

Unlike the stumbling vampire behind her.

I'd have been a lot happier on a sidewalk.

Which told me I needed to start including a lot more outdoor activity in my exercise regimen. I grinned, remembering the last time I'd been in an outdoors environment.

Back in February. In Nepal. Trekking through the Himalayas with Wirek to rescue a boy named Jack.

Jack had a gift for summoning spirits from the other side. The kid could do it as easily as I drew a breath. And naturally, some power-hungry folks wanted that power for their own. So they kidnapped the little guy. And Wirek and I had flown over to get him back. The trip was not without cost.

After we came back, we spent a few days camping and hiking all the way to Jack's new school in the Canadian Rockies. I missed the kid. And for someone like me who's not exactly a walking day-care center, that's a big step.

I sighed. I hadn't been out in the woods since that time.

Why not?

I frowned. Probably because doing so reminded me too much of the little guy. I wondered how he was doing. I wondered if he was having success gaining control over his ability to conjure up supernatural energies.

I made a note to call Jack when I finished this case. See how he was doing.

Monk stopped.

I stopped.

She knelt and took a handful of dirt, rubbed it between her hands, and then sniffed it. I watched the granules sift through her fingers and fall back to the trail.

Monk stood. She looked back at me. "You okay?"

"Never better."

"Your shirt is soaked."

I nodded. "Yeah. It's been a while since I've gone hiking."

She nodded. "We've got a ways to go."

"Okay. Well, lead on."

"It's uphill, Lawson."

"Yeah?"

"Off the trail."

Damn. "Okay. Well, so be it."

"You need a break, you just let me know."

"I can hold my own."

She grinned. "You sure about that?"

The look on her face told me she thought the old vampire behind her couldn't cut the mustard. Well, we'd see about that.

"Just keep walking," I said.

I followed her as we left the trail and began our ascent through the vegetation. I hoped those rumors about rattlesnakes weren't true. I'd never experienced snake venom, and wasn't sure I wanted to anytime soon.

Initially, I wished I'd brought a machete or something, but Monk simply parted branches and vines with deft swipes of her hand and we passed through the openings that closed behind us. I'd never seen anyone move through the woods so easily and with so little disturbance.

All around us, the wildlife hadn't halted. Crows weren't sitting on branches sounding alarms. I could hear the staccato-machine-gun-pecking of a woodpecker from my right. To the left, I could hear squirrels bouncing through the underbrush in search of nuts. And behind me, back the way we'd come, I could hear the faint roar of cars zipping by on the access road.

The air had grown cooler in the meantime, not so thick anymore, which I took to mean we were definitely climbing higher. While the Blue Hills aren't so much mountains, they do rise quite a bit in elevation, clearly visible from the center of Downtown Boston on a good day.

My thighs burned. As we climbed, Monk and I brought our bodies more into parallel lines with the slope of the mountain, leaning into it to better take the strain of the climb.

Well, better for me anyway. I don't think the ascent even registered with Monk. She hadn't shown any signs of sweating at all, something that only vaguely annoyed the living shit out of me.

We broke through a tree line and back into the blazing sun. Monk stooped again and spent a minute or two with the dirt. I turned and saw the Boston skyline off in the distance. We'd been walking now for almost forty minutes.

I hoped we'd find the Lunaspe soon. I still had to take care of getting Monk back to town and trying to find the poor thing some food.

I frowned. For someone who was supposedly so hungry, she didn't seem taxed in the least.

She stood. "You rested now?"

"Yeah. Fine. But what about you?"

"What about me?"

"You okay for this hike? Not tired or anything?"

She smiled. "Lawson, lycanthropes were born in the woods and forests and mountains. This is my home. This is where I thrive."

I nodded. "Glad to hear it. I just assumed that since you haven't eaten in a few days, you'd be feeling the strain of the hike."

She smiled. "And you're wondering why I'm not, is that it?"

"Yeah."

"Maybe you're thinking I'm not being honest with you? Maybe you're not quite sure who you've got with you in the middle of nowhere?"

Even if I had been thinking that, I wouldn't have

admitted it. "Actually, I was just thinking that you ought to be tired."

"Well, I'm not. And don't forget: I was with you when we got ambushed, remember?"

"How could I forget?"

She turned and started walking again.

I followed. "Are we close?"

"Soon."

I nodded and plowed on. I felt like the annoying bratty kid who's forever piping up from the backseat of the car, "Are we there yet?"

But damn, it was plenty hot in the sunlight. I wished I'd remembered to bring some water. I could even use a drink of juice right about now.

Wildflowers sprung up around our legs as we moved out further from the tree line. Small shrubs grew out of cracks and fissures in the boulders. Smaller pine trees with thin spindly trunks poked out toward the sun.

And Monk skirted them all with ease.

I felt like I was tripping every few seconds.

But I stayed with her.

After another ten minutes, Monk knelt again and did the soil trick. This time when she stood, she veered abruptly back toward the trees to our right. We dipped as we entered the cool shade again, slipping back down about fifty feet before Monk's improvised trail led us back up the hill.

I could hear voices over to our right.

Monk stopped.

I knelt, feeling my knee push into the soft earth beneath it. It felt good to rest a moment. I stilled my breathing, inhaling through my nose and exhaling through my mouth, long inhales and long exhales designed to bring my breathing back to normal.

Monk, ahead of me, simply seemed to shrink into herself. She stayed absolutely still, and I noticed her body seemed like stone.

I heard the voices again. We must have been near a trail. This time of summer, I knew there'd be hikers all over. Part of me had been surprised there weren't more cars back down in the pull-off.

And then the voices were beyond us.

Monk came alive again and looked back at me. With a nod she rose and we started climbing again. I guessed she wanted to avoid contact with anyone else, and that was fine by me. All I wanted to do was retrieve this artifact and get the hell out of Dodge.

We came to a rock face about thirty feet high, smooth rocks leading upward. Monk glanced around as if checking for an alternative route. She smiled.

"We go up."

I nodded. "Up we go."

She led, adroitly positioning her hands and feet, keeping three points of contact while she searched for the next hold. I followed. At least I knew something about rock climbing. And I wasn't really worried about a fall. I'd had them before. They could be handled easily.

We made it to the top of the rock face in about three minutes. Probably two minutes and fifty-five seconds longer than if Monk had been by herself. Us urban vampires always slow people down.

We came out into the sun a little further on and I noticed we were on something of a cliff, overlooking a drop of maybe three hundred feet straight down. If you fell from here, the only reception you'd get below were the jagged arms of treetops and stones waiting to slice you to ribbons.

No, thanks.

I turned toward Monk, but she was back on the ground. She did the soil test three times and suddenly nodded her head.

"What?"

She looked up at me. "It's here, Lawson. It's here."

Twenty-four

I looked but couldn't see anything unusual jutting out of the landscape. No bright flashing neon signs with thumbs extended reading "Lunaspe Here!"

Sometimes I think I just might expect too much from life.

"Where is it?"

Monk pointed toward the top of another outcropping of rocks. "There." She unfolded the copy of Jarvis's sheaf of papers and nodded. "The directions are fairly exact."

"Fairly?"

"Completely," she corrected herself. "It's over there. Don't worry."

"How we gonna get to that outcropping?" A chasm of perhaps fifty feet separated us from the outcropping that Monk had pointed out. Straight down, only jagged rock edges and thorny treetops waited for someone to mince themselves on.

Monk got low to the ground and began skirting the edges of the outcropping. The way I saw it, we'd have to backtrack and follow another path to the larger higher promontory.

Monk shook her head. "The directions of the map specifically say to find this outcropping first and then proceed to the higher one."

"When was that map written, you figure?"

She looked at me. "Maybe five hundred years ago."

"You think it's possible that in that small span of time, the landscape around here has changed?"

"Meaning what?"

"Like, for instance, maybe this big old chasm here wasn't a big chasm back when they wrote this."

Monk shook her head. "You know anything about geology, Lawson?"

"Sure. Geology is the study of rocks."

"Brilliant, Holmes. Absolutely brilliant."

"You've got a point. Make it."

She pointed down into the chasm. "You see the way the rocks are rounded in parts and jagged in others?"

"Yeah. I prefer the rounded parts myself. They damage a body less."

"Right. But they weren't always rounded. When the chasm was new they would have been jagged like the edges over there. So, I can tell looking at these rocks that in fact the chasm was here when the map directions were written. And that means there's a way for us to get to that outcropping without having to backtrack and lose time."

"Pole-vault?"

She looked at me.

I sighed. "Just trying to be helpful."

She went back to scanning the ground. From my angle, I couldn't see a damned way across the chasm. And I wasn't all that crazy about backing up and running for it either. Maybe if I'd just scored some good juice I could do it. But I'd been hiking the hell out of myself and my energy level wasn't optimal.

And neither was Monk's.

If she intended to get us across, she'd have to locate an easier, less taxing means of doing so.

It took her ten minutes before she let out a low whistle. "Lawson."

"Yeah?"

"Come take a look."

I eased over to the edge and followed her pointing arm. About ten feet down from the top of the cliff there was a small outcropping, a lip really, that ran around to the right, skirting the edge of the chasm. Unless you were specifically looking for a way to get across, the lip would never even register in your mind.

I looked at Monk. "A path?"

"Cut into the mountain. Yes."

"Technically, it's a hill."

She got to her feet. "That's how we get across."

"Great."

She eyed me. "Afraid of heights?"

"Me? Hell, no. I love 'em. It's just that I have this dislike of falling from them."

She nodded. "That's easily remedied."

"How so?"

"Don't fucking fall."

"Now who's being brilliant?"

She peered over the edge. "I'll go first."

I backed up. "Be my guest." In truth, the prospect of walking along some tiny lip of rock around to another outcropping didn't really appeal to me. But a job's a job.

At least that's what I tried to tell myself.

I flipped myself the bird.

Monk disappeared over the edge of the cliff. I hesitated and then walked to the edge. She stood about ten feet below me.

On the lip.

"Come on, Lawson."

"You sure that thing can take our combined weight?"

She looked down and then back up. "Nope."

"Great." I got down on my knees and eased a leg over the edge. My hands found small handholds carved out of the rock face, which from my earlier vantage point hadn't been visible. It actually made climbing down to the lip a lot easier.

"Jeez, Lawson—you got a great ass."

If I hadn't been clinging on for dear life, I might have found that funny. As it was, Monk grabbed my butt as I got down to the lip.

I removed her hands. "Satisfied now?"

She winked. "Not even vaguely."

"Small comfort."

She gestured. "Walk slowly. Give me some space. If it looks like it won't handle us, you make your way back here and get out."

"What about you?"

"If we find out it won't take our weight, I'll be the first to know."

She had a point. I watched her ease her way along the lip of the rock, first cutting back into the hill and then further along back out toward the second outcropping.

She looked back and nodded.

I took a step.

The lip held. I took another step and shuffled my way around the lip back in toward the hill.

I began sweating.

It wasn't so much the height that affected me as much as the fact that the lip was only about twelve inches out from the rock face. Up here, a sudden wind could rip me right off of the cliff face and bounce my body off the rocks below.

And there were just enough trees down at the bottom that I could quite possibly end up speared through the heart with a length of maple or oak. Not the best way for me to end the day. Or my life.

I took another breath and slowed my heartbeat with a long slow exhale. I eventually got around to the second outcropping. Monk looked at me.

"You okay there, Lawson? You're looking a little peaked."

"I don't like twelve inches being the only thing that separates me from a painful fall."

"Up we go." Monk turned and began using now-visible handholds to climb up toward the higher outcropping. I watched her go, and suddenly thought about repaying her compliment with one of my own. From this angle, her butt looked very attractive.

She glanced down. "So . . . you aren't all business after all."

"I'm just studying your climbing technique."

"Liar."

"Worth a shot."

She disappeared over the edge of the outcropping and I followed her up.

On top, she leaned back into the ground. She didn't look so good.

"You all right?"

"Hungry. Just give me a minute."

If I could have helped I would have. But lycanthropes don't do well on vampire flesh for some reason. They need human. In the same way, vampires don't do well with lycanthrope blood. I smirked. Poor humans always fell to the bottom of the food chain.

Monk closed her eyes and took several deep breaths. "Maybe I should have ambushed those hikers who passed us a short time back."

"Maybe. You gonna be okay?"

"I don't have a choice," said Monk. "We need that relic."

I looked around. "You sure it's here?"

"What the map says."

"You rest. I'll look for it."

Monk scrambled to her feet. "You don't know what to look for."

"What—you can't tell me?"

She grinned. "Lawson, you don't understand. You can't see it. Only a lycanthrope can."

"Huh?"

"The Lunaspe hides itself from all but lycanthropes. You'll see it once I figure out where it is and take it from the hiding place, but you could sit on top of it right now and never know it."

I sank to the earth and sighed. "Okay, well, guess I'll take a breather then."

"Shouldn't take me long."

I watched Monk stoop again and begin sniffing all the dirt she could find. I assumed there must have been traces of the Lunaspe that could be detected in the earth. The closer we got to it, the more Monk would be able to sniff it out.

I felt a lot like I was playing second fiddle on this trip. Monk knew where everything was, what to do, and all that jazz. I was the hired gun along for the ride. Along to make sure the Lunaspe didn't end up with the bad guys.

Part of me wondered what the good guys would do with it when they got their hands on it. Part of me didn't much want to know.

Monk suddenly shifted direction and came back toward a small white pine with a thick short trunk. It reminded me of a bonsai dwarf tree like the kind I'd seen so often in my trips to Japan.

Like the last time I'd been there.

With Jarvis.

Getting cornered by a band of vampires who controlled one of the most powerful Yakuza gangs in Tokyo didn't do much for my outlook on life.

Seeing Jarvis disappear into a building with four of them on his tail did even less for my mood.

When we hooked up again, I had no way of knowing if he'd dispatched them at all or whether he'd simply run away faster than they could chase him.

I knew my end was clean. I left six bodies behind me that night.

I sighed.

Jarvis.

I heard an audible gasp from Monk. I got to my feet and dusted myself off. "You got it?"

She'd disappeared among the mass of roots and shrubbery at the base of the white pine. But now she reemerged from the bushes.

Empty-handed.

I frowned. "Well, you were right, Monk. I can't see shit."

She shook her head. "No, Lawson. You can't. But it's not because of what I said. It's because someone's already been here."

"You—"

"It's gone, Lawson. The Lunaspe is gone."

Twenty-five

The ride back to Boston was not pretty.

I'd known Monk less than two days and I already knew she handled disappointment about as well as I handle hearing boy bands played on the radio.

Monk sulked the majority of the trip back to Boston. But she perked up as we entered the city limits.

"Where are we headed?"

I stopped. I needed a phone so I could call Arthur. Granted, it hadn't been that long yet, but I like to sometimes consider myself an optimist.

Arthur took a while to answer the phone. When he did, he didn't sound particularly friendly.

"It's me."

"Yeah."

I sighed. "Well?"

"Well, it ain't rosy, that's for sure."

"They know they didn't get me?"

"Whatever Niles tried to do, it didn't work. Jarvis came and went three times today so far and the day isn't even over yet. Belarus has been stomping around all over the building as if he's waiting for something to happen. And no one's mentioned your supposed death."

"That doesn't sound good."

"Sounds just like what it is, a bag of shite."

I hung up and called Niles. The phone rang for ten minutes. No one answered it.

I hung up the pay phone and started back toward the car. Monk sat very still inside.

I hopped in the front seat and shook my head. "Arthur says they know they didn't get me. It's not safe back in town."

Monk shrugged. "I might know a place."

"You?"

She looked at me. "You don't think it's conceivable I know a good place to go?"

"Up until now I thought the only place you felt comfortable was up on Mount Desert Island."

"It might suit you to know that I've traveled somewhat in my lifetime."

"Okay. I stand corrected." I started the engine. "Where'm I heading?"

"Mission Hill. You know the area?"

"Sure."

"There's an old generator on top of the hill. It's been abandoned for years."

"And you know this how?"

She smiled. "Lawson, do you know of other cities and safe places you can hide if you need to while you're there?"

"Sure."

"So, why are you finding this so unusual?"

"I never knew lycanthropes did this kind of thing."

"I'm feeling some prejudice here, Fixer."

I shook my head. "None intended. I'm just engaged in some serious learning here is all."

"Is that right?"

"Sure. And I'm wondering why the hell you didn't simply have me drop you off here the other night when we came to town."

"I didn't want to have to use this place unless I absolutely had to. I'm sure you understand the concept of safe houses."

Yeah, I knew about them. But it didn't make me feel any more comfortable that she'd held out on me.

Monk faced front again as we slid through Mattapan Square and caught the road that would take us back toward Forest Hills, Jamaica Plain, and then beyond to Mission Hill.

I watched the sun beginning to sink lower over the horizon. "It's getting late."

Monk nodded. "Sure is."

"You must be starved."

"Trying not to think about it actually."

"Sorry."

"Tonight's the full moon. Whoever stole the Lunaspe will try to use it tonight or else they'll have to wait until next month. I don't think they'll do that."

"Wait until next month?"

"Yes."

"Explain this ceremony to me, would you? I mean, they've got to do it someplace, don't they? Is there a ceremony they'll follow? Some consecrated area they'll do the thing?"

"There is a ceremony, yes. And they have to do it outside, preferably catching the rays of the moon through the amulet before reciting the incantation that will first harness the moon's power and then enable the relic holder to unleash it at will."

"But where would they do it?"

"According to the papers you got for me, the directions speak of a mountaintop and an altar that faces west."

"West?"

"The moon rises in the west, silly."

"Oh, right."

"Given that we're in New England, there are a lot of choices for the ceremony."

"They'd need some privacy."

"Yes, that would be a good thing."

"You got any ideas who would take it?"

"Seems pretty obvious to me, don't you think?"

"Jarvis?"

"And the other one."

"Belarus."

"Yes."

I nodded. We were back on the Jamaicaway heading down toward Perkins Street. I banked a right and we slid down toward South Huntington Avenue.

"But according to Arthur, they're still at the Council Building," I said. "That limits the location, given the length of time between now and midnight—isn't that when they'd have to do the ceremony?"

"Yes."

At the small Heath Street T station, I banked right again and further on I took a left, aiming us up a steep hill that led toward New England Baptist Hospital.

Monk pointed. "Take a right at the top."

"It's a one-way."

Monk looked at me like I had two heads, so I took the illegal right and then saw where she pointed. "Left into the driveway there."

We rolled over gravel in the drive and slid down toward the back of the red brick and iron plant. I looked up. "This place hasn't been used in years, huh?"

"Nope." Monk hopped out of the Mercedes and I followed.

Monk strode to the back of the plant and produced two keys from her pocket, slid them into the padlocks, and I heard the click as they came open.

She stood back, yanked the steel door, and gestured for me to go inside.

"You sure no one's home?"

She smiled. "Lawson, you need to be more trusting of people, you know that?"

I sighed and stepped up across the threshold and then down the steps into the plant. Monk stepped inside and closed the door behind us. Echoes of dings and clanks from the iron machinery bounced off the walls. I could hear the telltale steady drip-drip of bits of water leaking from pipes. Cobwebs at the corners of the ceiling forty feet above us housed what looked like a wide array of spiders.

Monk led the way downstairs. "Follow me."

We descended into the plant. I've been a lot of weird places around Boston. But the old water and electrical plants that still poke out of the city landscape always fascinate me. Stepping into them is like taking a giant step back in time. You can almost hear the ancient machinery trying to come back to life, you can smell the scent of must and mildew, and you can feel the sense of a different time.

Monk ducked through a doorway and I followed. It was dark down here, but Monk switched on a small lightbulb hanging from a think strand of twine. Light flooded the room we were in. I saw a small twin bed, a table, a small refrigerator, some chairs, and even a television set.

I chuckled. "Place looks like a college dorm room."

Monk shrugged. "I had to make it comfortable in case I ever needed it."

"You do this in any other cities?"

"A few. Boston's the nicest."

I shook my head. A lycanthrope safe house of all the damnedest things. "Well, at least we can chill out here for a while."

Monk looked at me. "Chill out?"

"Well . . ."

She stepped closer to me. "Is that all you want to do?"

I could feel the heat coming off her in waves, but it wasn't because of the temperature. Her eyes were dilating wide and black as she looked at me. If she stood on tiptoes, she could almost reach my lips.

I stepped back and broke the connection. "I could use a drink."

She smiled and walked to the fridge. "I have orange juice and Pepsi. Which one?"

"Can of Pepsi'll be fine."

She tossed one to me and I caught it, broke the seal, and took a long drag. I belched a second later feeling the bubbles burst out of my nose into the air.

"Nice," said Monk. She walked over to me. "Can I have a sip?"

"Get your own."

She put her hand around mine on the cold moist can. "Don't want my own. I want yours."

She tilted my hand and placed her mouth around the opening. I watched her lips part and her eyes close as she drank the soda in. A bob in her throat jumped each time she swallowed.

She tilted my hand back and sighed. "That's good."

I cleared my throat. "Yeah."

Monk laughed. "Are you always this tongue-tied around women, Lawson?"

"I don't know."

"Good answer." She pointed at the bed. "Want to lie down?"

The bed looked small. Maybe a twin at best. If we lay down together, there'd be no room. For anything to happen. Unless, of course, Monk happened to lie on top of me. Which seemed exactly like what she wanted to do.

I shook my head. "I'm not sleepy."

"I'm not talking about sleep, stupid."

"Insulting me is such a turn-on."

She laughed. "Bullshit. Lawson, I want you to make love to me."

"I know you do."

"I've wanted you from the moment I laid eyes on you. You've rejected me so far. But I know you can't keep doing that. I can see it in your eyes." She moved closer to me. "You want me."

I nodded. "Yes. I do."

Twenty-six

But I didn't touch her. Instead, I stepped back and glanced at my watch. "It's getting late, Monk. We've only got a few hours to figure out where the ceremony will be."

Monk took another step forward, occupying the space I'd just vacated. She put a hand on my chest. "Lawson."

"Yeah?"

"Let's not worry about that old relic for right now, okay? Can't we just have a little fun?"

I frowned. "You're telling me not to worry? This thing means more to your people than it does to me."

"So, why bother with it?"

"Because Belladonna told me it could impact my people as well. And I can't let that happen."

Monk nodded. "So honorable, aren't you?"

"I don't know about that."

"It's true." She pared the distance down some more. A thin layer of heated air stood between our bodies. "There's something about you, you know that? There's this sense of danger mixed with goodness that you exude like an aura."

"That so?"

"I find it very attractive."

I looked down at her eyes. They were even more

dilated now, as if she'd slid black contact lenses over her irises. She licked her lips and brought her other hand to my chest.

"Lawson."

"Monk."

She seemed to grow at that moment. The height between us shrank. I thought she must have been standing on her tiptoes. But that transition was so smooth, I couldn't imagine it being muscle power alone.

"Are you changing?"

She smiled. "Giving myself a little height is all."

Her head came level with mine. I grinned. "Too lazy to stand on your toes?"

Her lips brushed mine. Her voice dwindled to a husky whisper. "I like it better this way."

"Monk."

"No more talk, Lawson. We're a little beyond that."

I felt her lips touch mine again. This time they stayed there. I felt her press into me, first her mouth, followed by her chest and stomach and legs.

There was no more space between us.

I kissed her back, feeling the sudden surge of desire explode in my bloodstream. I wrapped my arms around her, continued kissing her, felt her tongue reach out for mine as we spilled into the twin bed plopping onto the creaking springs and musty blankets.

Monk moaned beneath me; I felt her legs part until she had one wrapped on either side of me.

I gazed into her eyes. She looked up at me and smiled. "Have you ever made love to a lycanthrope before?"

"Oh, yeah, sure, I do this all the time."

"Liar." She smiled again. "I'll be your first."

I felt her hand travel down my back toward my butt. She squeezed, pulled me into her as if we could complete the coupling while still fully clothed.

I slid my hand down toward her belly and then up under her shirt, running it over what felt like the white lace fabric of her bra. By touch she must have been a C cup. I grazed the top part of her cleavage with my fingertips, lightly. Monk sighed and kissed me again.

My mouth watered as Monk's hand released my butt and came around to my shirt. Her fingers deftly undid the buttons and it came off. She grabbed at it and tossed it into the far corner of the room.

She looked up at my chest rising above her and licked her lips. "You look wonderful."

I grinned. Monk didn't look so bad herself.

I went for her neck, tracing the tip of my tongue down along the sterno-cleido-mastoid muscle of her neck. I felt Monk shiver underneath me. I increased the pressure just slightly, almost cutting into her throbbing pulse, and then softened my tongue and lapped lower.

"Lawson."

Her voice tickled the musty air in the room like a feather on skin. I ran my hands under her back and got her shirt off next, exposing the delicate white bra underneath.

I stopped for a moment and drank in the view. Few things in life excite me as much as a woman in a nice bra. I looked at Monk and grinned. "I like your choice of underwear."

"You should see the panties."

I nodded. "That sounds like a plan."

I moved off her and she worked the snap on the jeans open. I unzipped them and caught a glimpse of the thin bikini waistband. This was getting better by the second.

Monk arched her back and the top of the jeans came off her hips and slid down by the top of her thighs. I helped her get them the rest of the way off, by tugging them off her legs.

I stopped at her boots.

She giggled. "Whoops."

"Held in check by L.L. Bean," I said with mock disappointment.

"They're Timberlands silly," said Monk.

I bent and untied the laces, freeing one first, then the other. Then I finished with the jeans and came back up on the bed.

Monk lay there, white bra, white panties, and white socks. The picture of sensual perfection—at least in my opinion.

Her eyes gleamed, looked a little moist, and her lips pouted full of rich blood flow.

"You're very beautiful, Monk."

She smiled.

I bent by the inside of her thigh, close by her knee, and kissed the spot of skin softly. Monk spread her legs on the first kiss and I felt her hands reaching for my head.

I slid down further, finding that special spot behind the knee that I knew drove some women crazy. Monk jumped a little, not knowing if it tickled or felt amazingly good. She settled on the latter and then moaned again. A little louder this time.

She moaned well.

Thank God.

I'd been with some women who grunted like

congested heifers during sex. It didn't do much for my arousal.

Monk's hands found the back of my head. I could hear her breathing coming faster now. "Lawson . . ." Her voice was still slight, but tinged with a pleading, plaintive desire.

I moved higher, kissing the inside of her thigh, kissing higher and higher until I felt her back arch under my hands. I came up to the panties and licked around the edges of the material before placing my mouth right over them and exhaling a stream of heated breath onto her juncture. I felt a surge of moisture soak through the cloth, and then Monk stabbed herself forward onto my mouth some more, her fingers grabbing handfuls of my hair, yanking, writhing, climbing, moaning, and then falling suddenly back to the bed.

I slid the panties off and slid out of the rest of my clothes. When I loomed over Monk again, her face held a blush that tinted the corners of her eyes with a delicate red shade.

She glanced down, saw me, and smiled again. "My, my, my."

"I've got good genes."

She nodded. "I'd say so."

I felt her fingertips lightly encircle me, stroking softly just the way I like it. She wrapped her hands around me and began stroking.

I closed my eyes and let myself slide into the rush of sensations. I let Monk guide me into her a second later, felt her moisture surround me, the heated furnace in both of us chugging out of control.

Monk reached her hands for my back again, and brought me down on top of her. Her legs wrapped around my hips. I felt her join herself to me then, sealing out any space between us the way she'd done when we kissed.

I kept the rhythm going, altering the depth of my thrusts every so often. I could see the gorge of blood rising in her chest, blushing her neck, seeping north to her face, watched her eyes close, her mouth open just so . . .

. . . and then the sudden wind of air rushing out of her as she sank back to the bed again.

"Lawson . . ."

I sank down between her legs again, tasting the fresh fountain that had come out of her. She arched her back instinctively; I reached for her hands and held them as she came twice more in the span of three minutes.

I came up, licking my lips. She met me halfway and kissed me hard, her own tongue licking around my mouth. I slid one of my hands toward the back of her skull, cupping the base of it, fingers in her hair as I tilted her head and kissed her mouth, licked her neck.

Monk's hands found me again and she began stroking me in earnest, her fingers slipping a little bit as she did so.

She looked at me. "Now?"

I nodded. "Yeah."

She lay back on the bed and I lowered myself again into her. We built slowly this time, the frenzied urge to couple having settled into a leisurely hundred-beats-per-minute slow jam.

Monk brought her head up to my chest and began suckling one of my nipples. I closed my eyes, enjoying the simultaneous tactile exploration going on both down south and up north.

Monk's tongue traced around my nipple, kissing

it softly. I could feel her hot breath against my chest. I could feel the liquid fire engulfing me below, sliding in and out of her forge.

Monk's hands gripped me and pulled me deeper into her, her legs clamped down. We were joined so completely, I found it difficult to work my hips.

But that didn't matter anymore.

I could feel my own fire rising in that space of time that lies between birth and death, that space between molecules, that gasp between breaths, and as I looked down at Monk, saw her beauty—her emotion—her lust, I closed my eyes once more and exploded deep.

I collapsed against her shoulder, inhaled the subtle perfume of her hair, breathed deep.

I really needed that. I thought about Talya and felt guilty for only a second. We were both professionals. I wouldn't hold it against her if she needed a nip in the sack while we were apart. I knew she wouldn't hold it against me either.

It had been a year, after all. Judging by recent headlines, I was doing better than a lot of priests who supposedly take a vow of chastity.

I could feel Monk's pulse drumming against my cheek. Her heartbeat had increased.

"Lawson."

I sighed. "Monk."

She laughed softly. "Lawson."

"Tired. Let me just rest here a moment."

"No."

I frowned. I wanted to sleep.

"Lawson."

I pushed myself back and looked down.

But Monk wasn't underneath me anymore.

Shiva was.

Twenty-seven

I rolled off faster than I would have thought possible. My gun and pants lay in a jumble across the room. Shiva just laughed at my efforts.

"Calm down, Lawson."

I found my gun and drew it out of the holster, aiming it at her. "Just stay where you are, Shiva."

She shook her head. "I could have killed you easily any time I wanted to, you know that, Lawson?"

As much as I hated admitting it, I knew she spoke the truth. I lowered the gun slightly. "So, why didn't you?"

"I already told you I'm not gunning for you. I want Belarus. And Jarvis." She smiled. "You look a little different during an adrenaline rush, huh?"

I glanced down and sighed. "You didn't seem to mind a few minutes ago."

"I sure didn't. Why don't you find your clothes and then we can talk about this."

I kept the gun loosely trained in her direction as I pulled on my jockey shorts and pants and then got my Hawaiian shirt on. I sat in one of the chairs and pulled on my socks and shoes.

Shiva looked the way she'd looked back at my house that night she'd come in impersonating Talya. The look really didn't suit her as much as the one she'd pulled off on the Boston Common and I told her so.

"I don't like this either, but I needed you to realize who I was and that was the most effective way."

"You could have chosen the other lady."

"I could have. I think I wanted a better effect. That same shock value from the other night. It tends to get your attention a lot faster."

"Yeah, well, you got it."

"Yes," she said. "I certainly did." She held up the tangle of clothes. "I need to change back to Monk now if you don't mind. Her clothes won't fit me like this."

"Be my guest." I sat watching the transformation take place. I don't really know what I expected to happen although I did expect something much more dramatic than I saw. I'd thought it might look a little something like the old Michael Jackson "Thriller" video.

It didn't.

Shiva's features simply morphed back into Monk's face. Her body shrank a little back to Monk's petite stature.

Shiva sat there pulling on the clothes. "Not as exciting as you pictured, was it?"

"Nope."

"Are you always honest, Lawson?"

"Most of the time."

"Unless it suits you otherwise, right?"

"Isn't that always the way?"

"For some people, yes."

"Are you getting at something here, Shiva?"

She shifted on the bed. I could hear the springs protest the movement. I couldn't remember hearing them that much while Shiva and I had sex.

"Belarus has the Lunaspe."

"How do you know?"

"Because he's the only one who could find it aside from me. He's the only one who had the map."

"Jarvis had the map."

"Jarvis is a fool. He doesn't know how to look for it properly. If Jarvis was all I had to worry about, he would have been dead ages ago."

"Why's it taken you this long already?"

"Because I needed him to get to Belarus. If I'd killed him earlier, Belarus would have gone into hiding."

"Now that he has the Lunaspe, what happens next?"

"Nothing changes. Belarus will try to use the Lunaspe tonight to draw down the power of the moon. Who knows—he might succeed."

"He might?"

She nodded. "Unless we stop him, Lawson."

I shook my head. "I've had more partners in the last few days than I thought possible. And you know what? I don't much care for any of them."

"At least you got laid with me," said Shiva. "Jarvis couldn't have given you what I just did."

"Thanks for the nasty visual." I slid my gun back into my holster. "Do you know where Belarus will hold the ceremony?"

"There's really only one place he can hold it, Lawson."

"And that is?"

She smiled. "Not yet. I don't want you shooting me and going after them alone. I have to be involved in it, don't you understand that?"

"You asked me a minute ago if I always told the

truth. You seemed satisfied with my answer. So, what gives?"

"I haven't been completely honest with you."

"Well. Knock me over with a feather."

She frowned. "Don't be sarcastic, Lawson. It wasn't the right time."

"And now—after we've had sex—it's the right time?"

"Sure."

"So nonchalant about this thing. It doesn't seem like it does matter that much to you."

Shiva frowned. "Don't mistake my laid-back post-orgasmic attitude for nonchalance, Lawson. I'm deadly serious about this. I must have Belarus and Jarvis."

"So, what weren't you honest about then?"

"Belarus," said Shiva, "is my stepfather."

"Oh, shit. You mean this whole sordid thing is some kind of whacked-out family affair?" I shook my head. I'd really stepped in it this time.

"And Jarvis is my stepbrother."

I leaned forward. "Belarus is Jarvis's father?"

"Yes."

"And together?"

"They've been hunting down the half-breeds, trying to consolidate power over the lycanthropes and vampires at the same time."

"And the Lunaspe?"

"They need that to do the job right. They can continue what they're doing, but it will take them too long. The Lunaspe will enable them to derive more power. Minds will bend to them. They'll win over the hearts of others like them and become unstoppable."

"Unless we stop them first."

She nodded. "That's the plan."

"I need a drink."

Shiva laughed. "More Pepsi?"

"No. Thank you."

She sat on the edge of the bed. "What do you say, Lawson? I can't do it alone. I've been trying for years. I need your help."

"You really want to kill your stepdad and brother?"

Shiva frowned. "Stepbrother. Make sure you understand that. And yes, I do want to kill them. You have no idea what they've done to me over the years."

"So tell me."

"Belarus, when he was a member of my family so many years ago, raped my sister and then urged Jarvis to do the same. When they were done, they took turns on me as well."

"What about your mother?"

Shiva looked down at the floor. "They'd killed her before they started in on us."

I let go a breath of air and shook my head. I'd always known Belarus seemed pretty scummy, but this was nasty shit.

"My sister never recovered," said Shiva. "She killed herself by injecting silver nitrate into her bloodstream. She died in agony. But it was nothing like the agony we went through together."

"What about your birth father?"

"Been dead for years."

"And so you embarked on this rampage to track them down?"

"I've spent years chasing them, Lawson. You know that. You know my history, my past. You know I mean business."

"Yes. I do."

"And now I have a chance. A final chance to stop it."

"Final chance? What the hell does that mean?"

Shiva tried a grin but it didn't take. "I'm dying, Lawson."

I glanced down at my crotch and she laughed. "No. Nothing like that. Fortunately. I wouldn't do that to you."

"Then what?"

"I have degenerative lycanthropy."

"Never been good with medical terms, Shiva. You'll have to break that down for me."

"Each time I change, each time the moon waxes and I yield to its power, I lose some measure of control over my abilities. My power to transform will eventually cease. My senses will dull. My metabolism will turn on itself and begin burning me up."

"I don't understand."

"Lycanthropes, even half-breeds, need to change, Lawson. When we change, we release the primal lunar energy that builds in us each month. We can change any time we want to, but if we don't change for long periods, the energy builds and consumes us whole."

"So keep changing."

"It's not that simple. Degenerative lycanthropy affects only a scant few in our population. It's some sort of evolutionary genetic defect or something. There's never been a cure. There probably never will."

"And you've got it."

"Yes."

"How long?"

"Until it kills me? Maybe a few weeks."

"How long have you known?"

"About a month."

"And that's why you came to Boston?"

"I've been trying to avoid coming here, thinking I could get to Jarvis and Belarus in other places. I didn't want to intrude on your territory, Lawson."

I grinned. "Why not?"

"Because believe it or not, your name is legend. You are known far and wide. Granted not by the vast majority, but in the secret circles, they speak of you in whispers. Fearful whispers. Not many wish to ever cross your path if they can help it."

I cocked one eyebrow higher than the other. "You are definitely a gifted bullshitter, Shiva."

She smiled. "I wish I was lying. I'm not."

Silliest thing I'd ever heard. I sat taking it all in. If Shiva really was dying, then there wouldn't be much to fear from her for long, even if she was bullshitting about Belarus and Jarvis.

"Lawson."

I looked up. "Yeah?"

"We need to go soon. Are you with me?"

I sighed, looking around the dank room and then back at her. "I got no place else to be, Shiva."

Twenty-eight

We emerged from the old water-treatment facility into darkness. The top of Mission Hill lay shrouded in shadows with the Boston skyline twinkling in the distance.

I slid into Wirek's Mercedes and started the engine. Shiva slid in next to me, still looking like Monk. I'd never realized how much having a shapeshifter in my life could easily mess up my mind. I was having trouble adjusting to the fact that Shiva was, in fact, Monk.

I was having even more trouble with the fact that I'd just had sex with her. I don't like thinking I'm having sex with one woman only to find out it's another.

Especially one I'd tried to kill.

I'd enjoyed myself, I wasn't denying that. But that enjoyment had come from sleeping with Monk. Not Shiva. Shiva, I wasn't crazy about.

I wasn't crazy about Monk either. Just sexually attracted to her.

We drove down the hill behind the Veterans Administration Hospital and banked left on South Huntington. Shiva pointed. "Head toward Jamaica Plain."

"JP?"

"Like you're heading home, Lawson. Yes."

I frowned. The idea of Belarus and Jarvis doing bad stuff in my neighborhood didn't thrill me. Actually, the idea of them doing anything anywhere didn't thrill me.

I thought about Talya again.

Maybe I did feel a little guilty for sleeping with someone else. We'd never had an agreement, that was true. But maybe by having sex with Monk/Shiva, I'd simply clarified my own feelings for Talya.

Still the same old romantic fool I've always been, I guessed. Nothing wrong with it, just so long as I didn't keep sleeping with women who wanted me dead.

Or vice versa.

But damn, I missed Talya.

Maybe when this whole mess was over, maybe I'd go about trying to find her. I could use a vacation. Maybe I could scam something so we'd be together. Maybe I could even keep it hidden from the Council.

"Lawson."

Shiva's voice brought me back to reality. "Yeah?"

"I said make this next right."

Perkins Street. I turned right and stopped further on at the intersection of the Jamaicaway and Perkins, waiting for the light to change.

"Go straight on through, okay?"

"Yeah."

"You okay?"

"Fine."

I felt her gaze on me. I turned and tried to grin. "I'm fine. Really."

She chuckled. "You're still trying to come to grips with the fact that we fucked back there, aren't you?"

"I don't think Monk would have said it like that."

"Who cares how she would have said it?"

"I got a question for you."

"Shoot."

I concentrated on following the winding road. "What'd you do with the real Monk?"

"What do you mean?"

I frowned. "Belladonna really did have an apprentice named Monk that she presumably sent with me when I was up there."

"What makes you think Monk wasn't just simply my creation?"

"You can't be in two places at the same time Shiva. You know that. I know that. There really was a Monk. Your disguise wouldn't have fooled Belladonna."

Shiva sighed in the haze of headlights. "You're right, of course."

"So?"

"You really want to know?"

"Yes."

"I had to kill her, Lawson."

"Why?"

"Why kill her? That's a funny question coming from someone like you. After all, you're a professional hitter."

"I kill targets that have jeopardized my society—my people."

"Is that what you tell yourself, Lawson? Is that what you tell yourself when the demons come at night? When the faces of your kills haunt you at night. Do you really believe it?"

"Yes. I don't kill indiscriminately."

"Well, then my hat's off to you. I killed Monk because she was a loose end. You would have done the same if you'd been in my position."

"Thankfully, I'm not in your position."

"You might find yourself there someday."

"Maybe. But you didn't have to kill Monk. She was an innocent."

"Lawson, you aren't naïve enough to believe that innocents don't get killed in this life. I know you aren't. Collateral damage exists in our world as much as the world of humans. Sure, we might like to say we try, but when it comes right down to it, we don't care all that much. As long as what needs to get done gets done, that's all we care about."

"You're wrong, Shiva."

"Am I?"

"Yes." I paused. "I care."

Shiva regarded me. "You're too honorable, Lawson. You know that?"

"It's been mentioned before."

"You might pay some heed to it."

"Or I might not." I accelerated on the light. "Which way am I going?"

"Toward Larz Anderson's."

"Larz Anderson Park?"

"Yes. You sound surprised."

"Is that where the ceremony takes place?"

Shiva shrugged. "I don't know yet."

"Doesn't seem like it would offer much concealment for those involved. After all, Brookline Police patrol the park after dark. People still go up there too. Dog walkers, drinkers, kids looking to make out. Hell, I got caught there once with my shirt off."

"That's nice."

I looked at her quickly. "It's not where the ceremony is, is it?"

Shiva sighed loudly. "Lawson, you're a real pest.

Why don't you just be quiet and see what happens when we get there, all right?"

"I don't like surprises, Shiva. I told you that already."

She laughed. "And God knows you've already had more than your share this jaunt, eh?"

"Are we meeting someone?" We passed Rockwood Street on the left and continued winding our way up past the school.

Shiva pointed. "The small street on the left. Take it."

I swung left and instantly a dense canopy of maple trees overshadowed the car. Beside me, Shiva cleared her throat.

"Pull over under there. The car will be almost invisible."

"Just so long as no one crashes into it. I'd hate to have to return it to Wirek as a banged-up jalopy." Sully would take great pleasure in trying to beat the snot out of me.

"Don't worry so much, Lawson."

I killed the engine and turned in my seat. "So. Now what?"

Shiva unbuckled her seat belt and unlocked the door. "Now, we get out and go see what we can see."

"You're not going to tell me anything, are you?"

"I already told you as much as you need to know, Lawson. Now stop worrying so much and follow me. The sooner we get this done, the sooner we can get the rest of it tied up as well."

She eased the door shut behind her. I watched her vanish into the darkness.

I sighed again, opened my door, and slid out after her into the waiting arms of ebony.

Twenty-nine

Larz Anderson Park took its name from one of the first U.S. ambassadors to Japan back about a hundred years or so. The town of Brookline took over the estate sometime in the mid-twentieth century, slapping a skating rink, an antique-car museum, and a lot of outdoor grills on the land for the benefit of the locals.

One of the biggest attractions of the place is the huge hill that draws kite fliers during the warm months, and roughly a gazillion sledders during the snowy days that pop up during Boston's winters.

Tall green grass reached up for Shiva and me as we walked along. My feet slipped every few steps, courtesy of the dew that made the footing slick.

Shiva moved us toward the line of shrubs and small trees that ran alongside one edge of the hill, all the way to the top. The move made good tactical sense, since walking out in the open on such a well-lit full-moon night meant we stood out against the backdrop of night.

And we'd make easy targets.

I frowned as we walked. If Belarus and Jarvis had planned their little Lunaspe ceremony here, I doubted they'd have a chance to get the thing completed.

It seemed silly, after all. Brookline Police patrolled Larz Anderson's with a feverish delight at catching people up here after dark. I think they just liked catching a few winks up here under the stars on slow nights. I couldn't blame them. I might have done the same thing in their position.

But I wasn't in their position.

I wasn't in a nice comfortable cruiser with the air-conditioning on.

Sweat soaked through the cotton of my Hawaiian shirt as we hiked up the hill through the wet grass.

Shiva stopped ahead of me.

I stopped as well.

She knelt and stayed absolutely still. I couldn't make out what she might have seen, but I'm not dumb enough to think I catch everything. I've got enough scars to prove I don't catch nearly as much as I should.

I heard the engine then. A low growl that cut through the dark like some nocturnal mechanoid creature out looking for dinner.

A cruiser appeared on top of the hill where the paved road wound its way around to a small parking lot.

The police had arrived.

You couldn't blame folks for wanting to lock lips and a few other choice body parts while gazing at the city skyline. It was the closest thing Brookline had to an Inspiration Point.

My mind flashed back to my own encounter up here many years in the past. Back when that spotlight had hit me, I'd been down to just my jeans. Somehow, telling the cop who wandered over to my window that I was stargazing just didn't hold up.

Of course, the woman with her head in my lap didn't help my case all that much.

But the cop grinned as he told us to get the hell out of the park.

I sighed.

Memories.

Shiva moved again.

Just as the cop car finished his route and dipped back down toward the lower access road. The smaller shrubs running alongside our left mandated that Shiva and I keep our own profiles lower.

I'm always amazed at how much is visible during a full-moonlit night. Ancient espionage texts always say the best time to do reconnaissance is during a moonlit night just like this was. Insertions on the other hand, are best done during the new moon—when it's inky dark outside.

I'm not much of a contrarian when it comes to this stuff. I like sticking with tried-and-true methods. Violating standards doesn't sit well with me.

Shiva and I were doing the opposite of what we should have been doing.

If we weren't incredibly careful, our element of surprise would evaporate—probably while we died.

At the top, Shiva and I huddled by a lone rhododendron and waited. Shiva seemed to sniff the air a lot. Maybe she could smell danger, I don't know. But the fact that she'd survived as long as she had meant she must have been able to sniff out hot spots in some manner.

At last, she turned back to me and nodded, then pointed across the lot toward a high stone wall. I nodded and Shiva went first, sliding across the lot in a smooth motion that I could hardly distinguish.

I went next and reached the cool stone next to Shiva. We didn't say anything, just exchanged a few hand signals. I knew from past experience that we were close to the columns and Japanese stone lanterns that still dotted the landscape up here. Maybe Belarus and Jarvis were up here.

But that location still didn't offer them much of an opportunity to perform their ceremony undisturbed. The problem was that despite the police presence, Larz Anderson's remained a popular nighttime haunt for people.

Part of me wondered what the hell we were doing here.

Shiva slunk down the edge of the wall until she reached the backside of it and disappeared around the corner. I frowned. I don't like it when people move out of my field of vision. It means the odds of a surprise coming my way increase tenfold.

I'm not a big fan of surprises.

I moved off after her, keeping my right hand on the wall as I stole down toward the backside of it.

My hair stood up on my neck.

I dropped and froze in the taller grass here.

A light suddenly exploded across the stone wall in the area I'd just been moving through. The light swept all over the wall, casting long shadows in the darkness.

I heard the crackle of radio static and frowned.

Another cop.

Jesus. Wasn't there a donut shop open somewhere that they could harass instead?

The light tracked back toward the end of the wall and then back in my direction again. If the grass was high enough, I wouldn't be seen.

I hoped the groundskeeper had been lazy lately.

The light disappeared.

I heard the car roll off.

I exhaled, feeling the sweat pooling around the small of my beck.

I got to my feet and hustled around the corner.

Shiva had vanished.

Shit.

I sank down for a minute and tried to get my bearings. The moonlight hadn't penetrated this darker section that much yet, and I had to wait for my eyes to adjust before I could see the details of the surrounding landscape.

I could make out the columns above me; the old granite stood silently in the darkness like fingers poking out of the earth. I turned and caught a glimpse of the Japanese stone lantern, and further on the garden monument depicting the five elements of Japanese mythology: earth, water, fire, wind, and void.

My ears picked up a host of sounds: the *tsk-tsk* of bats in the air searching for their body weight worth of mosquitoes, the scurrying of nearby mice and rats as they prowled close to the stone wall, the *thop-thop* of a rabbit in the woods close by.

But no Shiva.

I thought about how funny it would be to stand up and just holler her name and see who came running. Funny. Hilarious. And it would get me killed most likely.

I stayed put for another two minutes, ticking off the time in my mind and willing Shiva to reappear out of the shadows and lead me to where we needed to be.

But Shiva didn't reappear.

Damned rude of her not to.

I frowned. This is what I got for sleeping with a lycanthrope.

I slid down the backside of the wall. From my location, I could see the chain-link fence separating the ice skating rink from the rest of the land. When I was younger, the ice skating rink used to serve a really good pizza. Friday nights, I'd sometimes come up and skate with the crowd before enjoying a slice and a bit of hot chocolate inside the snack shack.

The snack shack had been replaced in recent years. Gone were their pizza slices, hot chocolate, and candy bars and soda. Now they served sparkling water and salads.

Some people have a real twisted definition of what progress is all about.

I moved across the open field toward the chain-link fence. During the summer, the rink was nothing more than a simple open cement floor.

Were Belarus and Jarvis waiting there to perform their ceremony?

Again, it didn't make much sense to me for them to do so. They had to be ready to scatter if the cops showed up. And as my experience tonight had already shown, things must have been very quiet elsewhere in Brookline for so many of them to be meddling around the park.

I squinted through the fence.

Someone was down there.

In the middle of the rink.

Shiva?

I frowned and eased my pistol out of my holster. My hands felt slippery from the sweat.

I crept along toward the gate. There should be a padlock barring entry to the rink.

I looked down.

The padlock was gone.

And the gate, although closed, was open.

I glanced at the hinges. Were they oiled? If I opened the gate, would it squeak and let everyone within five miles know I was coming?

I remembered that when Shiva had vanished, I hadn't heard a thing. That meant the hinges were probably fixed to keep them quiet.

I held the pistol ready, took a breath, and pushed my way through.

The gate opened without a sound and I moved through the opening quickly, closing the gate again behind me.

Stone steps led down to the rink's level. The ticket admission house of my past had been removed. The steps were wider now than they had been all those years before.

Which left me out in the open.

And I didn't like it.

I crouched by the side of the steps along the wall and risked a peek over the lip toward the rink.

There was definitely somebody in the middle.

But who?

I couldn't make out who it might have been. The figure's back was to me. The only thing to do was get down, check the place out, and see who was on the rink.

I crept down the steps and reached the wooden rink boundary wall. Above me, the heavy-duty Plexiglas shield obscured my vision, but I could see around the immediate vicinity.

The place looked clean.

I took another glimpse of the figure on the rink and saw it seemed perfectly still.

Maybe it was dead.

Maybe unconscious.

I took a breath and eased to the right, following the curve of the rink. Underneath my feet, the thick rubber matting laid down to allow skaters to walk without damaging their blades now enabled me to move quietly.

I noticed the night sounds had disappeared.

The bats and rats and rabbits seemed to have deserted me too.

Figures.

I brought my other hand up under the butt of my gun, keeping it in low-ready position with the barrel just off the horizon. I could bring it to bear quickly on any targets that presented themselves.

I hoped I wouldn't need to.

If I fired my gun now, I'd have a host of donut jockeys on me like rabid parents shopping for Christmas toys.

I didn't need that.

Overhead, the moon continued its upward arc into the sky. It really did seem particularly bright tonight. I wondered if this case was simply amplifying my awareness of it.

I frowned.

Moon be damned. I had a job to do and I was going to do it.

I completed my circuit around the rink and found no one else. The entire time, the figure in the middle of the rink hadn't moved. I figured it was time to move onto the rink and see who was out there.

I stepped onto the concrete.

In the middle of the rink I'd be exposed. Painfully so. I took another look around, searching for sniper vantage points. It would be tough. They'd have to be higher than the rink itself in order to have a good downward firing position. The only places I could make out would have been back at the chain-link gate entry or on top of the shed.

Neither seemed likely. The moonlight would have compromised them. And I couldn't see anything.

I turned back and looked at the figure. It seemed wrapped up in some kind of coat.

I took another step out toward it, half-expecting the night air to explode with gunfire and half-expecting to feel a thousand slugs rip into my body.

Neither happened.

I reached the body.

Nudged it.

It fell to the ground.

Turned over.

Shiva.

Her eyes were wide and white. Her eyebrows jumped at me and I could hear her trying to shout behind the gag someone had stuck in her mouth.

I stooped.

Started to turn.

And promptly got a solid shot to the back of my head that dropped me down to the concrete rink surface.

I sank into oblivion.

Thirty

I don't care what anyone else tells you—getting whacked on the skull hurts like a bastard. Judging by how my head throbbed when I finally came back to the land of the coherent, whoever had knocked me senseless must have used a crowbar the size of North Dakota.

I tried to roll over and promptly received a kick in my back for my effort. Some people are so damned rude.

I opened my eyes slowly—my stomach churned like a restless volcano. The hit to the head would surely have given me a slight concussion—if not something more serious.

Part of me wanted to puke my guts out.

But a bigger part just wanted me to get my hands on the sonofabitch who did this to me.

"Welcome back, Lawson."

I knew the voice. I wished I didn't.

Jarvis.

I opened my eyes a little bit more. Jarvis stood over me, cologne dropping off him in waves like dry ice in a bad horror flick. I was really beginning to hate this guy.

"Jarvis. You traitorous piece of shit."

He knelt down. "We could have killed you, you know that?"

"Ah, yes, the cowardly route. Just like you to kill someone when they can't even fend for themselves, is that it?"

"Whatever it takes. You know that. It's what we were taught. It's what we do."

"Sometimes it's okay to have standards, you know. Untie me and I'll explain it to you."

He laughed. "I don't think so."

I shrugged. "Can't blame a guy for trying."

"You know, I've always wondered how you always seem to be able to maintain such a good sense of humor about being in desperately bad situations."

I sniffed. "I get myself into so much shit, Jarvis, seems like it only makes sense to learn how to relax and enjoy those times."

"I see."

"Don't bother trying to understand it. I wouldn't expect anyone who runs from danger to understand."

"Excuse me?"

"I never believed you about Tokyo. I know you ran. You left me there to fend for myself. You couldn't handle the Yakuza punks if you tried."

"You don't know a damned thing, Lawson. Now don't piss me off or I'll have to kill you ahead of schedule."

"Where's Shiva?"

He laughed. "Oh, yes, I almost forgot about her." He turned, and I struggled to see where he was going. I could see the pistol sticking out of a holster on his belt. The sight of it didn't make me feel all warm and fuzzy inside.

I twisted on the ground. I was in what looked like a cleared circle of earth. I could feel a breeze and knew we must have been up somewhere high.

But where? I couldn't make out the Boston skyline anymore. But overhead, the moon looked high in the sky. And still as radiantly powerful as ever.

"Lawson."

I twisted again, spit out dirt, and looked. Shiva, still dressed as Monk, stood over me. She wasn't tied up anymore.

Great.

Jarvis must have noticed my expression because he laughed again. "Looks like someone's just beginning to figure things out, eh?"

Actually, I didn't really have much of an idea as to what was going on other than the fact that Shiva had apparently double-crossed me. Or was it triple-crossed? However many times we were up to, the end result was the same: She'd played me.

Well, that was fine. It just meant I'd be able to kill her with a clear conscience.

"Shiva tells me you were quite the paramour, Lawson."

I shook my head—my stomach churned some more. "Jarvis, you have any idea how stupid it sounds hearing you use that kind of silly language? You sound like you scored a word-a-day calendar for Christmas last year and you're trying to stick to it."

Jarvis frowned. "Shiva mentioned you were a good fuck."

I nodded. "Better. Makes you sound tougher too." I looked at Shiva. "Don't you think?"

She shrugged. "I don't much care really what he sounds like."

I flexed my wrists against the ropes holding me. They held fast. "So . . . what happens now?"

"You die," said Jarvis. "Eventually."

"Always been a big fan of 'eventually.' Personally, I like 'a hundred years from now eventually' even more." I glanced at Shiva. "Everything working out like you thought it would?"

"So far. Yes. A little skip here and there. I'm not concerned about it, though."

"Gee, that's great." I looked back at Jarvis. "So, since I'm apparently due to die, would you mind cuing me in on what you've been cooking up?"

"You haven't got it yet?"

"Sometimes I'm a little slow on the uptake. Besides, you really enjoyed knocking my brains out back there. My head isn't really sharp right now. Give me a break and spell it out for me, would you?"

I saw him look quickly to Shiva. She must have been running the show. But she must have nodded because Jarvis cleared his throat and started talking.

"Shiva told you that Belarus and I were the bad guys."

"She was apparently telling me the truth in one respect."

He nodded. "Yes. Me. I am the bad seed, I'm afraid."

"When did you turn, Jarvis?"

"Just after Tokyo. You're right, of course, I never could have handled those Yakuza on my own. I didn't even want to. My goal was to lure you there and get you killed. You shouldn't have been able to handle them either. Especially since I'd given them wooden blades earlier that day."

"You're a traitor, Jarvis."

He nodded. "You mentioned that." He smiled. "I

caught up with Shiva—or rather, she caught up with me, just after that event. She had information on the Lunaspe."

"Why would that matter to you? You're a vampire."

"No. Shiva told you I am a half-breed and she's right. Why do you think I wear so much cologne all the time? My scent needs to be masked or else people would know I wasn't all vampire."

"And you use cheap cologne to do it?"

"Whatever works."

"So, you decided to go after the Lunaspe. That's it? What about Belarus?"

"Belarus is nothing but an old fool."

"Tell me something I don't know."

"His participation in this little exercise was necessary to draw you out. We knew the location of the Lunaspe was in Massachusetts. Long ago, the lycanthrope tribes in the area buried it here. But Boston is your stomping ground, Lawson. And we didn't want to tangle with you if we could avoid it. Far better, I think, to have you as an ally. And that's just what we did."

I frowned. I hate it when people successfully fool me.

Jarvis continued. "Shiva's map had ancient Geralach writing on it that neither of us could translate. But you, Lawson, with your wonderful Elder friend, gave us some clues. And when that Limey bastard Arthur told you to go to Maine and see Belladonna, that was the opportunity we'd been waiting for."

"You sent Shiva ahead?"

"Yes. She killed the one you call Monk. She took her place. Didn't you notice how far back she stayed when you were at Belladonna's house? If she hadn't, Belladonna might have smelled something wrong. But Shiva merely assumed Monk's place. Once Belladonna translated the map and the directions, the rest was easy."

"And the story she told me about you and Belarus hunting down and killing all the half-breeds?"

"Bogus, of course. As closed a society as the half-breeds are, word would certainly have filtered out that someone was systematically killing them off."

"And Belarus isn't a half-breed, I take it?"

"One-hundred-percent vampire."

I glanced at Shiva. "Not your father either?"

"Nope."

"What about you two morons? Are you related?"

"She's my half sister," said Jarvis.

"Great." I looked around. Shiva was setting out what looked like special stones around the circle. "So, what are you two planning to do with this Lunaspe anyway?"

"Draw down its power, of course," said Jarvis.

"Yeah, I got that. But what about afterward? What then? You didn't go through all this trouble just to find a relic, get some lunar power, and then take off. Did you?"

"No." Jarvis looked at Shiva again, who stopped and came back toward me.

"The heads of both the vampire and lycanthrope societies are weak, Lawson," she said. "We will assume command of them both. Jarvis will head the vampire society and I the lycanthropes."

"How nice. A brother-and-sister team. Warms my heart to know this is all a family affair."

Shiva smiled and walked to Jarvis. I watched as

she kissed him hard on the lips, bit him, and then licked at the blood oozing from his wounds.

I guess it really was a family affair.

"You two are some of the most twisted saps I've ever had the displeasure to know. Anyone ever tell you that?"

"No one who wasn't about to die," said Jarvis. He wiped his hand over his mouth and smiled. "You should see us in bed. It's wild."

"No, thanks. Incest gives me heartburn. But hey, you two go ahead. Don't let me stop you. Just untie me and I'll be on my way."

Shiva chuckled somewhere off in the darkness. "I don't think so, Lawson."

"Those Fixers you killed, Shiva. That wasn't a hit team of half-breeds, was it?"

"No."

"You've been lying to me quite a bit, haven't you?"

"Absolutely."

"I really hate liars."

"Too bad."

I flipped over again, trying to flex my ropes a bit more. I thought I felt some give, and kept rolling around. Jarvis looked up.

"Stop moving, Lawson."

"Just trying to see what you guys are up to. I'm kind of at a disadvantage down here on this dirt. Maybe you could sit me up against something?"

Jarvis sighed. "Fine. Whatever." He came around and helped me sit up with my legs in front of me. My ankles were bound with the same rope. I could see it looked like a twine cord. Probably not a lot of give to it either.

Jarvis leaned me against a tree stump and then went back to arranging the rocks Shiva was placing around the circle. I went back to working on the ropes holding my hands.

My pistol was gone. I was willing to bet Shiva had it in her belt. If I could get free and get my hands on either Jarvis or Shiva, that would be good enough.

Shiva came walking back into the circle. "It won't be too much longer, Lawson."

"Tell me something, Shiva. Why did you sleep with me? I mean, it wasn't like you needed to. What was it? Old Jarvis there not as good in the sack as you'd like?"

Shiva glanced at Jarvis. "He's fine."

I laughed. "Hair is fine, Shiva. Lovers are either awesome or they suck." I nodded at Jarvis. "What is it—thirty seconds of blitzkrieg passion and then he drops to sleep like a bad stone?"

"Shut up, Lawson."

I nodded. "Maybe you guys should try the Kama Sutra. I hear it works well for couples with sexual problems. Of course, it could be the ugly fact that you two are, after all, brother and sister." I grimaced. The thought alone made me want to hurl.

"That has nothing to do with it, Lawson. We love each other."

"Yeah. I'll bet."

Jarvis walked over and said something to Shiva in Geralach. It sounded like he had a throat full of phlegm and was about to spit it out. Shiva answered him back. "Just do it."

I nodded. "Just as I thought."

Jarvis turned. "What?"

"Nothing."

"You got something to say, Lawson?"

"I was just noticing that it looks like Shiva wears the pants in the family, literally."

"We're equals in this regard, Lawson." He stalked away.

I looked at Shiva, who was crouching nearby. "You're gonna drop him too once you get what you need, aren't you?"

"I need him," she said. "I won't kill him."

"But the thought crossed your mind."

Shiva said nothing. I kept working the ropes. I watched them both lay out more stones. I couldn't tell what sort of design they were making, but it was complicated by the number and positioning of them.

I broke one of the ropes finally and breathed a sigh of relief. If I could just get the rest broken.

"We're ready."

Shit.

I looked up.

Shiva stood over me.

Smiling.

I grinned back. "Great, that's just great. What happens now?"

"Now you will die. In the ceremony."

"Jesus, you guys need a sacrifice? That's so . . ."

"Pious?"

I shook my head. "I was thinking lame actually."

"Well, it will make you happy to know it won't just be you we're sacrificing tonight."

"No?"

She smiled again. "No." She spoke over her shoulder. "Bring him in."

I shifted and then saw Jarvis dragging another figure into the circle of stones. Jarvis struggled to heft the body, but he finally got the bound figure into the circle and then stood, wiping sweat from his brow.

"Guy's heavy."
I looked.
And sighed.
"Oh, for crying out loud."
Belarus.

Thirty-one

I wasn't happy to see him again. And I doubt he was happy to see me. But I was even less happy about being tied up with Jarvis and Shiva looming around waiting to kill us both.

Shiva nudged Belarus in the back with her knee. "How are you feeling, Belarus?"

Jarvis yanked the balled-up sock out of Belarus's mouth. Belarus spit a wad of saliva tinged with blood to the ground and frowned. "You will both die for this. You realize that, don't you?"

Jarvis chuckled. "Somehow I don't see much chance of that seeing as how we've got your star Fixer tied up as well."

Belarus glared at me. "I should have expected this kind of incompetence from you."

"Nice to see you too, Belarus." Some people. I kept working on the rope knots. "How'd you get yourself so deep into this mess anyway?"

"I kept him paranoid, that's how," said Jarvis. "Tell the guy enough lies about Shiva coming to Boston to gun for him and even the most steadfast folks will just shrivel up and wet themselves."

"I did not wet myself," said Belarus.

Jarvis nodded. "Of course you didn't. That dampness on the front of your trousers just magically appeared there. That's cool. I can accept that."

As funny as I found the idea of Belarus pissing his pants, I had more important things on my mind right now. Namely, breaking the ropes holding my hands.

Time was a factor right now. A big one. Even if I got my hands freed, I'd still have to get my feet undone as well and then wrestle a gun away from either Shiva or Jarvis.

I wasn't crazy about tackling either of them actually.

Belarus rolled over. "So, what now?"

Shiva leaned close to him. "Well, honestly, we're going to do what Jarvis told you I'd do to you anyway. I'm going to cut you open."

Belarus's eyes went wide and white. I wondered if he was pissing himself again. I sighed. Shiva looked at me.

"Something to say, Lawson?"

"Why kill Belarus? You've got me. You don't need him. Let him go."

Personally, I couldn't believe the words came out of my mouth. Even if they did go for it, there was no way Belarus would ever sing my praises posthumously. Must have been that damned honorable streak in me again.

Sometimes I hate that thing.

Shiva smiled. "Perhaps you think it's because Belarus is the head of the Council? Maybe you think that us killing him will somehow impart a greater significance to the ceremony?"

"You tell me—it's your shindig."

"The honest truth, Lawson, is that he was convenient. Belarus wouldn't let Jarvis out of his sight once we thought we'd blown you up. When word got out that there'd been an explosion and you might have been killed, Belarus went nuts."

"And what about later?"

"When you came back to Wirek's apartment to get me?" Shiva shrugged. "Made no difference to me. I'd kill you when we were ready. Getting you up to Larz Anderson Park where Jarvis was waiting wasn't hard at all."

I turned to Jarvis. "Reminds me: How come I didn't smell you back at the rink?"

"I took a shower," said Jarvis.

"Well, nice to see that the personal-hygiene quest is working out for you so well."

Jarvis sniffed again. "Lawson, you're a real card. People must tell you that all the time, huh?"

I nodded. "Usually right before I kill them."

"I guess tonight's a little different, huh?"

I smiled. "The night's not over yet."

"For you it is."

I turned back to Shiva. I needed to keep them talking. "So, two sacrifices. Why does it have to be two?"

"One to represent the drawing down of the lunar power and one to represent the formation of one mind under the Lunaspe. Jarvis and I will share the power equally. Once the lunar power is drawn down, we will absorb it in kind. Your deaths will enable the power process to occur."

"You two geniuses have certainly figured everything out, huh?"

"Yes."

I looked at Jarvis, who had built a large fire in the center of the circle. Flames leaped about catching sticks and twigs and making pops and snaps in the night air.

"So, how are you going to assume command of the Council anyway? Won't it look a little unusual to have you just show up and proclaim yourself as the new leader? Especially if Belarus here turns up dead?"

Jarvis smiled. "The power of the Lunaspe will help me bend the necessary minds and spirits to my will. They will shortly see that accepting me as their new leader is a far better choice than anyone currently sitting on the Council."

I nodded. "And that works the same way in the lycanthrope Council, Shiva?"

"Pretty much. Of course, if there are any strong enough to withstand the power of the Lunaspe, we will simply kill them."

"Well, sure, that would make the most sense." Another rope broke behind me. They must have tied individual knots to make it harder for me to try to escape. By feeling, I could tell there were two more remaining. I kept flexing.

"It's really not that hard to imagine, when you think about it," said Jarvis.

"What is?"

"The idea that our two societies should be merged into one."

Belarus looked pale. "You're going to merge the societies?"

Shiva laughed. "Of course. That's been part of the plan since the get-go."

"You can't," said Belarus. "You can't merge lycanthropes and vampires. We'd never last. Plus, the thought of heathen lycanthropes polluting our society . . ." He trailed off.

I grinned. "Guess Belarus might have some racism issues to work through, eh?"

Belarus glowered. "You can't honestly think this idea would be any good, Lawson. You know what the cost would be. Lycanthropes and vampires living together is unacceptable, by anyone's standards."

"I don't know about that. Seems like it might just be a fairly decent idea. After all, if we could make the world one big happier place, there might not even be a need for Fixers."

"That," said Belarus, "might be the best thing to come out of it. But lycanthropes should not be mixed with vampire society."

"Doesn't look like you've got much say in the matter, Belarus."

Shiva cleared her throat. "Lawson is correct. You don't have any say in the matter. Neither of you do."

I looked up. "Hey, leave me out of this. I'm not a racist. I hate racists. Racists suck."

"I could have you terminated on insubordination charges, Lawson," said Belarus. "Do you know that?"

I shook my head. "You go right ahead and do that, Belarus. I'll wait right here for you, okay?" I shook my head. "You are such an idiot."

"What?"

Shiva stepped between us. "All right, that's enough. You two stop fighting. You sound like a couple of kids."

"He started it."

"Lawson!"

I shrugged. "Just trying to help."

Jarvis shook his head. "I doubt that very much."

I broke another knot.

Almost free.

Just one left. I felt much closer now. I kept flexing. My wrists ached and the rope was biting into my wrist. I could smell the copper of sticky blood. I hoped the smoke and fire would camouflage the scent. If Shiva and Jarvis caught a whiff, it'd be the end of my escape attempts for sure.

Belarus was eyeing me with a mixture of anger and curiosity. Maybe he could see my muscles straining or read the desperation in my face. I didn't much care.

I didn't like Belarus.

But I liked the idea of dying even less.

Shiva's voice broke the night. "Is it ready yet?"

Jarvis sighed. "You're so impatient. The fire needs more time to catch. Otherwise, we'll be doing the ceremony to a bunch of dying embers."

"Time, dear brother, is short. Midnight is coming and the moon's about as high as it will get tonight. We need to do this soon or we risk losing the opportunity for another month."

"Yeah, yeah," said Jarvis. "I know. I don't want to wait another month either."

I smiled. "Plus, you'd have to feed us and listen to us bitch and moan for thirty days too."

Shiva shook her head. "Your ability to make light of this situation amazes me, Lawson."

"I'm an amazing guy. Oh, sorry. You already knew that judging by the way you moaned my name this afternoon." I looked at Jarvis. "Your sister fucks like she hasn't been laid properly in years, Jarvis."

He stepped closer to me and slapped my face with a backhand strike that knocked me hard. I slid to the side and tasted blood.

"Shut up, Lawson."

"Hit a nerve, Jarvis?" It didn't come out like I wanted it to sound. It's tough to do so when your mouth is swelling and your tongue's a mess.

"He's trying to get you angry, Jarvis. Don't pay attention to his methods."

Jarvis looked back at the fire. "Almost ready."

"That's good," I said righting myself. "We wouldn't want any premature combustion happening here. It'd make a mess of the whole place."

Shiva chuckled. Jarvis whirled. I think I scored pay dirt with that comment. He kicked me in the stomach. I retched and puked up a small amount of bile. It burned my mouth and stung my throat. I swallowed and bit my tongue to stimulate some saliva flow. I flushed as much as possible and smiled in spite of the pain.

"Jarvis, you wear your emotions on your sleeve a bit too much, pal."

Jarvis turned and looked at the fire. Finally, he nodded. "It is time, sister."

Shiva smiled. "At last."

She drew a knife and started walking toward Belarus.

Jarvis came for me.

Thirty-two

There's something to be said for determination.

After years of training and being in bad situations, I can faithfully report that it is only by going through some extremely crappy real-world scenarios that you develop that internal strength, desire, and discipline needed to prevail in the face of certain death.

Nowadays, New Age gurus and lazy people try to make excuses that let them avoid the bruises and sweating and constant bone-grinding pain of hard living and training.

It's bullshit.

There are no shortcuts to the necessary mentality that will enable you to persevere in hostile situations.

You skip out on the sweat, you pay in blood.

I broke the last rope.

As Jarvis came within range, I launched my bound feet up toward his groin—an act that strained my already aching stomach.

He sidestepped and drew his pistol.

I reached up and got my hands up around his wrists and clamped down. I used my body weight to pull him into me for a head butt off his orbital bone. There was a sickening crunch as his bone

broke—instant swelling ballooned his eye shut—
and he dropped to the ground.

I grabbed the pistol out of his hands and aimed it
at my feet, flicked the safety off, and fired a round.

It was risky. Hell, it was damned desperate. But I
was out of time and out of options.

The round burned into the ropes, sawing
through them as the tip of the round fragmented
and shards of wood bit into the cords. I jerked my
legs in opposite directions and broke the last few
strands of twine.

Free.

Jarvis tackled me from behind, sending us both
sprawling into the dirt, just shy of a big rock. The
gun went flying. I rolled over and he came up
astride my chest.

"You ever seen the mount position, Lawson? It's
unbeatable." Jarvis began raining punches down
on me.

I blocked the punches and drove the thumb tips
of my hands into his floating ribs. As he grunted, I
jerked my hips up at the same time dislodging him.
I got to my feet and turned.

"You always did fall for useless propaganda,
Jarvis. No position is unbeatable."

He came off the ground launching a kick at my
head. I twisted and caught the backside of his heel
just shy of my jawbone. Still, I tasted blood. I'd be
paying my dentist a visit if I got out of this alive.

I couldn't see what Shiva was doing and that concerned me. I hoped Belarus could at the very least
keep her busy while I dealt with Jarvis. Then again,
knowing Belarus, that would be too much to expect, let alone ask.

Jarvis kicked again, but his range fell short. I

caught his heel and began a joint lock on the ankle. He swore under his breath and jerked his body out of my grasp. Ankle locks are always a bitch to pull off—for me anyway.

He got to his feet and we squared off. I feinted with a front snap kick to his groin. He went for it and I used the feint to bridge the distance between us, sending a palm heel strike right onto his nose.

I heard another crunch and blood poured out of his nostrils, slicking his face with crimson.

He swore again, not so loud this time.

Jarvis backed up. I followed. I saw movement out of the corner of my eye. It registered as Belarus and Shiva fighting, but I couldn't waste time on them right now. Jarvis wouldn't let me get away with that.

Jarvis looked a little shaky on his feet. Seeing his own blood for the first time probably rocked his world some.

Good.

I closed the distance down again and threw a right jab, intending to follow through with a cross and a hook to his head.

Jarvis ducked the jab and sent an elbow strike into my sternum. I staggered back, sucking hot lead into my lungs. Combined with the earlier taste of bile, I was really enjoying my body juices today.

Jarvis came in. "How'd that feel, Lawson?"

I sucked more wind. One thing about bad guys is they always feel this undying need to narrate their attempt to kill you. I hate that shit.

I threw a sidekick into Jarvis's knee as he smiled

at me. He saw it too late, and lifting his leg only put it into my optimum range even more.

The knee joint shattered and Jarvis screamed out, collapsing to the ground with his useless limb underneath him, folded at an odd angle.

Blood and sweat ran off as he gritted his teeth in pain. He wasn't moving now.

Better.

I dove for the pistol that had gone into the dirt when he'd tackled me, closed my hand around it, and came up already drawing a bead on Jarvis's chest.

One round. One round would end him forever.

Thank God.

I drew the barrel down.

And stopped.

Jarvis had a gun on me.

My gun.

He smiled in spite of his pain. "Forgot that I had this, didn't you?"

"I would have thought your sister would have taken it."

"She doesn't like guns."

"Figures."

Jarvis grinned. "You broke my fucking knee, Lawson. You know that?"

"Generally what happens when you combine a locked-out joint with the power of a kick with body weight behind it."

"You going to kill me now?"

"That was the plan."

"Was?"

I shrugged. "Well, you are holding a piece on me. My piece, I might add."

"Be pretty insulting to get shot with your own gun, wouldn't it?"

"Probably wouldn't go down as one of my best nights, no."

Jarvis smiled. His nose whistled a little. Small gurgles of blood continued to seep out of it. "I'm in a lot of pain here, Lawson. I can't keep this gun on you forever."

"So, put it down."

"You'll shoot me."

I nodded. "It'll be quick."

Jarvis took a breath. "Maybe I should just shoot you now, huh?"

"So we both die? What kind of sense does that make?"

"Makes better sense than just me dying."

"Depends on your perspective." I could see the sweat and blood making him blink rapidly. They probably burned his eyes.

"We had some good times together, Lawson."

"You had good times, Jarvis. I've never really liked you. You're too cocky, too suave with the ladies. You're too much of everything."

He took another breath. I watched him look at the side of my gun, turn it just so slightly.

I drew the hammer back on the pistol I held.

Jarvis smiled. "So, this is how it ends, huh?"

"If it has to be this way. Yes."

Jarvis nodded. "So be it." I watched him start to thumb the hammer back—

I squeezed the trigger of my gun as I started to roll to my right.

The round firing sounded like a huge explosion puncturing the night air. From the distance we'd been at, the bullet thundered into Jarvis's chest as his own round fired and struck the ground an inch away from me.

The bullet I'd fired blossomed immediately inside Jarvis's chest, sending wooden fragments splintering throughout his thorax and heart.

It wouldn't take long.

Jarvis slumped back on the ground, moaning. Pink froth bubbled out of his mouth. I watched his canines extend to the full length—the death-throe action that was even more telling than fully blown pupils.

I leaned over him, took my own gun out of his hand, and then looked around.

Belarus and Shiva were gone.

Shit.

"Lawson."

I turned back to Jarvis. He was almost dead.

I sat down next to him. "I'm here."

"She's gone, isn't she?"

"Yeah. Took Belarus and scrammed."

"You won't find her."

"No?"

"Contingency plans . . . we had a few of them . . . professional to the end, you know?"

I frowned. I figured Shiva would have plenty. I looked back at Jarvis. "Do the right thing, Jarvis. Tell me where she'll go now."

He tried to shake his head. It didn't work. Instead, more blood and pink froth came out of him. His chest was a mess of dark blood and torn flesh.

"I can't . . . do that."

"You'll die protecting her?"

He smiled. Dried blood cracked on his lip saliva dribbled out of one side of his mouth her. Don't you understand that?"

Yeah. I did. I knew what love was. I knew because of Talya. I knew because doing the right thing doesn't always mean doing the thing that made me feel good. I knew because of the pain and suffering that so many people find the courage to live through every single day.

I looked down at the ground. Jarvis's gun lay in the dirt. I picked it up and turned it over.

He'd gotten himself a small caliber Walther PPK. The James Bond gun. Figured. I almost smiled.

I dropped the magazine out of the grip and then ratcheted the slide to clear the chamber of the live bullet in it. It spun out, catching a glint of the fire flames in the casing before tumbling to the ground beyond the firelight.

I slid the magazine back into the gun.

And then I slid the gun back into Jarvis's hand.

"Here's your piece, Jarvis."

His eyes were bright with tears. I watched his hand close around the grip. Even now, he still had some strength in him. Vampires don't relinquish their hold on life without battling every step of the way.

Jarvis felt the coolness of the metal in his hand and smiled. "Thank you, Lawson."

I stood. My own gun was at my side.

In the dark night, I watched Jarvis breathe his ᵃath, heard it waft out of his mouth and scat- ᵘr winds.

Jarvis."

Thirty-three

The situation sucked.

It took me almost two hours to get back to the Council Building. First I had to hike down from the top of the Blue Hills where Shiva and Jarvis had staged their little ceremony, without breaking my legs. Then I had to thumb my way back into Boston. That meant flagging down a motorist on a lightly traveled road at night. By the time I lucked out and scored a lift into town with a gas-pedal-allergic driver, more time than I wanted to had elapsed.

Arthur met me at the door, his shotgun in hand. "Where ya been?"

"Almost dying," I said. "Shiva's got Belarus."

He nodded. "I know."

"You know—how?"

He held a belt up in his other hand. "This belongs to Belarus. It's got a homing device in it that we can use to locate him in the event of something like this. All the Council members have them. I found this in the lobby here a few hours back."

I sighed. "Jarvis is dead. I assume he kidnapped Belarus while Shiva was luring me out to where they ambushed me."

"Wanker. Never liked him anyway," said Arthur. "What happens now?"

I reached for the phone. "I need Niles here. He's

my Control. He might have to run interference for me while I figure out how to rescue Belarus from Shiva."

"You'll need help."

I looked up from the phone. Arthur hadn't asked a question. He'd stated a simple fact. "Should I assume from the way you're holding that shotgun of yours that you intend to tag along anyway?"

He shrugged. "Someone's got to make sure you don't take the opportunity to drop two into Belarus while he's in a touchy situation."

I grinned. "I'm shocked you'd even suggest such a preposterous notion."

"I'll just go and fetch some of my things then."

He disappeared downstairs. I rang up Niles.

"Yes?"

"It's Lawson. I need you in town here at the building five minutes ago."

"What's going on?"

I told him and he didn't say a thing. He just hung up. I checked the clock. It was just after two-thirty in the morning.

Shiva'd missed her chance to draw down the lunar power for this month. But she'd taken Belarus. As far as I was concerned, she could have the sonofabitch. What made me frown was why she'd even bothered with him. He was just extra poundage to drag with her. She could have left him back in the Blue Hills and simply disappeared into thin air.

But she hadn't.

Which struck me as odd.

Arthur emerged from the basement dressed in black fatigues and with a watch cap on his head. He looked like an SAS trooper and I told him as much.

"Fine lads those boys from Hereford are." He

nodded at me. "Besides, once you get changed, you'll look the same as me."

I looked down at my clothes. They looked like hell. Leaves and grass clung to me aided by sweat and blood. The branches during my downhill trek had shredded my shirt and jeans.

And I hitchhiked looking like this? My luck must have been changing.

"'Sides," said Arthur, "if we're able to move tonight, we don't want to show up in the dark, do we?"

"Good point."

Arthur eyed me. "What's bothering you?"

"Shiva's actions on the hill. She didn't have to take Belarus with her. Hell, the guy weighs a lot."

"Wouldn't matter to her. Being a lycanthrope and all, she could easily lift him."

"Yeah, but why bother? I was already occupied with Jarvis. Belarus was tied up on the ground. Why take a hostage when she didn't need to?"

"To improve her bargaining position?"

"She's already got what she needed, though. She has the Lunaspe. She's got nothing to bargain for. It doesn't make any sense."

"Granted." He leaned back against the door-jamb. "What are you thinking?"

"What if Belarus wasn't kidnapped after all?"

"You're suggesting he's in on this?"

"I don't know. Look: Shiva came to me and said that this whole thing was concocted by Jarvis and Belarus for the purpose of destroying all the half-breeds and then solidifying control of both lycanthrope and vampire societies."

"When did she tell you this?"

"That doesn't matter. What matters is that until

she turned on me, everything looked like it was pointing in that direction. When we were up on the hill, Jarvis and Shiva told me it was all a lie."

"But now you're not so sure."

"No. I'm not. Worse, I'm starting to think I was used to take Jarvis out of the equation."

"Why?"

"I don't know. Maybe he was getting to be troublesome. Maybe Shiva was double-dealing with Belarus."

Arthur frowned. "What a mess."

"Jarvis and Shiva were brother and sister, did you know that?"

"Of course not." Arthur sighed. "Means that wanker was a half-breed. That explains his fetish for that cheap cologne."

"I know. I don't understand how he could have gotten past the Council on his centennial being so."

"Unless he had help," said Arthur.

I looked at him. "It might be true."

He nodded. "You might be able to kill Belarus after all."

"I wish that made me happy."

"It's not supposed to, lad."

"What about the Lunaspe?"

"What about it?"

"Belladonna told me that it was only able to draw down the lunar power during the full moon. Tonight was the full moon. But she missed her chance. Shiva will have to wait another month or so for the next full moon, won't she?"

Arthur sucked his teeth. "Hold that thought." He dialed a number on the phone and spoke quietly for a few minutes. When he hung up, he turned to me.

"It's a bloody different calendar."

"What?"

"The lycanthropes use a different calendar than we do. I mean, it makes sense, doesn't it? They're more obsessed with the moon. We don't even care about it. They base their calendar on the strength of the moon."

"Which means what?"

"That tonight wasn't the real night of the full moon, according to their calendar. Tomorrow is."

"You mean tonight."

"Yeah, that's right. It's morning now, ain't it?"

"Uh-huh."

"Belladonna—that was her on the blower—says that Shiva would need to do the ceremony tonight."

"But we have no idea where."

"No," said Arthur. "But we'll need to find out."

"The question is, does Shiva stay out in the woods or wherever she'll do the ceremony? Or does she come back into the city and hole up for the day and move tonight?"

"You," said Arthur, "seem to know her better than anyone else."

Sure, I'd only slept with her a few hours ago. I shook my head. "I don't know her well enough to predict what she'll do."

"And Jarvis is dead."

"Yeah."

"We're fucked, Lawson."

Niles rushed in through the kitchen door. "What the hell is going on?"

I looked at Arthur. "He's got a key?"

"This one does," said Arthur. "New order from the Council: The station Control gets a key."

"About time they did something smart." I turned to Niles and filled him in as best I could.

He stood there shaking his head when I was finished. "I can't believe Belarus would betray the Council."

"He's betraying a lot more than just the Council," I said. "He's compromising the entire society. If he is dirty, then he and Shiva mean to destroy everything."

Niles frowned. "Belarus has a long distinguished record of service in our society, Lawson. Are you sure he's dirty?"

"I'm not sure of anything. All I know is both Shiva and Belarus are gone. Shiva has the Lunaspe. She didn't need to take Belarus with her. But she did. I'm theorizing, yeah, but it's the only thing that makes a damned bit of sense."

"All right. All right." He looked at me and then stared at Arthur's black fatigues. "What are you planning to do?"

"We've got to find them, obviously. We need to take the Lunaspe back. Maybe we can destroy the damned thing before it causes any more heartache."

"Do you have any idea where they are?"

"None."

Niles actually grinned. "Do you always work like this, Lawson?"

"Nah. Sometimes I know even less."

Niles looked Arthur up and down. "You're ready to go, I take it?"

"You betcha," said Arthur.

Niles nodded. "You have any more of that gear downstairs in the armory?"

Arthur's eyebrows shot up a full two inches. Mine did the same. "You aren't serious."

Niles turned to me. "I'm absolutely serious. You

two can't do this alone. At the very least you should have superior numbers before you go into action like this. It's written in all the tactical textbooks I've ever read."

I chuckled. "Niles, have you ever seen the business end of a tactical situation?"

"Not a damned one. But I'm sure willing to learn. Especially when it comes to preserving our society."

I glanced at Arthur, who shrugged. "He's right about that."

"Yes, he is."

"No sense keeping the boy from his dreams, Lawson. He wants to tag along, it's fine with me."

I looked at Niles. "You realize what you're about to step into here?"

"Yes," said Niles. "And I'm ready."

"We'll see about that," I said. I looked at Arthur. "May as well get him suited up."

Thirty-four

Even with the three of us standing in the Council lobby looking like a hostage-rescue team all set to storm an embassy, our prospects sucked. Shiva and Belarus had apparently disappeared. We had no idea where they could be.

And time kept slipping away.

"What about that water-treatment facility over on Mission Hill you told us about?" asked Niles.

Arthur frowned. "She'd be a damn fool to go back there now that Lawson's been there."

"Maybe she thinks we wouldn't look there because of that very reason," said Niles. "It might be worth a swing by just to confirm it."

I nodded. "We can add it to the list."

Arthur looked at me. "List?"

"You have an address for Belarus?"

"Sure."

"We'll hit there as well."

"And if they're not at either place?"

I frowned. "I'd rather not think about that. We've got about twenty hours to find them and see what this mess is all about. If we don't get lucky before then, well, something will be happening anyway."

"Something bad," said Arthur.

I grinned. "When was the last time a 'something' actually turned out good for you?"

"Been a long time."

I nodded. "Me too."

Belarus lived in a large brownstone on the lower end of Marlborough Street. Large bay windows looked out onto the street. Flowering dwarf dogwoods sprawled under the windows, coating the air with a perfume.

We passed through the iron gate quickly. Darkness luckily remained on our side. And the hour was early enough that the dog walkers hadn't crawled out of bed yet.

Thank God for small favors. The sight of three vampires decked out in full hostage-rescue garb probably wasn't the best thing to see first thing in the morning.

I bent and examined the lock. I had pulled out my picks when Arthur tapped me on the shoulder. I looked back.

He held a key.

Leaning close to my ear to whisper, he said, "All the Council members are required to keep a key at the main building now."

"Why?"

"After the debacle with Arvella, it was decided there should be another level of checks and balances."

More refreshing news. Arvella had been a Council member who'd gone bad on my last jaunt. I'd had to storm her estate out in Newton. I could have used a key back then.

Arthur opened the door and we passed into the front lobby.

I took a quick glance at Niles. His eyes were wide

and white but he seemed okay. A thin trail of sweat oozed down his face and he gripped the modified Heckler & Koch MP5K a little harder than he should have.

Arthur and I stacked by the inside door. We'd decided to hit it hard with Niles acting as rear security. Arthur would unlock the door and then we'd crash through.

Noise wasn't much of a factor at that point since Belarus owned the entire building. An alley on one side of his house meant we only had a neighbor to his left who might react. And at three-thirty in the morning, a time when humans are at their deepest point of sleep, I doubted that would happen.

Arthur checked the lock and then slid the key into it.

He looked at me.

I looked at Niles.

Niles nodded.

I nodded.

Arthur turned the key. I could hear the bolt slide back with a dull thunk. Arthur immediately rose and moved behind me. I had my MP5SD butt in my shoulder and muzzle at low-ready.

I took a breath.

Eased off the door frame.

And then shoved myself into the door.

It popped easily and swung open. I went left immediately while Arthur swung right.

The door had opened into a reception hall with a coat rack and long table. Paintings on the wall attested to Belarus's love of modern art. I spotted an Andy Warhol and a Keith Haring that registered as my eyes swept the room.

But the room sat empty.

Arthur said quietly, "Clear."

We moved.

Ahead of us, a flight of stairs led up, but we had to clear the lower level first. We moved through the living room and the dining room.

Both empty.

In the kitchen, all the pots and pans hung over a central rack lofted above the stove area. No dishes waited to be washed. No food smells hung in the air.

I frowned. I didn't have a good feeling about this.

We cleared the rest of the lower level and stacked again at the bottom of the stairs.

Climbing stairs on an assault is tough. Your area of vulnerability is high. The point man aims forward and up, taking out targets that might present themselves directly ahead. The man behind him aims up and to the rear, firing on targets that might try to use the height to ambush from the rear.

Arthur put one hand on my shoulder and used the other to aim his MP5SD as we moved as one unit. Niles would come up after we got to the top of the steps.

Arthur squeezed my shoulder and we took the steps. I had the benefit of using both my hands. Fortunately, Arthur's MP5 could be fired and controlled using one hand since the recoil was almost nonexistent, especially after it had been customized for vampire use.

Thick red carpeting helped muffle our boots as we crested each step. I kept my breathing even and level as much as possible. Behind me, I could hear Arthur breathing at the same rate. The old guy might have been old and retired, but he hadn't lost his edge yet.

At least not that I could see so far.

We got to the top of the steps and moved immediately right, checking a closed door. Niles came up and sat by the top of the stairs, covering our backs while we stacked outside each closed door we came to.

Each room we cleared, we came up empty.

We moved to the left of the stairs outside another room. The door here looked thicker than the others. Arthur frowned and pointed at the hinges.

"Outside of the door," he said. "Damned thing opens out."

I nodded. We couldn't stack the way we had at the other doors. Since the door opened out, and the staircase was immediately to the side of the door, there was no room to stack beside the door-jamb. We'd have to pull the door open and then rush in.

Not a good tactical situation.

One person sitting inside could simply shoot us as we rushed through. I looked at Arthur and then down at his vest. I smiled and pointed.

Arthur looked down and smiled too.

It wasn't a great idea, but it would help us.

Hopefully.

Flash-bangs are special light and noise concussion grenades of the sort that are thrown into rooms before human hostage-rescue teams storm them. The combination of brilliant light, explosive sound, and a concussion wave helps overwhelm terrorists and hostages alike, making it easier to rush the room and gain quick control over it.

We'd use a flash-bang here.

I quickly arranged the setup. Niles would yank the door open and flatten himself behind the door as he did. Arthur would toss the flash-bang, and I would cover him from further down the hall, aiming over him at anyone inside.

It wasn't a great plan, but working within the confines of tight space and the door setup, it wasn't all bad.

Niles readied himself by the doorknob.

I slid back down the hallway, turned, and aimed. I'd aim as Arthur threw the flash-bang, close my eyes as the thing exploded, and then reopen them right after that. If I timed it right, my eyesight wouldn't be affected.

If I timed it right.

I'd used flash-bangs a few times in the past. It takes constant training right on top of the things to grow used to the explosion, thunder, and bright light that accompany them.

It had been a few years since I'd used one.

Arthur looked at me.

I looked at Niles.

Niles nodded.

I nodded.

Arthur pulled the pin.

Niles yanked the door.

Arthur threw the flash-bang as I aimed.

I closed my eyes.

Heard a thud.

And a bounce.

Bounce—

Bounce—

Arthur's voice, "Shite!"

And then I felt the explosion of the flash-bang detonating in the hall with us. My ears exploded and I felt myself lifted up and thrown back into the wall behind me.

I hit the ground hard; wind rushed out of my lungs. I sucked air.

I tried to sort myself out. I heard Arthur shouting. Was he shouting at me?

My ears felt clogged with balls of wet cotton. I struggled to my feet, trying to bring my MP5 up and ready just in case we'd just walked into some kind of ambush.

But I didn't think we had.

I heard Niles's voice then, dimly, as if he was speaking through about fifteen yards of aluminum foil.

I felt Arthur's hands on me, dragging me up to my feet, felt him stuff my MP5 back into my hands.

"Lawson!"

I exhaled. Sound was coming back. I looked at him. Clouds of smoke hung in the hallway.

"What the fuck?"

He was still shouting, but I only heard it as if he were speaking normally. "The flash-bang bounced. It came back and exploded almost right in front of you!"

That would account for me feeling like I'd gotten kicked in the balls, ass, and throat all at the same time. I nodded.

"What did it bounce off of?"

Arthur frowned. The clouds of smoke were beginning to clear. I could see down the hall.

Arthur fished a flashlight off of his vest and switched it on. The powerful light cut through the haze.

Toward the door.

Beyond it.

Niles jerked his head away.

Arthur swore again.

I swallowed hard.

Jesus.

Belarus was just inside the room.

Suspended somehow from the ceiling.

Arms and legs akimbo.

Naked.

And disemboweled.

His intestines spilled out of him, dangling in long moist lines toward the floor.

Somewhere ahead of me, Niles puked.

And if I hadn't recently gotten reacquainted with my own purging instincts, I might well have done the same thing.

Thirty-five

It took Niles about five minutes to regain control over his heaving. I couldn't blame him. Seeing someone's intestinal tract draped like a Christmas tree garland around a room can demolish an iron constitution.

While Niles went to the bathroom to splash some cold water on his face and calm down, Arthur and I moved into the room.

"Cripes, what a stench."

"He's been dead a few hours by the look of it," I said.

Arthur shook his head. "Ain't no way for a vampire to die, Lawson."

I nodded. Along with the horrific disembowelment, Shiva'd left a huge chunk of wood protruding from Belarus's chest. Arthur peered closer at it and sighed.

"Good God, man, you know what she staked him with?"

"No."

"It's a goddamned bedpost. His bedpost if I remember what the four-poster down the hall looks like."

"Sick bitch." I sighed. "We gotta cut him down."

Arthur nodded. "I got a knife. I'll take his right arm if you want the left."

I stood on an armchair and reached for his left hand. A leather handcuff with spikes held it in place; a chain running from the handcuff bolted into the wall.

I sighed. "Looks like some S&M sex play went seriously wrong here."

Arthur continued swearing. "I'm not into that scene any, Lawson, but even I know most people don't get their bollocks off disemboweling lovers."

"That's even if Shiva and Belarus were lovers. What she told me, Belarus was her stepfather."

"If I were you," said Arthur, "I'd pretty much bin anything that beast told you. It's likely all a bunch of lies."

"True, but there might be some grains of truth in what she told me as well."

"How do you figure that?"

"Shiva's not a dummy."

"No, she's a bloody heathen beast who deserves a slow agonizing death. I mean, I didn't much care for Belarus either. Big tosser if you ask me. But he didn't deserve *this*."

"What I mean is that she'd base any of her lies on some measure of truth. Any professional knows that a lie is so much better when it's built on a foundation of truth. Even if it goes off on some bizarre tangent, there has to be some truth there."

"No need for the remedial lesson, Lawson. I remember them all well."

"Just thinking out loud."

He nodded. "Well, your problem now is trying to decide which of those silly bullshit lines she fed you were true at all. Me? I happen to think someone like Shiva doesn't even give a damn about the truth. Whatever her mission was when she started, she's certainly lived up to her name, hasn't she? The Destructor. Indeed."

"Yeah. She sure has." I positioned my knife. "You ready?"

"Yeah."

We cut the restraints and Belarus's body fell to the floor, splashing noisily into the pool of blood and excrement beneath him.

Niles reappeared in the doorway. Arthur looked at him.

"You all right, lad? You look white as a ghost."

Niles ran a hand over his hair and tried to smile. "I've never seen anything quite so horrible in all my life."

"Stick around long enough and you'll see plenty more," I said.

His eyes looked sad. "Was that supposed to cheer me up?"

I shook my head. "There's nothing that's going to cheer you up after you've an image like this plastered on your mind's eye, Niles. This is what my job deals with. Like it or not, you're my Control and you'll see this kind of crap from time to time."

Arthur broke in. "Actually, I'd be really cheered up if I could have two minutes alone with Shiva."

I grinned.

Niles smiled.

Arthur chuckled.

It was over too quick, that momentary break in the tension. I pointed at Belarus. "We ought to cover his body."

"Hang on," said Niles. "I'll get a bedsheet."

He disappeared, and returned a moment later with a dark navy sheet from Belarus's bedroom. Arthur and I draped it over the mess on the floor.

Dark blood oozed out from under the sheet, but it was at least somewhat contained for the time being.

I looked at Niles. "You'll need to get a cleanup crew over here."

"Yeah. I'll take care of it."

Arthur watched him go. "He's all right that one, ain't he?"

"Yeah, he's turning out pretty okay, all things considered."

"Have you met his boyfriend yet?"

I shook my head. "Arthur, you know the only thing that matters to me is that the people I work with are competent and get their jobs done when they need to get them done. Sexual preference doesn't matter. Niles could have seven legs and mate with Cameroon frogs for all I care—as long as he does his job, and does it well, that's all I care about."

Arthur chuckled. "Cameroon frogs?"

"Best I could come up with on short notice. Besides, it's late and I'm tired."

Arthur shook his head. "That's some head you got on your neck there, Lawson."

"Only to be used for the purposes of good, I assure you."

"Oh, naturally."

Niles came back in the room. "Cleanup crew will be here in under an hour."

I checked my watch. "We need to get out of here before then."

Arthur started for the door and we piled downstairs. We were just about to leave when the phone rang.

We stopped.

Arthur looked at me. "Who'd be calling at this time of morning?"

"Cameroon frogs?"

Niles started to back up. "You want me to get it?"

I stopped him. "No. See if the answering machine picks up."

Arthur and I walked to the living room and stood over the phone. Niles stayed by the front door. Arthur looked at me.

"You think?"

I shrugged. "Why would she call?"

"Why not?"

The ringing stopped and the answering machine picked up. Belarus's voice droned on for almost a minute.

Then there was a pause.

And her voice filtered out of the metallic grill. "Pick up the phone, Lawson."

"Jesus, this one doesn't let up." Arthur's eyebrows shot up. "Might's well see what she's got to say, huh?"

"Might as well." I picked up the receiver. "Shiva."

She laughed in my ear. "How are you?"

"Nifty. Just fucking swell."

"Did you like my handiwork?"

"I don't foresee any gallery openings for you, Shiva. Your work has too limited an audience—psychopaths only."

"Too bad, I was going to a sort of *Silence of the Lambs* motif. I thought it worked quite well."

"You forgot the wings, psycho."

"That's it! That's what I forgot. I should have called you first and checked it with you, huh?"

"You got a reason for calling me, Shiva? It's late and I'm tired of your shit."

"You're no fun, Lawson. Well, actually, that's not quite true. I thought you were kind of fun in bed when we fucked like animals. Did you enjoy that? The sweaty grunting? I love a good primal fuck."

"Get to the point already."

"Why? You have someplace else to be? What did I interrupt—you going home and trying to figure out where I might be hiding? How you're going to find me?" She laughed again. "This phone call is the best chance you've got."

"How do you figure that?"

"Because if you're nice to me, I might just tell you where I'll be tonight."

"You expect me to swallow that kind of crap after all the other bullshit you dropped me on?"

"Sure, why not? You fell for everything else, after all."

I shook my head. "I'm not going to tolerate insults now. I'm hanging up."

"I wouldn't do that if I were you, lover boy."

"Why not?"

"Because you'll miss the best part."

I sighed. "Shiva, you've got something to say, say it already. I don't feel like playing twenty questions with a head case like you."

"You're a spoilsport, you know that?"

"What I am," I said, "is tired. I'm exhausted from having to crawl down from the Blue Hills and then hitchhike back to the city and then storm a house and find the head of the Council butchered in a way no vampire should ever be butchered."

"You presume to judge me because I killed Belarus? Lawson, you're a hypocrite. You kill routinely in the course of your job. We're no different."

"I preserve the Balance. If that means I have to terminate some evil to preserve society, then so be it. It has to get done. And someone has to do it. I don't recall leaving any of my targets with their guts strewn all the room."

"You're getting morals, Lawson. I never thought that would happen to you."

"I've always had morals, Shiva. You just don't know me well enough to understand them. Fucking me doesn't give you some extraordinary insight into my psyche."

There was a pause on the phone. "Maybe you're right."

"Yeah, I am. Listen, why don't you tell me where you are right now so I can come on over and introduce you to some of my other morals?"

She laughed again. "I don't think so, lover boy. It's not that easy. Besides, God knows who'd you show up with. Probably that old fart Arthur and that silly faggot Control of yours."

I frowned. How had she known about Arthur and Niles being here with me?

"You there, Lawson?"

"Yeah." I motioned for Arthur to get to the front door and look. "I'm here."

"Good because I want you to listen carefully now."

"Go ahead." The hairs on the back of my neck stood up.

"I have your friend Wirek."

"Bullshit."

She laughed. "I thought you might say something like that. Hold the line."

I heard a scrape and then a low voice. "Lawson."

"Wirek? Jesus Christ."

"She told me to tell you something only you'd know about so you know it's me."

"Go ahead."

"Remember in the Himalayas? The blood bread we ate that Saano gave us?"

Shit. "Yeah, pal, I remember. You hold on, okay? I'm coming for you."

Shiva's voice reappeared in my ear. "Are you satisfied now, Lawson? Are you satisfied this isn't just another bit of bullshit on my part."

"Yeah. You got my attention." I gripped the phone tightly.

"Good. You come alone tonight, you understand? If I even think someone's with you, Wirek dies a horrible death. And don't think I won't have the capacity to do it, because we both know I will."

"Where?"

"Eleven o'clock. There's a hill in your neighborhood, in the Arnold Arboretum, that has a nice little roundabout at the top."

"Bussey Hill?"

"That's the one."

"I know it."

"Good. You be there at eleven o'clock. And Lawson, I am intimately aware of the surrounding area. Don't think about showing up hours early and attempting any kind of ambush. I'll see it a mile away and your dear friend Wirek will never see the light of day again. Do we understand each other?"

"Yes."

"Wonderful. Oh, there's just one final tidbit I'd like to leave you with."

"What's that?"

"I left a little something behind when I departed Belarus's place earlier tonight."

"Yeah?"

"Yes. By my clock, you've got ten seconds before that entire house explodes—"

I ran for the door, shoving Niles and Arthur out with me. We fell down the steps and toppled behind a car just as the entire brownstone detonated.

Shards of wood, glass, metal, and Belarus rained down on the street. On us. As the roar subsided, I kept my head down low.

And wondered if things could get any worse.

Thirty-six

The Arnold Arboretum is a 265-acre botanical park in Jamaica Plain. Designed to be the crown jewel of the Emerald Necklace by Frederick Law Olmsted, the park is home to exotic species of trees, plants, and shrubs from all over the world. All of them meshed together in a seamless green patch that almost lets you forget the city's right outside.

It's a gorgeous place. And I've met more than a few beautiful women while strolling the lilac paths.

But tonight wouldn't be about meeting women.

It'd be about killing a particularly evil one.

Throughout the park, trails and paved roads run all over the place. There are lesser-known pathways as well, but I figured Shiva'd had time to discover them all. 265 acres is big, but it's not impossible to learn quickly.

Paved road ran all the way to the top of Bussey Hill, terminating in an almost circular drive that bled into a small seating area with a grass knoll and gravel path. Looking off in one direction, you can see the city skyline. Looking off anywhere else is just a nice view. Overhead, there's not much cover.

The Arboretum's generally deserted at night, although I've prowled a few times there late at night and known other prowlers were there as well. Maybe they were like me, just working on their stealth techniques. Maybe they were evil. Whatever they were, we left each other alone.

And that was fine with me.

I got to the park at about ten-thirty. I slid past the main gate near the visitor center and immediately disappeared into the pine knoll behind the building. I paralleled the gravel path running down the backside, and then crested a small series of hills by the Dana Greenhouses, where the Arboretum staff tends to a respectable collection of Japanese bonsai trees.

The path ended by running back into the paved road further on. From my vantage point, I could see Bussey Hill rising ahead of me, the summit roughly three hundred meters in front of me.

I couldn't see anything.

Not that I expected Shiva to simply stand at the top and wave me on. She'd gotten this far by playing it smart.

And playing me stupid.

I frowned and thought maybe one of us had been played better than the other. Hell, I'd been a fool for most of this jaunt.

I had two choices for my ascent: I could either head straight up the side of the grassy hill—a more strenuous route, or I could simply walk the paved road in a more leisurely winding route.

I checked my watch. Ten minutes had elapsed. I'd easily make it by eleven either way.

I took the paved road.

I passed lilac bushes, wandered through the haze of delicate perfume.

My night vision enabled me to see all around the park and I saw nothing, which vaguely unnerved me. Even at this late hour, a spare dog walker or two usually strolled through the park. The absence of dog walkers might be nothing. But knowing Shiva, it meant something.

Around me, I couldn't detect much in the way of nocturnal noises either, another unusual sign. 265 acres can provide homes to a lot of wildlife. Gray and red foxes hang out here. So do a family of hawks. Rabbits, raccoons, possum, maybe even a weasel or two.

Nothing.

The night air stood still, the humidity hung heavy around me. I figured that might be it. It's always easier to hear when the air is cold and crisp. The animals might have been out but I was having trouble hearing them.

Or maybe they were smarter than me—maybe they'd simply vanished. I wish I could have done the same.

I don't have a lot of friends, being a Fixer and all. It's tough, simply put. My lifestyle precludes certain social activities. It's tough ordering a round at a bar and having your beeper go off. "Whoops, gotta run and kill someone." Somehow, I always imagine that as being a real conversation killer.

But Wirek was something else.

I'd met him after the death of my mentor Zero last year. Wirek was a last-ditch effort back then, someone I would have avoided like a splintery plywood panel if Zero hadn't requested I do it. Wirek had been a staggering drunk back then. A former Elder, driven to drink by the hypocrisy and bullshit of political infighting and opportunism in the vampire society.

I smiled again. Humans thought they had a monopoly on everything.

Wirek'd cleaned himself up in the subsequent months. A recovering drunken asshole is what he liked to tell people he was. By the time I needed his help again, Wirek was ready to kick some ass—quite literally in fact.

And we did.

Both here and over in Nepal. It wasn't easy, it wasn't what he'd been trained to do, but he did it. In fact, Wirek had pretty much been a damned good help to me every time I needed something.

And it was my fault the poor guy had gotten himself kidnapped by Shiva. After all, I'd dragged both Jarvis and Shiva to his apartment on Beacon Hill.

He was probably cursing my name in all the two hundred languages he spoke. And I couldn't blame him.

So being here tonight was the least I could do. I sure as hell wouldn't let someone like Shiva have the satisfaction of killing him.

Especially since I'd probably need his help again.

And his friendship.

I thought I saw a flicker of movement by a green park bench further up the path. I adjusted my eyesight so I was looking at the landscape from the corner of my eyes.

Vampire eyes are like humans', meaning we have both rods and cones. At night we both use the rods at the outer edge of the eye to see better. Vampires just have a lot more of them to see with is all.

But I saw nothing more.

Maybe I'd imagined it.

Part of me was hoping I was imagining this whole caper.

Maybe I'd wake up tomorrow in bed with a beautiful woman next to me, warming me with the softness of her flesh. She'd roll over with those limpid eyes and tell me what an incredible lover I'd been. And then we'd go at it all over again.

The other part was yelling at me to stop being stupid.

I listened to that part.

I reached what I knew would be the final curve in the path. My stomach was doing somersaults the way it always does before I head into combat.

It's typical. It's what happens. There's no way you can ever adjust to the sudden flood of adrenaline spiking your system like a football jock spiking the punch at a high school prom. Adrenaline is supposed to make you jumpy. It's supposed to fire you up and get your reflexes alert. It's supposed to make you feel like you need to take a serious dump and simultaneously feel constipated at the same time.

So, if someone tells you they're used to combat, they're lying.

Badly.

Nowadays, I simply recognize the fact that it's happening inside of me and keep going. Because it's all I know how to do.

Dense shrubs draped over the curve. I could hear a mosquito go whining past my ear. I resisted the urge to reach up and swat it. I didn't want Shiva seeing any sudden movements—she'd likely think I was drawing my gun.

As a result, she'd waste Wirek.

I came around the corner and paused.

Again, I could sense no movement ahead of me.

Nothing stirred up here on top of Bussey Hill. I looked around. The Boston skyline twinkled in the moonlight.

Overhead, the moon cast long shadows and

illuminated the surrounding area. Combined with my night vision, it almost looked like daylight.

But Shiva had better vision.

After all, she was part lycanthrope. And lycanthropes are designed for hunting the woods and forests more than vampires are. If vampires are the cosmopolitan society, lycanthropes are the redneck clans. Although I doubt any of them would agree with that assessment.

Shiva came up behind me in my blind spot. I sensed her approach and it was all I could do not to move.

"Hello, Shiva."

She stopped and then leaned forward, pressing something into my back just above my left kidney.

"Good evening, Lawson."

"Nice night."

"It's glorious."

"You going to do the ceremony here then?"

"Yes."

"Lot of dog walkers around here at night, you know. Some of them might just stumble in on your lunacy—forgive the pun."

"Hysterical. But we won't be bothered. Not tonight."

I frowned. What had she done to cut down on the traffic in this place? I wanted to ask, but I also wanted to see what she had planned for me.

"Where's Wirek?"

"Safe. At least temporarily."

"I want to see him."

She laughed in my ear. "I don't much care what you want, Lawson."

"Sure you do."

"Excuse me?"

"You know you want me to see him. It'll make this little game of yours that much more fun for you, won't it?"

"You know what I want, vampire?"

"Your dead brother back?"

She sniffed. "I could care less about him. Lovestruck fool that he was."

I grimaced. "Can we not get into that again? I'm trying to keep my dinner down."

"Did our relationship offend your sensitivities, Lawson?"

"That's one way of phrasing it, I suppose."

"He was convenient. A necessary tool to get where I needed to go. Haven't you ever done that? Haven't you ever simply used someone to get something you needed?"

"Sure. But not a family member."

"You should try it."

"I don't have enough family to try it on."

"Poor Lawson. You're such an antiquated man. No family, honor-bound to do the right thing, and yet . . ." She trailed off.

"What?"

"Well, with all that honor, I'm wondering how you're reconciling the fact that you slept with me."

"I scrubbed my crotch with bleach and sandpaper. I'm hoping that helps."

She laughed again. "And what about the memories of what we did floating through your mind?"

"Well, I figure you'll either end that nightmare for me, or else I may look into abusing a little over-the-counter medication at some point in the near future."

"I see."

"Where's Wirek?"

She jabbed me in the kidney. "Just walk, Lawson. You'll see him soon enough. And then we'll get into what I have planned for you tonight, okay?"

"Planned?"

"Yes."

"I thought you just wanted to kill me."

"Oh, I do. I do want to kill you, Lawson. In the worst way, as a matter of fact. Remember that time we tangled all those years ago?"

"Wasn't that long ago."

"Long enough."

"What about it?"

"I let you live, you know that?"

"Must be my charming personality."

"I don't know why I did, really. You were so bent on killing me. I think I'd never seen that kind of relentless dedication to a job in anyone else. Maybe I even respected you for it."

"Great. Respect from you I don't need."

"When I got the jump on you, I could have finished you off then. We wouldn't even be having this delightful talk right now. But something made me stop. Something made me want to keep you around. And now I know why."

"Because I'm a good lay?"

"Not even close. You're here because you will serve as an adequate demonstration as to what the power of the Lunaspe can accomplish once it's been drawn down."

What the hell did that mean? "That doesn't sound like much fun. Might be better if you just kill me now."

"Don't be silly, Lawson. I wouldn't dream of dragging you up here this late at night just so I could kill you quickly."

We kept moving and finally reached the grassy knoll. I heard him before I saw him. Actually, I heard the ropes creaking as they twisted.

Shiva's voice in my ear. "You see? He's still very much alive. For now, at least."

And then I saw him. Wirek was strung up. Hanging by his wrists, suspended from a tree branch in the center of the grassy knoll. I could see dark blood crusted around his mouth. One of his eyes looked swollen shut.

"He put up a bit of a fight," said Shiva. "I had to teach him a small lesson."

"You damned near killed him by the look of it."

"That's nothing compared to what I'll be doing to you soon enough, Lawson."

Thirty-seven

"It's simple really."

I frowned and finally managed to stop staring at Wirek's suspended body. "What's simple?"

Shiva held up the Lunaspe and for the first time, I saw it. A medallion of gold inscribed with what looked like ancient script running all along the edge. It caught in the moonlight and seemed to glow.

"You told me it was made out of iron. You lied about that as well?"

"It was made out of iron. But when it senses the approach of the ceremony, it changes."

"Metal doesn't change."

"Maybe not conventionally. But during mystical ceremonies it certainly can."

"Magic?"

"If that term makes you feel better about it, sure."

Great. Every time I get mixed up in something magical, things go from bad to worse.

Shiva held the medallion aloft. "See? Even now it senses the moon."

I frowned. "All right already, what makes this simple?"

Shiva looked skyward, still keeping a gun leveled

at me. I had no idea if it was a Fixer gun like my own or one of her own creation.

"I will draw down the power of the moon using the Lunaspe. And then you and I will have a contest. The winner gets Wirek."

"And gets to live presumably."

"Certainly. What good is a prize if you don't live to enjoy it?"

"Indeed." I looked at the gun. "That a Fixer piece?"

Shiva shook her head. "I borrowed the concept, but then I improved upon it. After all, my work has taken me into realms not only frequented by vampires, but other creatures as well." She smiled. "Speaking of which, take your gun out using just your thumb and forefinger."

I did, keeping them both in the trigger guard. My pistol dangled from my finger.

Shiva nodded. "Toss it into the bushes."

I frowned. "So some little kid can find it tomorrow morning? How about I just hand it to you?"

"So conscientious, aren't you?"

"Someone has to be. God knows there aren't many in the world who are." I reached over.

Shiva took the pistol. "Feels heavier than the others I've handled."

"I packed heavier loads for tonight. What about yours?"

"I use special bullets that explode both wood fragments and silver nitrate once they penetrate. It's almost like a two-stage rocket. When the rounds penetrate, a small charge goes off exploding the contents into the bloodstream."

"Nice touch."

"Works on either vampires or lycanthropes."

"Or half-breeds."

Shiva smiled. "Yes. Half-breeds it's particularly effective on. Actually kills them faster."

"I'll keep that in mind. Maybe I'll have the chance to use it on you, huh?"

"I wouldn't worry about that if I were you, Lawson."

"Well, I worry about the darnedest things."

Shiva glanced up again. Could I rush her? I frowned. No. Her position was too far away. She'd be able to squeeze off a few rounds before I could cover the distance. Especially since she probably expected me to do just that.

I held off.

She looked back at me. "Just in case you're thinking I could be overpowered, you should know that Wirek has a small packet of explosive strapped to his back, shaped to explode through his heart."

I looked over at Wirek. He nodded slowly. "I suppose it's fragmentary?"

"Yes. Full of wooden splinters all eager to shatter Wirek's thorax. Isn't that nice?"

"You really are a sick bitch, Shiva."

She laughed. "Very true. I am that. And you know? I love being just the way I am."

The Lunaspe seemed to be glowing even brighter. Shiva noticed it too, and smiled. "At last. The time grows near."

"Tell me something: If you knew it was really tonight, why go through the elaborate staging last night?"

"I needed to get rid of Jarvis, of course."

"So why not just kill him?"

Shiva frowned. "Jarvis had the Lunaspe. I

couldn't get it unless I told him that last night was the right time to do the ceremony."

"And you expected me to jump him?"

"Of course. I knew you would. Who do you think tied your ropes?"

"You want me to thank you for that? You didn't give me much slack to work with."

"Ah, but I gave you enough, didn't I? And the timing worked out perfectly. You broke free at just the right moment. I imagine Jarvis went to his grave thinking he'd never even been set up to take the fall."

"What about Belarus? What was the truth behind that? Was he ever involved?"

"Belarus is no longer an issue. He's dead."

"Yeah, but I want to know."

"We can't always get what we want, Lawson."

"Why are you protecting him?"

Shiva laughed again. "I'm not protecting him. He was never worth protecting."

"Was he dirty?"

Shiva regarded me for a moment. "He wasn't. I tried to corrupt him. It didn't work. He had too much honor. Like you. Another damned fool. He was a half-breed, you know."

"Jarvis told me he was one-hundred-percent vampire."

"He lied."

"All this lying." I sighed. "Must be some kind of family thing, huh?"

"Half of Belarus wasn't vampire. But he refused to acknowledge it. He only wanted to be vampire. When I came to him, I begged him to help me."

"He didn't know about Jarvis?"

"Of course not. He would never have consented to having Jarvis protect him if he had known."

"So, he didn't help you and you killed him."

"Yes."

"You slept with your brother—"

"Half brother."

"And you killed your father."

"Stepfather."

"Whatever."

"Yes. And like I said, my stepfather was too honorable to do what was right."

The thought of Belarus being honorable didn't do much to improve my overall opinion of the man, but he'd died horribly and at least being true to the cause. I had to give him a nod for that.

"What about the sacrifice thing you said last night?"

"Oh, that was just bullshit. I thought it would add a nice bit of embellishment."

"Do you ever tell the truth, Shiva?"

"Certainly. For example, if you don't do exactly what I say, the truth of the matter is that Wirek will die, possibly you as well."

"I'm not refusing anything yet."

Shiva held the Lunaspe aloft. "You see how it catches the moon rays? It's almost time." She nodded toward the knoll. "Stand over there. Close by Wirek but not too close. I know all about your background in explosives."

I walked toward Wirek and winked at him. It wasn't much and Wirek was a realist like me. He could see things were bad. There wasn't a lot I could do right now and he knew that. Our best bet was to wait and see what Shiva had in store for us.

She followed about fifteen feet behind me. She was careful to maintain that distance.

I stood by Wirek. Shiva stood in the center of the knoll and slid the Lunaspe around her neck. It rested in between her breasts. I frowned and shut out the images of their pale softness.

As soon as the Lunaspe came to rest on her, it glowed even more. Bright golden and yellow auras began radiating outward. Shiva looked down and then up at me.

"Remember, Lawson, even if it looks like I'm incapacitated, that bomb is still wired to blow up unless I deactivate it. So, don't even think about trying anything funny."

"Wouldn't dream of it, Shiva. Just get on with this crap already."

She smiled and looked up toward the moon. She closed her eyes and began a slow rhythmic chant that sounded like a combination of growling and barking combined with a guttural-sounding dialect of Arabic. It came out harsh. Full of hard consonants.

Shiva's voice rose. A breeze kicked up around us, chasing the humidity away. Dust and small gravel rocks swirled and bounced all around us. In the middle of it, Shiva stood alone, untouched by the hellish wind beating the ground around Wirek and me.

My eyes stung. Tears flowed as I tried to keep the dust and rocks out of them. It hurt like hell. I could hear Wirek moaning next to me. He was probably afraid the bomb would detonate if a stray rock hit it the wrong way.

He might have been right.

Shiva's voice carried over the gale, and then

abruptly it died back down. Instantly, the wind died down as well.

And then everything returned to normal.

I brushed a hand across my face. It came away dark with dirt and mud.

Shiva looked fresh as dew. And she was smiling.

"It's done."

I sighed. "Great."

She nodded. "I can feel it, Lawson. I can feel the incredible power surging through me. It's as if a thousand electrical wires are connected to me right now. Juice flows in every one of my veins. I'm pulsing."

"Nifty. Glad it worked out for you. How about releasing Wirek?"

"And now I really feel like seeing just what it is I can do with all this new power."

Uh-oh.

She turned to me. "We're at stage two, Lawson."

"What's stage two?"

"Stage two is really simple. Just like I said." She turned and pointed to a small path leading off the top of the hill. "You go down this path."

"And do what?"

She smiled at me. "You run, Lawson. You run."

"I hate running. How about I walk?"

"You'll have five minutes. Three hundred seconds to cover as much ground as you possibly can."

"What happens after five minutes?"

"I come after you."

"And what—we fight somewhere? Is that it?"

"If you can stay alive for one hour, then you win. Wirek goes free. You live."

"You laid out a game course in the Arboretum?"

"This entire park will be our playing field

tonight, Lawson, You have 265 acres in which to lose yourself. Whether you choose to run or hide is up to you. If you can do that for one hour, then you win. That's the game."

"How do you know someone won't wander in here to walk their dog? I'd prefer to keep innocents out of any field of fire."

"Again with the honorable thing."

"I'm a creature of habit. Sue me."

"Well, have no worries about the public. Have you heard of electronic pain field generators?"

"Sure. They use sound and light to generate pain within a certain radius."

"Exactly. I set up electronic pain-field generators at the entrances to the park. Surely you noticed there is no activity in here tonight?"

"Yeah."

"The pain-field generators inhibit human and animal activity. It becomes too painful to walk in here tonight. We're alone. Believe me."

"So that's it? I get a five-minute head start. You try to hunt me down in some silly rendition of *The Most Dangerous Game?*"

"I don't think it's a silly rendition, Lawson."

"You should try looking at it from my perspective."

"No, thank you."

"All right."

"You understand the rules?"

"Yeah. I got them. What guarantee do I have that you'll even honor the agreement if I do make it through an hour's worth of play?"

"You have my word."

I sniffed. "Pardon me saying so, but your word means shit. You've been bullshitting me silly since this entire thing started. Forgive me if I'm not so ready to embrace your word as being honorable."

Shiva nodded. "How about this?" She removed a small black box from her pocket. "This is the detonator to Wirek's bomb. You survive an hour and you get the detonator."

"Doesn't do me any good without the code to deactivate it."

"True, but it's something. And it's all you'll get. Otherwise, I have no guarantees that you won't simply head off and then come right back without playing the game."

"And it's all about the game, is that it?"

"Of course. That's all life is anyway, Lawson. Just one big game. One big chance to beat everyone else."

I frowned. "I always hated organized sports."

"Well, here's your chance to make up for lost time." She pointed down the path. "I will give you five minutes. They won't do you much good, I'm sure. But you will have five minutes to get as much of a head start as you can. And then I'll be coming after you."

I looked down at the pathway and then back at Wirek. This time he winked at me.

I was right before. The wink didn't do a damned thing to boost my spirits.

I looked at Shiva. "I'm ready."

Shiva nodded. "Your five minutes start right . . . now."

Thirty-eight

I ran down the steps almost tripping over the vines that stretched across the concrete treads, clogging them. I hopped down the rest of the steps and landed at the bottom feeling the shock in my right knee.

There wasn't much time to consider my options. I didn't have the luxury of choosing an easy path. I dove straight ahead for the transplanted bamboo grove the Arboretum staff tends to.

A few nocturnal creatures too small to be affected by Shiva's pain-field generators scampered out of the way, vanishing under the rustling leaves.

For a moment, I felt like I was back in Japan, what with the long tall stalks of bamboo stretching up on either side of me. I wished I was. I could use a vacation.

Five minutes didn't give me a lot of time. And that was if Shiva really intended to play by the rules. I didn't expect her to. So I figured I had maybe thirty seconds before she got so antsy that she'd toss the stopwatch and come after me.

One tactic employed during escape and evasion is to find a good hiding spot and wait for the hunters to pass you by. At that point, you've successfully penetrated the line and can work your way out moving behind the hunters.

Another tactic is to hide and wait for the hunter force to give up. At that point you can continue on your way, with a lot less stress.

Neither of those options would work for me tonight.

I had no doubts Shiva would be able to sniff me out of any hiding space I found. And with the best hiding spots, there's usually only one way in. Get cut off and it's all over.

I'm not a big fan of "all over."

I wasn't exactly sure what kind of power or attributes the Lunaspe would give Shiva, but I was willing to bet it would enable her to hone in on my location with ease. That meant my only chance would be to try and outrun her.

Have I ever mentioned how much I hate running?

Thank God I'd tanked up on juice before coming out tonight. It was probably the smartest thing I'd done since this whole mess started.

The bamboo grove sloped away down the back side of Bussey Hill. I wove like a slalom skier, dashed and slipped down the gravel path, tore across the paved path at the bottom of the hill, and ducked under more rhododendron shrubs.

Ahead of me, a brook carved a zigzag route through the ground. During the spring thaws, it normally swelled with rushing water. I used to build dams in it when I was younger.

During the summer months, the brook shriveled in the heat and humidity. And Boston hadn't had a lot of rain this year. The brook had dwindled to a trickle.

Mosquitoes whined in my ears, drawn by the lure of both my heaving chest that spewed too much carbon dioxide and the drumming pulse beat in my neck. I might as well have hung a neon sign around me that said "dinner."

I ignored the buzzing Stukas and drove on.

Another hill loomed ahead of me. It vaulted out of the earth at a sharp angle of ascent, broken up with craggy peaks, jagged handholds, and slippery moss-covered rock faces. Climbers liked testing and honing their skills on this hill. It could be challenging at times, but professional climbers never had a problem.

As for me, I'd climbed the silly thing so many times, the route was ingrained in my brain. I knew the handholds and footholds so well that in the dark of night my hands and feet honed in on them with ease.

I skirted the base of the cliff and found the small pathway that would take me up about thirty feet. From there, I'd have to take it slower.

Speed was obviously paramount; I could have just run straight on the path, but that wasn't the point. I wanted to try to use the natural obstacles of the Arboretum to my advantage. I was banking that Shiva's knowledge of the area was more limited than my own. And climbing hills might even tire her out some.

Maybe.

I found the handholds and started up. My boots found the soft earth and I climbed fast. I ignored the steady whine of bloodsucking dive-bombers and kept going.

A sound jumped up from below me.

A branch cracking?

I discarded it and kept climbing. Even if Shiva was already on my tail, there was nothing to do but keep going.

I made the top of the cliff and stepped into the blazing moonlight. I felt like the entire area was awash in halogen, so powerfully did the moon illuminate everything.

I kept low.

Shiva might conceivably be able to see me from her position on top of Bussey Hill. I doubted she was still there, but I didn't want to take any chances. If she got a bead on my direction, she could flank me, cut me off, and put in a perfect ambush.

The landscape at the top of the cliff consisted of mounds of volcanic rocks jutting out of the hill like bent crooked fingers of death. Misstep and they'd wrench an ankle. Or worse.

I threaded my way as carefully but as fast as I could. Maybe Shiva would get tied up in this igneous minefield.

Ahead of me, a rabbit darted out of my way, vanishing into the shadows. Lucky little guy.

I hopped down the back side of the cliff and wound my way back into the thick pine forest. Underneath, the soft earth cushioned my footfalls. I moved silently.

Sweat poured out of me. My heart hammered in my ears. It was all I could do to keep my breathing under control.

At last, I passed a big outcropping of rocks and found the marker I'd left here earlier in the day. I knelt for five seconds and cleared the branches and small rocks I'd piled on.

There.

In a small bag, I yanked my pistol and my cherished bokken out. Holding them in my hands made me feel a lot better. Being unarmed makes me nervous when I'm being stalked by a half-vampire half-lycanthrope who's been imbued with some sort of unholy power.

Under the cover of trees now, I slowed my progress. Five minutes had passed by now. Shiva would definitely be on the trail, scenting the air for me. Even without the Lunaspe, she'd be able to track my scent. I just hoped the circuitous route would tire her some.

I headed down the gentle slope, jumped over the gravel path cutting through this neck of the woods, and landed on the other side.

I wanted to make a giant loop of the park. That meant I'd have to cross back on the main path at some point. But I wanted to do it where I had little chance of being seen. I had to get as far away from where I'd started as possible and then do it.

I chose to cross near the gate close to the Jewish Rehabilitation Center that bordered this part of the Arboretum. A lot more trees grew in that section, providing ample concealment in the shadows and long dangling branches that stretched toward the paved road in places.

I crouched by the road and waited.

Timing played a key role here. Since this area bordered a road, I'd wait for a car to go by. Not only would its engine make enough noise to cover my run, but the headlights might also hurt Shiva's night vision if she saw me.

I heard another noise some distance behind me. My heartbeat increased.

If it was Shiva, I was sure she was making the noise deliberately. A lycanthrope can move even quieter in the woods than a vampire can.

She was probably enjoying herself tonight.

I wished I was.

A car whizzed by and I jetted across the paved path into shrubs on the other side.

Since I was armed, the natural instinct would be for me to wait and set an ambush—kill Shiva as she came for me. But I couldn't risk it. Not with Wirek still strapped to a pack of some explosive.

I'd kill Shiva and her final act would be to detonate the explosives strapped to Wirek's body.

Unacceptable.

I had to play the game by her rules as much as possible and hope she would honor the agreement if I did make it through the hour.

I checked my watch.

Thirty minutes were gone already.

At this rate, the contest wouldn't last long.

I crept up the side of the smaller hill and headed back into the trees. I heard bats whizzing overhead; the air punctuated with their *tsk-tsks*.

Ahead of me, I heard another sound.

But this wasn't natural. It sounded like someone trying to be quiet.

I knelt down slowly. In the darkness, sudden movement draws the eye. All actions have to be slower.

I heard the sound again. I frowned. I didn't think Shiva would make this much noise.

I waited.

And then I saw him.

Niles.

He was walking along the path. I watched him trying to pick his way down the path without crunching stones underfoot. He wasn't enjoying much success. He carried a long rifle in his hands. I could see the silhouette of the scope from my vantage point.

He walked past my position and I grabbed him. I

cupped my hand over his mouth, and it's a good thing I did because he started to cry out. I dragged him down into the shrubs, hoping the commotion wouldn't draw Shiva even faster, and whispered into his ear.

"It's Lawson. Lie still!"

He stopped moving. That was a good sign. I knelt close to his ear again. "What are you doing here?"

"Arthur suggested we help you out."

"If she catches wind of you, she'll kill Wirek!"

"Arthur insisted."

I frowned. I was glad to see Niles. And I was happy to know Arthur was out here somewhere as well. But I couldn't risk Wirek's life on them. If Shiva found out, she might well blow Wirek up right away.

I whispered into Niles's ear. "I'm sorry."

"For wha—?"

I pinched the nerve plexus by his neck and felt his body go limp and heavy as unconsciousness swept over him. I hid his body under the bushes, stowed the rifle nearby, and then took to the trail again.

If Niles was on this side of the park, maybe Arthur was somewhere closer to Wirek. My heart took a small leap. Maybe Arthur knew how to disarm the explosives.

Then I remembered Arthur had been retired for a long time. He probably wasn't familiar with the newest detonator technology.

I'd have to hope Shiva played fair.

Even though I doubted she would.

I took a step and heard a gunshot ring out behind me. Dirt and gravel kicked up by my foot. I ran.

I heard laughter behind me. Shiva's laughter.

I hated her all the more for it.

I ran hard through the trees, wind rushing in and out of my lungs like a bellows. My hands gripped the bokken and pistol, but I knew my palms were slick with sweat. I could feel it pooling in the small of my back. My heartbeat hammered away in my chest and ears.

Shiva wasn't worried about noise anymore. I could hear her behind me, stomping like mad.

Another shot rang out.

I ducked as the round whizzed past my head.

Shiva apparently didn't care about shooting someone in the back.

I broke out of the forest and hit the main path. Straight ahead of me Bussey Hill loomed again, but if I went straight, I'd be exposed on the hill with little cover. Shiva could kneel and pick me off at her leisure.

If I was going to die tonight, I'd make her work for the kill.

I ran downhill on the paved path, picking up speed by the lilac bushes I'd passed earlier. At the base, I broke right hard by the water fountain and cut back up Bussey Hill by a small path I know about.

Perfume cloyed at me as I slipped through the bushes.

Quiet.

I couldn't hear Shiva anymore behind me.

Had I lost her? Maybe the lilacs covered my scent some.

I kept climbing.

I risked a look at my watch and saw fifty minutes had passed.

Just ten to go.

Count to six hundred, I told myself, and it will be all over.

And then I heard more laughter behind me.

"Nice try, Lawson" floated over the bushes. Shiva couldn't have been more than fifty feet back.

I kept climbing, altering my path to a zigzag motion, trying to not follow a routine.

I could feel her aiming the gun at me. I spun right and dodged another bullet that came exploding out of the barrel of her piece.

I ran again, tearing through more bushes. I aimed my own pistol back behind me and squeezed off a single round. I wasn't really aiming to kill her, not yet, but she didn't know that. And if she knew I was packing, she might just back off some and be a little more wary.

It must have worked because the laughter stopped.

I kept climbing.

I could see the top of the hill now.

The moonlight bathed everything in a soft bright glow.

Another shot rang out, and it hit the dirt an inch away from my right foot. I shifted and aimed back at where I thought Shiva would be and fired.

I kept running.

I reached the top and checked my watch. I still had three minutes.

Three minutes.

An eternity.

My heart sank.

I looked back at the way I'd come. I didn't see anything.

I turned back.

Shiva stood in front of me.

Her gun aimed at my heart.

She smiled. "By my clock, you've still got two

minutes in the game, Lawson. And here we are."
She pointed. "Put those weapons down."

I let them drop to the ground. Shiva broke into
a big smile.

"Are you ready to die, Lawson?"

Thirty-nine

The look on her face irked me the most. I hate self-righteous people.

"Spare me the lengthy speech, Shiva."

She frowned. "You won't indulge me?"

"Near as I can tell, I've been indulging you ever since you showed up on my steps."

Shiva nodded. "Fair enough. I suppose the least I can do is make it quick. You played a good game, though."

"Is that supposed to make me feel better?"

"I don't care if it does or not. Your time is up."

She took a step back and brought the gun up, aligning the sights and getting it fixed on my heart.

I waited.

I could see Shiva's finger begin taking up the slack from the trigger.

A single shot rang out in the darkness.

The pistol flew out of Shiva's hand with a loud clang. She whirled, looking for the source of the shot.

Arthur walked out of the darkness.

"'Evenin', Lawson."

"Boy, am I glad to see you." I knelt and picked up my pistol and bokken.

Arthur smiled at Shiva. "Spoiled your fun, have I?"

Shiva frowned but turned to me. "I still have the

detonator, Lawson. And Wirek is still my prisoner. You kill me and he dies as well."

"Ah, that's right," said Arthur. He reached into his pocket and withdrew something. He tossed it to Shiva. "That's your little bomb there, ain't it?"

Shiva's face fell as she caught the packet of explosives.

I looked at Arthur. "What'd you do with Wirek?"

"I left him right where he was. I figured I had to make it look like this bitch still held the cards, right?"

"That must have made him happy."

Shiva looked up at me. "This isn't finished, Lawson. Not by a long shot."

I shook my head. "You never know when to give up, do you?"

But then she moved faster than I've ever seen anyone move before. It must have been the Lunaspe.

She backhanded Arthur in the jaw, spun, and grabbed his rifle, tossing it away. Then she slipped inside Arthur's arms and threw him into the bushes.

I brought my gun up. It was time to end this.

I aimed and fired instinctively.

And heard the hammer fall on an empty chamber, the click echoing across the top of the hill.

Empty.

Lifeless.

Shit.

"No bullets, Lawson," said Shiva. "I found your little hide earlier today. I removed the bullets from the magazine and left just one in the chamber. I didn't think you'd notice in the heat of the chase. Guess I was right, huh?"

I'd foolishly neglected to check when I recovered

the gun. Looking back on it, I thought it did feel a little light.

I dropped the pistol and gripped my bokken. "Doesn't matter to me. I can kill you easily enough."

Shiva smiled and bowed from the waist.

What th—?

She danced away, flicking her wrist at me.

I ducked, holding the bokken in front of me vertically in what's known as *kongo no kamae*. I caught one of Shiva's wooden shuriken off the blade and it flopped harmlessly to the ground.

Shiva dove to the left, vaulting into the darkness.

She spun and two more shuriken came flying at me. I parried these as well, but then she threw three more.

One of them barely missed nicking my neck.

I ran at her, cutting down the distance between us. I chopped diagonally down at the side of her neck. I needed to incapacitate her arms so she couldn't throw any more of those shuriken at me.

But Shiva backpedaled out of range.

I moved with the bokken, feeling the energy that had been imbued in it by the weaponsmith who'd made it for me so many years ago.

I ran after Shiva, lifting the bokken so the point aimed between her eyes. I'd drop and thrust through her chest at the last minute. She'd never see it.

Shiva stopped.

Whirled.

And faced me head-on.

She held nothing in her hands.

I feinted and then dropped the blade, aiming for her heart—committed the energy and drove it straight in toward her chest.

Shiva ducked and came in under the bokken.

It was a classic unarmed defense against a sword technique that I'd been taught a long time ago. But Shiva's knowledge of it surprised me.

And the heel of her palm slamming into the bottom of my jaw hurt like hell. She turned and tore the bokken from my grasp. I heard it go skittering off in the darkness.

"I picked up some *muto dori* in Japan, Lawson. You like?"

I couldn't answer because she'd already launched a renewed attack on me. She kicked at my knee, but I twisted just enough to deflect the kick. I drove my own hand down onto her neck, chopping hard on her trapezius muscles.

She grunted and dropped, pivoted on her knee, and swept my legs out from under me. I went down hard on my back, wind rushing out of me.

Shiva straddled my chest and began pummeling my face with her claws. She went for my eyes.

I brought my arms up trying to shut her down. She went over the top of them and kept raking my face.

I bucked my hips to dislodge her and she rolled off, finding purchase a few feet away from me. We circled each other.

And then it happened.

Shiva's body began to morph. Change.

Except she wasn't morphing into someone else. She was changing into some sort of . . .

Creature.

Fur broke out along her arms and neck. Her eyes glowed yellow and her hands became grizzled claws topped by needle-sharp nails.

Her voice growled like a lifelong smoker gargling

sandpaper. "Now, you'll fight a true lycanthrope, Lawson. Someone who has the power of the Lunaspe on her side."

Shiva lashed out with another kick, but it was out of range and it missed me easily. So I thought.

I felt a biting sensation across my shin and glanced down. Shiva's feet now had claws too. And they'd sliced through my pants and into my skin with ease.

I hoped she didn't have rabies.

I closed and feinted left with a jab and tried to catch her with a right hook to the head.

She brought her hand up at the last moment, but I still caught some of her jaw. She reeled away, crying out with some kind of guttural bark.

I moved in, but she turned and dove for my legs going for another tackle. I backpedaled and dropped my elbows down on her furry back, driving them into her spine as hard as I could. I heard another grunt erupt out of her.

She twisted out from under me and rolled away.

Her jaw had elongated some more. She had a mouth full of incredibly sharp teeth. She almost looked like the stereotypical werewolf, but she wasn't.

She was something much deadlier.

I clawed at the ground trying to get up myself. My right hand felt the wooden bokken. I yanked it up in front of me just in time.

Shiva launched another shuriken at me. She must have found one when she rolled. I deflected it.

The shuriken bounced away again.

Shiva began chanting and in the darkness, I could see the Lunaspe begin to glow around her neck. It bloomed bright golden yellow. It stung my eyes to look at it. I squinted, feeling tears roll out of my eyes.

My vision clouded. Sharp images dissolved into a dark opaque mass of shadows.

I couldn't see shit.

I kept the bokken in front of me. I kept moving.

I heard Shiva laughing. "I told you, Lawson. I told you it wasn't over."

Something like a wind rushed over me and I pivoted, bringing the bokken up. I heard the thock of another shuriken bouncing off the wooden blade.

I stumbled. Tears ran out of my eyes, but I couldn't fix Shiva's position.

A kick landed in my stomach and folded me over. I rolled back over, barely able to hold onto the bokken. I came up and felt my body jerk itself left again as a rush of air went flying past my ear.

"You can fight blind, Lawson? How interesting."

I dodged right again. I jerked the bokken up and still I couldn't see. I flipped it sideways and cut down, feeling it chop into flesh. Shiva grunted.

"Nice shot."

I tried to use her voice to pinpoint her, but she kept whirling away in front of me. More punches landed in my solar plexus. I sucked hot fiery wind that tasted like boiling molasses overflowing my lungs.

Shiva laughed again.

And still, I couldn't see anything.

I pivoted, brought the bokken up, and cut down. But I only caught naked air.

"Missed me."

Another kick caught me square in the small of my back. I stumbled forward trying to catch myself before I landed on my face.

My eyes stung. It was like looking into the sun.

"The Lunaspe protects me, Lawson."

I cut behind me, shifting as I did so. Again, I caught air. Shiva was invisible. And I couldn't catch her.

I felt the flat of a small square catch me on the face and Shiva cursed. Her shuriken hadn't penetrated my skin.

I couldn't last much longer.

I brought the bokken up and tried to regain control over myself. I shut my eyes, trying to close out the intense yellow flames that burned them.

My breathing slowed.

My heart rate stilled.

The drumming in my ears lessened.

And inside myself I felt something. Something unlike anything I'd ever felt before. A clarity.

A moment.

An opening.

I turned then, brought the bokken up, and dropped to one knee . . .

Plunged forward.

And felt a sudden heaviness on the blade—a sickening slide through skin, muscle, cartilage, and juices.

I heard a gasp.

Felt warm blood running down toward my hands.

I shoved one last time, with the last ounce of energy I had, and heard the crack of bone.

I'd nailed her.

"Lawson."

It came out as a gurgle.

I opened my eyes.

My vision returned. I could see.

Shiva was stooped. Frozen in time, bent over, and my bokken jutted out of her chest. I'd impaled her heart.

Her eyes were moist.

Pleading almost.

"How?"

I shook my head. "I don't know."

I turned the blade, hearing the squishy sounds of a torn thorax as it moved with the wooden blade. I let Shiva slide off the bokken toward the ground. She rolled over, her chest heaving blood now. She glanced down at herself and tried to smile.

"I meant it, you know."

Blood pooled around her, but the ground drank it up fast. "What?"

"You really were a good fuck."

I smiled in spite of everything. "Glad I could oblige."

I felt Arthur's presence next to me. He pressed something into my hand. I knew what it was just by touch. I looked down at Shiva.

"You know what I have to do."

Her body had changed again. She was human-looking again. But I'd never seen this woman before. She saw my face.

"This is me, Lawson. The real me."

Her long black hair was matted with sticky blood. Dirt streaked her face. I could see the blood crusting on her lips. But there was no doubt she was beautiful.

Somehow, I wished she was ugly. Maybe I wouldn't have felt so bad.

She coughed. Pink froth bubbled up out of her mouth. "You don't have to do this, Lawson. I'm finished anyway."

I tried to smile. "You know it doesn't work that way."

She smiled too. "We had a good run."

"You had a good run. I've been playing catch-up the entire time."

Shiva nodded. I could see her pupils expanding like spilled ink. "I'm glad it's you."

I knelt and stroked the back of her hair. I tightened my grip and then swung my right hand, cleaving her head from her neck with one cut of the large knife Arthur had given me.

I heard a final gasp escape Shiva's mouth.

And then it was over.

I looked down at her head. "I'm glad too."

Forty

Arthur brushed himself off and retrieved his rifle.

I watched him come back. "One helluva shot you made there, Arthur."

He nodded. "Yeah, not bad, eh?" He looked down at the tear in his pants. "Damned shame about these, though. Only just got a shipment of them in. Those bean-counting wankers'll be plenty pissed."

I wasn't about to let his modesty win the day. "And you disarmed the bomb strapped to Wirek too. I'm pretty impressed."

He shrugged, but I could see the pride in his face. "Yeah, well, it's not every day a retired bugger like me gets to see himself a bit of action now, is it?"

"I suppose not."

"And speaking of Wirek"—he thumbed over his shoulder—"I suppose we oughta let the poor bugger down, eh?"

"Guess so."

We walked over to where Wirek still hung. By the frown on his face through the silver-gray duct tape, I could tell he wasn't happy.

Arthur cut him down and freed his hands. Wirek yanked the tape off and screamed as he did so. "Sonofabitch!" He rubbed his mouth. "Damn, that hurt like hell."

"On the plus side," I said, "you won't have to shave for about a month."

He looked at me. "Lawson. Where in the hell is my goddamned automobile?"

Uh-oh. "Relax. I'm sure it's safe."

"Where is it?"

"About a mile away."

"When did you see it last?"

"Uh . . . yesterday."

"And you still think it's there?"

"Oh, sure."

"You aren't convincing me. I just want you to know that." Wirek looked at Arthur. "I can't believe you just left me hanging there. What if she'd just decided to pop me and be done with it?"

"Had her in my sights the entire time," said Arthur. "Besides, she had to think you were still tied up nice and tight. Otherwise, she wouldn't have reacted the way she did."

Wirek sighed. "Yeah. I suppose you're right. At least she kicked your ass good, though." He chuckled.

Arthur frowned. "She did *not* kick my ass."

"Sure looked like it from my perspective," said Wirek. "Threw you like an old sack of potatoes."

"All the blood's pooled at your feet, Wirek. Brain probably hasn't had any oxygen in hours. You don't know what you were looking at."

Wirek nodded. "Whatever you say." He pointed at Shiva's headless corpse. "She dead?"

"Unless half-breeds can take a stab through the heart, decapitation, and live to tell the tale, yes." I sighed. "Really sorry about bringing her to your house, Wirek."

"Yeah. We gotta talk about that. No more unannounced visitors, okay? When she came over and grabbed me out of my own home, oh, man, was I pissed."

"Hello?"

We all turned. Niles was hiking up the hill. Arthur chuckled. "Wondered what happened to the bloke."

I took a breath. "Uh . . . yeah. He was making a lot of noise on the trail. I had to sort of knock him out."

Arthur looked at me. "Sort of?"

"If Shiva'd seen him, she would have blown Wirek up. I didn't know you'd disarmed the package of explosives. I wasn't even expecting you guys to be here. Remember, when I left, I said no help?"

Arthur shrugged. "Sometimes my hearing goes. I'm an old bastard, you know."

Niles came up and let his rifle slide down butt-first. "Lawson."

"Yeah?"

"What the hell did you do that for?"

"Your own good," I said. "But thanks for being here. I really appreciate it."

Niles looked at Arthur. "Funny way he has of showing his thanks. He knocks me out with some gimmicky vital-point thingy."

"No accounting for some folks, Niles," said Arthur. "We tried, we did. We tried to help him. And what thanks do we get? I get thrown in the bushes"—he eyed Wirek—"and you get knocked out." He shook his head. "I tell ya, it's a crying shame the state of our world."

Niles nodded. "I could use a drink."

Arthur grinned. "Have I got a drink for you, mate. Have you ever heard . . ."

Wirek and I watched them walk down the paved path. I glanced at Wirek. "You okay?"

"I'll be okay once I get some feeling back into my arms. Hanging like that was not something I think I'll take up as a hobby."

"Good to know."

"I need some sleep."

I nodded. "Me too."

"She's gone, huh?"

"Yeah."

"And the Lunaspe?"

"Still on Shiva's body back there. What the hell are we supposed to do with it?"

"I don't know."

"We can't leave it there. Don't want someone picking it up."

"Maybe Arthur knows someone who can take care of it."

I looked at him. "Is that such a wise idea? If a lycanthrope has the amulet, they might be tempted to use it. And if word got around that it was recovered, who knows how many would try to get it."

"What are you suggesting?"

"Bury it. Burn it. Hell, I don't know."

"You want to go get it?"

I nodded and walked over to Shiva's corpse. The Lunaspe came off easily enough. Shiva not having a head anymore made taking the amulet off a cinch.

The Lunaspe still glowed in the moonlight. "Kind of nice, though, huh?"

"Forget it, Lawson. We have to get rid of it."

"Doesn't work for us anyway, remember?"

"Yeah." Wirek looked at Shiva. "What about the body?"

"Niles can get a cleanup crew over here. Place'll be clean by morning."

"Did you really sleep with her?"

I looked at him. "She tell you that?"

"Yeah."

I sighed. "Yeah. I did. Of course, I didn't think it was her at the time."

Wirek chuckled. "That's what they always say when it turns bad."

"Don't you start."

Wirek walked away to join Arthur and Niles. "Start? Me? Lawson, trust me, I am just getting warmed up. You'll be working your way out of this for years."

"Great."

Wirek ran to catch up with Niles and Arthur. I looked down at the Lunaspe and then up at the moon. It was trekking east, beginning to dip lower in the sky.

I wondered what would have happened if we hadn't stopped Shiva.

Then I realized I didn't want to know.

In the end, it didn't matter a damned bit. As long as the job got done, that was what counted.

I pocketed the Lunaspe and started walking home.

Forty-one

The death of Belarus and ensuing fallout over the Council not having an appointed leader threw things into a temporary turmoil. So much so, the Council recalled Wirek to help them sort the matter through, which made me feel good. I'd pressed Belarus a few months earlier to bring Wirek onto the Council—to fill the space vacated by the traitor Arvella. Now there was a good chance that would actually happen.

If anyone deserved a spot on the Council, I felt it was Wirek. But the old guy made it clear that even if he did accept a position, he'd still live in his crummy apartment.

"Place is my home, you know? I can't just up and ditch it because my job has changed."

I glanced around the dingy, litter-strewn hallway and just grinned. What people call home sometimes mystifies me as much as it makes me a sentimental fool.

I had lunch with Niles a short time after the Shiva incident. We met at the same greasy spoon in Harvard Square where he'd first briefed me. I watched him plow through a hamburger with cheese oozing off the sides and slurp a giant Cola.

"Niles?"

He looked up. Grease and cheddar ran off the corner of his mouth. "What?"

"When we met a week or so ago, you said that stuff would kill you. Now you're chomping your way through it like there's no tomorrow. What's the deal?"

He smirked. "I'm through denying myself. I think I rediscovered my zest for life when we were hunting Shiva. Besides, a gooey cheeseburger can't really hurt us, can it?"

"Not that I've seen. No."

He nodded and went back to eating. I cleared my throat and took a sip of my drink. "You know, Niles."

He looked up. "Yes?"

"When I first met you, well, I didn't think too much of you."

"I know it." He used a napkin to wipe off a bit of ketchup.

"I mean, you looked like one of those fast-track brown-nosers who has all the bells and whistles but none of the field experience that a real Control needs to make sure his operatives stay safe. I thought you'd fall to pieces as soon as the defecation hit the ventilation——"

"The what?"

"Shit hit the fan."

"Oh." Niles looked at me.

"But I was wrong."

"You were?"

I nodded. "You proved a lot to me during this time out. You didn't have to do much of what you did. But you did it anyway. I know you didn't have a lot of field experience. But you didn't let that stop you from doing the things that any good

Control would have done. Hell, you came out and risked your life with me on more than one occasion. That took a lot of courage. There aren't a lot of men in your position who would have done what you did. And I just wanted to say thanks."

Niles smiled. "I was scared shitless, to tell you the truth."

"We always are," I said. "Any Fixer who tells you otherwise is just lying. Being scared comes with the territory. No matter how many times you go through it."

"But you do it anyway," said Niles. "You go through it. That amazes me."

"I do it because I have to do it. I didn't pick this profession, I was born into it. We all were."

"Don't you sometimes wish you could be something else, though?"

I nodded. "Yeah. Sure do. But I guess when you've been around as much as I have and you see what could happen to the good in the world if you let evil go unchecked, you begin to take a certain degree of pride in your work."

"I can understand that."

"It's not ego. It can't be ego. I'd be dead by now if it was. After all, we aren't heroes; we aren't talked about. Hell, most people don't even know we exist. But we're there. And sometimes we're the only thing that keeps the bad from beating the good."

"That was almost poetic."

"Catch me after I've had some Bombay Sapphire and tonic. I can get downright scary."

Niles grinned. "Thanks, Lawson. I appreciate you saying that to me. I'm really glad you did."

I extended my hand across the table. "I hope you'll stay on, Niles. I could use a good Control. It's been years since I had one I could count on with my life. And I'd be plenty honored to have you looking out for me."

He shook my hand. "The honor's mine, Lawson. It truly is."

I got home late that night.

After lunch with Niles, I drove slowly through the city, stopping on Mission Hill to look at the city lights. I stayed there for a long time. There's something unmistakably beautiful about a city skyline at night. You can look out and see the buildings, the twinkling lights that pierce the night, and almost imagine they can disguise the filth and decay and the evil that you know is always there.

I watched the Citgo sign light up and fall dark in its usual sequence of electricity-hogging rhythm. I watched cars drive by, their headlights flashing—brief moments of illumination in an otherwise dark world.

And, of course, I watched a few pretty nurses walk out of New England Baptist Hospital and head for home.

One of these days, I might even wave to a few of them.

I smiled, started the engine of my rental car, and headed back to Jamaica Plain.

Wirek's Mercedes had been impounded by the Brookline cops since they'd assumed someone had abandonned an $85,000 car. I'd make a point never to walk past Sully's on Newbury again. I didn't need the aggravation.

At the top of my street, I slowed down. Parking's been a real pain in the ass lately. Part of me hoped the local grass-roots-we-weren't-around-in-the-60's-but-we-can-be-activists-too neighborhood group would push for a "resident parking only" zone so I'd be assured of a guaranteed place to park each night.

Then again, knowing how the city bureaucracy works, I wasn't holding my breath.

I parked and got out of my car.

I looked up and saw Phoebe asleep on one end of my couch. The couch sits in the living room by the window and affords a good view of the street below. Around Phoebe, the cushion looked like it was swallowing her. Might be time for a diet for that cat.

I started up the steps but stopped.

Something felt . . .

"Lawson."

My heart jumped.

I turned around.

That voice.

I came down from the steps. My pulse raced. I think I felt flushed. I wanted to close my eyes and pray for this to be real. I didn't need more disappointment. Not after what I'd been through recently.

A line of shrubs runs down the side of my house.

Talya stepped out of their shadows.

Just the sight of her made my heart flip-flop.

But I stopped her.

"Last year—where did we make love?"

She frowned. "In Cambridge. At the Charles Hotel."

"Was I good?"

She smiled. "Fanfuckingtastic."

"Come here." I hugged her tight, breathing in her perfume. "God, I missed you."

"What's with the twenty questions? Are you trying out to be a game show host?"

"Someone impersonated you recently."

"Impersonated me? What? How is that possible?"

"That's not the worst part."

"It's not?"

"No. The worst part is that I fell for it."

"You fell for it?" She pulled back. "I'm shocked to hear you say that."

I smirked. "Well, it's been a while since. . . ."

Her eyes crinkled the same way they did a year ago. A playful smirk jumped across her face. "Since what?"

"You know, since we last had . . . uh . . ."

"Sex?"

"Yeah."

She regarded me in the darkness, but I could see the smile blossoming even more. She pulled me into her and kissed me on the lips. I tasted her, the real her, for the first time in a year.

And God, she tasted wonderful.

Talya pulled away. "Did that do anything to refresh your memory?"

I frowned. "A tiny bit. Maybe we could do that some more. I've got a feeling with a little time and effort, you'll be able to completely restore my memory."

She laughed. "This way, Mr. Patient. The doctor will see you now."

I kissed her again. "That's the best damned thing I've heard in a long time."

Talya just laughed and disappeared up my steps.

I watched her for just a second, admiring the view, and then started after her.

Please turn the page for an exciting sneak peek
at the next thrilling installment of the
Lawson Vampire series,

THE SYNDICATE,

coming in October 2003 from Pinnacle Books!

One

Darkness enveloped everything.

I couldn't see a damned thing.

Even with my incredible vision, the cloud of blackness hid everything from me. I felt vulnerable. I could be attacked from any angle and never see it coming.

"Lawson."

The voice was a sick harsh whisper coated with the promise of extreme violence. I wheeled around, searching for the source. None revealed itself.

Again the voice spoke. "Do you remember me?"

Something about it seemed familiar. Something about it tickled the back of my mind. I could feel the adrenaline coursing through my veins. I could hear my heartbeat drumming against my bones.

And I knew.

Cosgrove.

He laughed then and it seemed to echo off unseen walls all around me. I pivoted, jumped, and threw myself from position to position hoping to stay one step ahead of him.

"You remember. Don't you?"

My throat felt tight. Suffocated. Squeezed between the forefinger of fear and the thumb of hesitation. "I killed you."

An unseen punch crashed into my jaw and

snapped my head back. I felt my teeth grind together, tasted blood—it was a helluva shot.

I brought my hands up to ward off the secondary
blow, but none followed the initial strike.

"You didn't kill me, remember? I warned you
about that. You chose not to listen. I told you I'd be
back. I swore my vengeance."

I shook my head. It wasn't possible. I'd staked
and decapitated him. There was no possible way he
could ever come back. Not after what he did. Not
after what I did in return.

A kick to the groin doubled me over. I felt my
bowels drop toward my feet but sucked them back
in, steeling myself and hoping he hadn't just
crushed my testicles.

"Do you believe me now?"

"NO!"

The shout that erupted from me did a lot to restore my confidence. If I could only see through
the darkness. If only I could see him.

But the darkness didn't clear. Instead, it suddenly
became unbearably hot. I felt a rush of energy go
by my right side. I jumped. Another energy burst
zipped past my left side.

"Lawson."

The voice had changed. Cosgrove had vanished
seemingly. He'd been replaced by something
softer. But I knew the softness was only a disguise to
mask the pure evil residing behind it.

Something slammed into my chest. I flew back
and hit the ground somewhere beneath me. Wind
jumped out of my chest. I heaved and struggled to
get to my feet. Colors swirled around my eyes.

"What about me? Do you remember me, Fixer?"

I tried to stand. Another bolt of energy slammed

into my chest. I flew back again and felt my shoulder crack when it hit the ground.

What the hell was going on?

"Say my name, Fixer. Say it!"

I'd seen her killed, too. It couldn't be.

"Arvella?"

Her laughter wafted through the air like an evil mist. "Very good. I'm so glad you remember me."

"You're dead. I saw you die."

"Maybe you didn't. Maybe I fooled you. Maybe now I've come back for my vengeance."

Impossible.

Another voice joined Arvella's. "I'll bet he doesn't remember me."

Another man. The vague hint of an accent told me who it was immediately.

"Petrov."

A shot rang out. I felt a hot burning sensation sear my right biceps. I grunted and spun, fishing behind my right hip for my own gun trying to ignore the pain.

But my gun wasn't there.

I was unarmed.

"I couldn't toy with you," said Petrov. "I could kill you as easily as I draw a breath. Look at you. Already wounded and we haven't even begun yet."

We?

A whisper tickled the back of my neck. "You were such a good fuck."

I whirled.

Shiva.

A low growl suddenly sounded in front of me and I felt a claw slash across my chest. Sharp fingernails cut open my flesh. Blood poured out my body. I could feel the throbbing sting of sudden pain. I could smell the rush of fresh coppery blood.

My head hurt. My arm was hurt bad. I could tell the wooden fragments had nailed an artery. A few minutes longer and I wouldn't be much of a problem to anyone.

"You're dying, Lawson. You're almost dead now. We told you we'd be back. We told you that you'd never be rid of us. This is your day of reckoning. Welcome to hell."

Cosgrove's laughter erupted once again. I always did hate hearing that sick bastard laugh. Arvella's spirit-invoking chants emanated from somewhere off to my right. I could hear Petrov chuckling as he ratcheted the slide on his gun, chambering another round to finish me off. And Shiva's growling came from behind and all around me.

More voices joined them. More evil vampires I'd long since executed for crimes against our society.

All of them had come back.

All of them had returned for their revenge.

My past had finally caught up with me.

"This can't be. This can't be possible. I saw you all die. I killed you. You're all dead!"

They spoke with one voice. "You can't kill us, Lawson. You can never be free of us. You can never be free of what we have all become to you."

The pain in my body increased. My head felt light. Their voices echoed inside my skull.

My stomach rumbled.

Woozy.

I sank to the ground.

Retching.

Heaving.

Bleeding.

Was I dying?

Was it all true?

Had they all come back from the dead? Had they all come back to take me off to hell?

The darkness abruptly began to clear. Slowly it became a lighter shade of gray. The voices receded in volume. The pain in my head lessened, but only slightly. I could sense something happening on the fringe of my consciousness.

A figure stood in the gray mist.

Smaller than a full-sized man.

The mist cleared some more and I could make out a few details. I could see his face.

I winced.

He was horribly disfigured.

He smiled at me, his teeth coated with fresh blood.

He mouthed something that I couldn't make out.

What was he trying to tell me? What was his message?

My head exploded in pain again. I cried out and felt myself sinking toward the black fuzziness once again.

I passed out.

For a while, I had no thoughts. I had no sensations. I floated in limbo, exhausted, bloody, and almost dead.

I woke to the sound of incessant ringing.

The phone.

My head throbbed like I'd just gotten back from a ten-day pub crawl with my good buddies Jim Beam, Johnny Walker, and Captain Morgan. My stomach felt like I was going to give birth to a blue whale through my mouth.

I sat up quickly and instantly regretted it. I looked down, convinced that there'd be claw marks across my chest.

Nothing.

I looked at my arm.

No gunshot wound.

I breathed deep.

Another dream.

A bad one at that.

What the hell was making that damned noise?

I slid my legs over the edge of the bed and felt my bare feet touch cold wood floor. I needed to start wearing socks to bed.

I got up, stifled the urge to puke my guts out, and padded out of my bedroom.

I used to have a telephone in my bedroom but I'd ditched it a few months back. There are times when I like to sleep unaffected by a ringing telephone.

Now I was actually glad the stupid thing had woken me up. I didn't want to have to go on with that dream for much longer.

I padded down the hallway and took the stairs to the second floor to my office. My leather swivel chair accepted my body with a small squeak of surrender. The phone on my desk flashed obnoxiously.

I needed to get a phone with a better ring. This one sounded like an old cold war alarm.

I picked the receiver up.

"Yeah?"

"Lawson?"

"Yeah."

"It's Uncle Phil."

My eyes opened a bit wider. I don't have much in

the way of family. Uncle Phil was one of the few relatives I had left. His call was a complete and total surprise. I almost forgot about my intense headache and vomit-ready gut ache.

I checked the clock. Six in the morning.

"It's a little early isn't it?"

"I need your help."

"What's up?"

He paused. His next words faltered and stuttered out of his mouth in a broken staccato sentence. "Are you . . . still—you know—a . . . Fixer?"

"It's okay to say the word, Phil."

"Well, are you?"

"Last I checked."

His voice emanated relief. "Good."

"Is something wrong?"

"I think so. Yes."

I felt like a dentist yanking on a particularly stubborn wisdom tooth. "Anytime you want to tell me what it is, Phil."

"It's Marilyn."

My cousin. Phil's daughter. Last I knew, she lived in New York City. "What about her?"

"She's missing, Lawson."

"How missing? Like she hasn't called you or something?"

"She hasn't been seen in over a week. Her roommate doesn't know where she is. She hasn't called. I'm worried to death about her."

"Maybe she's gone somewhere."

"She could be dead. Kidnapped. I don't know."

"Calm down. It's probably not something so bad as that."

"I'm beyond remaining calm, Lawson. I don't

know who else to turn to." He paused again. "I've only got one question to ask you: Can you help me?"

Family, even the little I had left, was important to me. As such, I only had one possible answer.

"Yes."

Feel the Seduction of
Pinnacle Horror

HORROR FROM PINNACLE . . .

___**HAUNTED** by Tamara Thorne
0-7860-1090-8 $5.99US/$7.99CAN

Its violent, sordid past is what draws best-selling author David Masters to the infamous Victorian mansion called Baudey House. Its shrouded history of madness and murder is just the inspiration he needs to write his ultimate masterpiece of horror. But what waits for David and his teenaged daughter at Baudey House is more terrifying than any legend; it is the dead, seducing the living, in an age-old ritual of perverted desire and unholy blood lust.

___**THIRST** by Michael Cecilione
0-7860-1091-6 $5.99US/$7.99CAN

Cassandra Hall meets her new lover at a Greenwich Village poetry reading— and sex with him is like nothing she's ever experienced. But Cassandra's new man has a secret he wants her to share: he's a vampire. And soon, Cassandra descends into a deeper realm of exotic thirst and unspeakable passion, where she must confront the dark side of her own sensuality . . . and where a beautiful rival threatens her earthly soul.

___**THE HAUNTING** by Ruby Jean Jensen
0-7860-1095-9 $5.99US/$7.99CAN

Soon after Katie Rogers moves into an abandoned house in the woods with her sister and her young niece and nephew, she begins having bizarre nightmares in which she is a small child again, running in terror. Then come horrifying visions of a woman wielding a gleaming butcher knife. Of course, Katie doesn't believe that any of it is *real* . . . until her niece and nephew disappear. Now only Katie can put an end to a savage evil that is slowly awakening to unleash a fresh cycle of slaughter and death in which the innocent will die again and again!

Call toll free **1-888-345-BOOK** to order by phone or use this coupon to order by mail.

Name_____
Address_____
City_____ State _____ Zip _____
Please send me the books I have checked above.
I am enclosing $_____
Plus postage and handling* $_____
Sales tax (in NY and TN) $_____
Total amount enclosed $_____
*Add $2.50 for the first book and $.50 for each additional book.
Send check or money order (no cash or CODs) to: **Kensington Publishing Corp., Dept. C.O., 850 Third Avenue, 16th Floor, New York, NY 10022**
Prices and numbers subject to change without notice. All orders subject to availability.
Check out our website at **www.kensingtonbooks.com**.

When Darkness Falls
Grab One of These
Pinnacle Horrors